D0467422

INDIAN SUMMER

INDIAN

Also by John Knowles:

A SEPARATE PEACE

MORNING IN ANTIBES

DOUBLE VISION: AMERICAN THOUGHTS ABROAD

SUMMER

BY JOHN KNOWLES

RANDOM HOUSE · NEW YORK

 Published in New York by Random House, Inc., and simultaneously in Toronto, Canada, by Random House of Canada Limited.

MANUFACTURED IN THE UNITED STATES OF AMERICA

Typography by Jeannette Young

For T. N. W.

with profound gratitude

. . . his actions, like everyone else's, being generally dictated by previous actions the prime motive of which has already ceased to exist.

MARCEL PROUST: *Remembrance of Things Past*

I

THE PRIVATEER

Demobilization sounded like the best word in the language in 1946.

Before it took place, as the war proceeded toward its close, "Victory" ships, dozens and dozens of them, painted a raw camouflage green, floated heavily in the Hudson River, filling the great waterway for miles, anchored there until the signal came to move in unison down the river, through the Narrows, and out into the Atlantic, to England or Naples or Cherbourg, to whatever funnel fed the front as it moved, always closer and closer to Germany.

Over the English Channel splotch-painted bombing planes passed like frozen birds, inexorable, riding as if on their own deep roller of sound, and as they came over the coast of continental Europe, in the streets below, ambulances sped and wardens ran, and anti-aircraft muzzles moved in their miniature tracing of the airplanes' movement; elsewhere armored cars and tanks and guns, guns which were always on wheels, advanced or retreated across deserts and mountains and through barnyards and slums. In America long, late trains straggled across the country, stopping for meaningless hours in the middle of some pasture, but sooner or later rejoining the world of movement, which existed everywhere then, as though the war were a great migration to the greener grass on the other side of every fence; also in America automobiles, as soon as the necessary gas had been hoarded, immediately began traveling and kept on until the last drop had been used up. Everything that had the energy to produce movement gave all it possessed, including human beings, who walked, marched, and crawled, advancing or retreating or drilling or running away or pacing, up and down, up and down. To stand still then was to be consumed by boredom and apathy, or to be annihilated. The people who stayed still were in concentration camps or dead.

When the hostilities suddenly ended, and the gigantic hush at last fell, and the surviving lights went on, millions of people began moving in a huge counterconvulsion, homeward. They sailed and trailed and flew and raced and crawled and walked and were carried, finally, home.

After that the United States quickly proceeded to demobilize.

Ex-Sergeant Harold Kinsolving 11128886, of the Army Air Force, walked out of the discharge center, into the hot, flat street of Wichita Falls, Texas, tossed his heavy duffel bag in the air, shouted, "I'm goin' *home!*" and turned a face-brightening grin on three pedestrians. "Home!" They smiled and said, "Good for you" and "Fine."

Harold, or Cleet as he was called, had the respectable color of skin for young men in 1946, faded yellow. It was as though fate was working to make the two enemies in the Pacific more and more resemble each other in appearance, as they had come to do in tactics: Pearl Harbor, and the reply four years later: Hiroshima. But now the danger of malaria, and so the yellow-staining atabrine pills, had been left behind in the festering South Pacific with all the rest of the bottomless boredom and depression of the war, and ahead everything was of course going to be just as bright as the sky over Wichita Falls was that morning: a luminous, philosophical blue.

Some kind of magnanimous, complete way of life was opening for him. He didn't know it, he felt it. There had to be; it was the way things were. A big wave rolling out of the sea encounters finally a shore to rush its energy out upon, every last shred of its potential rolling through the crash and ripples to the ultimate lacy fringe at the high-water mark, and he, Cleet Kinsolving, confidently expected to find a place where he himself could roll out his life full force.

"Which way is the East Coast?" he cheerfully asked a man in shirt sleeves with a long thin cigar, who was standing on the hot sidewalk; he asked it matter-of-factly, as you could ask, "Which way is the men's room?"

"Well? The East Coast'a what?"

"The East Coast. *The* East Coast. You know, Washington, New York."

"Oh. The North. Well there's Route Sixty-six?"

But Cleet decided then to do it systematically, with planning aforethought, since he had never done anything that way before and this seemed a good time to start. He bought a large and very heavy atlas, which had maps not only of Texas and the United States but also of Zanzibar, the Sporades, and Tonga. He ambled along to the outskirts of town, set his duffel bag down beside the highway, heading toward Oklahoma, fanned himself with his cap, put it back on his head, and began poring over the atlas.

First, of course, he found a page devoted entirely to Connecticut and located Wetherford, his home town, on the Connecticut River. Wetherford was very small and insignificant. So he turned to the double-page map of the United States and that did indeed spread very satisfactorily in all its spaciousness, coast-to-coast and Canada to Gulf, quite a panorama looked at this way, as though from a space ship, quite a field of action, where anybody could find a place to roll out his life full force.

He was very clear about what this meant: to be strong, to be happy, to be physically tired at night, to have love and sex at one and the same time, to be proud of himself.

Sometimes he thought that these were the simplest and most easily attainable goals in the world, too simple, as a matter of fact, unambitious, run-of-the-mill; but at other times they seemed as unreachable as the North Star.

Well, you never got anywhere unless you started. A small green truck was coming along. Cleet put the atlas into his duffel bag—who could tell to what ends of the earth his search might lead him?—grinned, and cocked his thumb.

Since he was yellow-skinned and in uniform, Cleet was picked up by one car as soon as another had let him out, and all of the people were friendly and talkative. There were no exceptions to this, and as he made his way with one after another open-faced and congenial American soul it began to come home to him that really life and people weren't so bad, at least life and people in America, or at least in this part of America. He didn't remember them as being anything like as kindly back in Connecticut, or in other parts of the country where he had trained in the Air Force. Perhaps he just hadn't noticed, or he had taken it for granted. But it didn't seem so; it seemed that they were genuinely an improved breed in these parts, or else it was because he himself had changed. He was twenty-three years old and looked older, and people now were treating him like the adult he was, with almost a deference, for some reason. It was a peculiar feeling. He had gotten so used to thinking of the world as bad, very very bad.

There had seemed to be no one in it except Hitlers and Hirohitos and Tojos and Mussolinis and Pétains and Quislings and Lavals and Goebbels' and Himmlers; and only slightly less bad, because of their weakness, Chamberlains and appeasers like that; and then a scattering of heroes—Roosevelt and Churchill and Commander Kelly and what was that chaplain's name who did something and a few others—a sprinkling of heroes which only made the mass of the human race look even blacker by contrast.

Now, utterly confounding all of that deluge of badness the radio and the newspapers had engulfed him in since he could read and hear, were to begin with the Japanese, of all people, with many graceful and gentle qualities. And now here were the American people themselves. During his four years in the Army Air Force the American people had been represented by the other enlisted men around him, and a more foul-mouthed, lazy, suspicious, malingering, pessimistic, anemic, low-down bunch of cruds it would be hard to picture; then there had been America's corps of noncommissioned officers, loud-mouthed drunks, one and all; and finally the officers and gentlemen by act of Congress, who were either unsuccessful business types that Cleet's tycoon friend, Mr. Hugh Reardon, could have spotted at half a mile, or brats. The American civilians whom he had encountered during those four years had been mostly wandering girls in platform shoes, with lots of hair and lots of problems, chiseling bar owners, and salesmen, and sprinkled once again over this grimy swarm of badness had been a few heroic types—Marlene Dietrich, who had entertained at his camp once even though she was very famous and didn't have to, one good pilot he had served under once, and one nice girl he met in Salt Lake City.

But now, really cut loose into civilian America, he found it flowing with really very good people who seemed to like him and want to be helpful. He was approaching Oklahoma City in the 1940 Pontiac of a book salesman when this occurred to him, and he took a tremendous breath, as though he had been breathing only something like mustard gas for the past four years.

"Do you know what?" he suddenly said to this man. "I'm planning to start up a little cargo airline between Washington State and Alaska."

"Where'd you get that idea?"

"It just came to me one day. Because Alaska has had all kinds of new equipment and airfields and bases put up there because of the Japs—the Japanese when they invaded the Aleutians. Now it's ready to really get going with its postwar development and it seemed to me a private freight airline up there from Seattle would come in really useful and make some money and work out. What do you think?"

"Bad territory for anything, if you want my opinion. Just from reading. I never have been to the place. But who lives in a territory like that? Nothing but Eskimos and ignorant people like that, who won't have any use for an airline."

Cleet, who was one-quarter Indian, passed over the ignorant-Eskimo remark, although he was fairly sure Eskimos were Indians; he had passed over such remarks all his life. "Indian giver!" Neil Reardon had once taunted him, and a second later they had both looked shocked; things like that he was always having to pass over because, well, they just seemed to him off the point; other people had a right to their opinions; he didn't expect everybody to be like himself. So he replied that he still thought there was a big potential up there.

"And where are you going to get your capital to start this airline?"

Cleet said that was a big problem but he had one or two ideas.

Then they started discussing the salesman's field and he gave Cleet a couple of recent books.

Cleet leafed through them without great interest, and then the salesman reached into the back seat for another book. "Here's one that's really moving. It gets publicity all by itself, we don't pay for it. You know, commentators on the radio, editorials, the best kind of publicity, and all for free. The author works very hard for it too. He's on a lecture tour in the Midwest right now, and that helps." He handed over the book, which was called *We're Home.* What a coincidence: it was Neil's.

Cleet held it for a moment and then said kind of casually, "I know the author of this one."

"Is *that* right? Well, he's really a seller. How well do you know him?"

"We grew up together."

"Is that so!"

"Yes." Out of some kind of pride or shyness Cleet didn't add that he had been the best man by proxy at Neil's wedding, that he knew every last secret of Neil's life, that he was in fact the closest friend in the world that Neil Reardon had.

"Listen." The salesman almost stopped the car at the thought that had come to him. "If you know him so well *he* can back your crazy airline to Alaska. Why his old man is worth about five hundred million dollars, isn't that right?"

"That's about right."

"Well then. That is, if you really *do* know him. Not wanting to pry."

"Sure." Cleet grinned and nodded. "Yeah, I know him very well. He's a very good friend of mine. He *could* back an airline, I guess. Yes, he could."

That night, to save money and for the fun of it, he slept under a bridge near Guthrie, Oklahoma, and the next morning caught a ride into Kansas with a semiprofessional baseball player, on through Wichita in a farm truck, which did not go to Kansas City as he had assumed, but instead let him off in the dead of night somewhere west of St. Joseph, Missouri. The farmer had at least deposited him near some tourist cabins, and Cleet, feeling progressively less the outdoors man as the fatigue had deepened in his muscles throughout the day and evening, paid four dollars for one of the tiny cabins. Bed, he thought to himself, a beautiful, wide, clean, firm yet soft, stable yet giving, one hundred per cent hygienic American-type bed. He collapsed on it without undressing, to see if it felt as voluptuous as it looked; it did, and he was asleep.

The next morning he woke up because his head was in a patch of sunlight, or rather he did not so much wake up as withdraw from sleep and move steadily into consciousness and a sense of firmly embedded energy which the sleep had renewed, an energy gathered inside his body in relaxed, strong reserves. He had, for some reason, never felt quite as well as this before. Christ, he thought, I believe this is the day I conquer the world or something like that.

The cabin was so small it seemed designed for Pigmies, and when Cleet stepped out onto the abbreviated screened-in porch, he found that the place was set deep in shrubbery and bushes, a shabby little brown shingled elf's hut. He liked this cabin. It appealed to a deep streak of sympathy in him, the streak which made him devoted to mongrel dogs, fall almost insanely in love with a girl because she was very slightly cross-eyed, and secretly envy schools where the football team lost. This peculiar, undersized Midwestern cabin somehow struck the same streak of sympathy. He was even inspired with a name for it: Hirohito's Hut. He didn't know why that seemed exactly the right name for it either.

There was a wide unkept lawn and some large trees in front of it, then the highway, and on the other side of that, a neat little airport, looking like a golf course or a croquet lawn, with a little red two-seater plane and two biplanes. Behind it the wide country rolled mile after mile, a vast patchwork of fields and clumps and lines of trees, large farmhouses and large barns here and there, a shine of fertility about it all, in the bright optimistic Midwestern sun. I like it, Cleet said to himself.

His eyes had become used to open spaces in the war, and he had grown to like them very much. Straight-laced, perpendicular, Colonially oriented Wetherford seemed especially cramped next to country like this. There was a narrowness about Wetherford; the land was all in bits and pieces based on deeds hundreds of years old, the plot boundaries practically set in iron by their ancient lineage. Here the land and its lines looked more casual, freer; there was a feeling that a few hundred acres could easily be sold and attached to some other farm; possessions were looser; he sensed a give and take and flow here which was completely absent in the rigid world he had grown up in.

It was farmland. Cleet had always thought he ought to be a farmer; one set of grandparents were. He needed fresh air, and he liked the idea of producing something. Unfortunately there was a monotony to farm life he didn't take to, a ceaseless repetition of the same chores he couldn't put up with. And then, a farmer stayed in the same place all of his life. In the middle of the war it had come to Cleet that if only farmers operated with airplanes instead of tractors he would be ideally happy; he also thought how crazy the idea of a flying farmer was.

He put on his Army khaki pants, a white T-shirt, and loafers and went across the highway to see what was going on at this uproariously funny excuse for an airport; he had loved it on sight. Peace, he sighed to himself as he went through the weeds on the far side of the highway, it's wonderful. *This* is what civilians have for airports, and that double-winged thing there, which looks like it came in a box from Toyland to be assembled at home, that is what they call an airplane.

There was a man in the shed there, and Cleet began talking to him, casually at first. And then without warning the man mentioned that the biplane was used for dusting crops.

"What?" said Cleet.

"Crop dusting."

"You mean, you," Cleet's voice became a little constricted, "farm with it, you, with the airplane, you farm?"

"I guess you could put it that way. We fly over the fields around here, spray them with insecticide, we–is anything the matter? Why are you grinning at me that way?"

"You just changed my life, that's all. Nothing important. You just changed my life."

Later he calmed down enough to view this miracle, flying farming, from a slightly more pragmatic standpoint. "Do they give these pilots any place to stay, like that tourist cabin over there or anything?"

"No, the boys have their own places where they stay, and when they're moving around they put up some place or other, the owners don't do that."

"Doesn't matter. I mean is food included at all?"

"Food? No, of course not. What do you think this is, the Army? You got your discharge. This is civilian life."

"Well the only thing is, I realize the pay wouldn't be very much."

"It depends on what you mean by much. Most of the boys gross about ten thousand the first year–"

"What!"

"And some of them get up to around fifteen or twenty thousand once they get their hand in."

Cleet turned abruptly away and began to walk toward a plane as though he had just noticed something about it he wanted to examine. His face was flushed with excitement and he didn't want the man to see.

Then he turned back and said, "I'd like to be one of these flying farmers."

"Flying farmers, that's a funny way of putting it."

"Thank you." Cleet always became very formal when important issues were at stake. "Can you tell me who I see about the job?"

The man, who was fattish and had a round face, said, "As a flying farmer?"

"Yes, sir."

"As a matter of fact, you'd have to see me to fly one of these particular planes here. I own these planes here. I'm Alex Eubanks."

"Well, my name is Harold Kinsolving and I served four years in the Air Force, and I'm not going to lie to you and say that I was a pilot because I wasn't, I was a gunner, but the trouble wasn't with my ability to fly. It was just mathematics and some navigation and those fields of study. I don't see why that part would be very important in the kind of flying you do here."

"Not a pilot," the man said reflectively.

"Yes but I—well, I think I have quite a bit to offer, if energy counts, and I certainly would be *dedicated* to it. You'd be able to see that right away."

"How's your vision?"

"Perfect. That little sign over there across the road, in the window of the tourist camp office there, can you read it?"

"As a matter of fact, no, I can't."

"It reads 'Hot Water Showers.'"

"Do you expect just to walk in here cold and get a job, just like that?"

"Well yes, because this just happens to be exactly what I want. I got discharged and I thought maybe I'd have to spend six months or so looking before I'd find my life's work, and then I just woke up this morning and walked over here and here it was! So naturally . . ."

"Yeah but we don't just go and hire people like that. I've got a pilot for my second plane. No openings, you know how it is."

"Do you need somebody to do maintenance, for instance?"

"That's a long way from flying."

"It is, but you have to start somewhere."

"Maybe some of the other places around here could hire you to fly."

"Maybe, but first I've got to get a job. You know, anything. What about keeping the lawn mowed? Driving that pickup truck? Uh—"

"Do you want to hang around here and do everything I can use you for, and get forty bucks a week for it?"

"Sure. That would be wonderful. That's just what I'd like to do, at first."

"I thought all you boys were *war-weary*."

"Yeah," said Cleet immediately, in his richest, levelest tone, "but what you've got here is peace."

During the next few days the war quickly, amazingly quickly, began to telescope into a kind of stale repetitiousness in his memory. He recalled the huge open airfields, with the horizon shimmering with heat and the grass between runways sighing in the wind, rows of squat planes, rows of hangars, rows of barracks, rows of Quonset huts, rows of men. All that part was on the boring, ugly side, but always overhead there were the vaults and domes of sky, where doubled up like a fetus in his gunner's bubble, he had traveled, and all of this flying had for him the strange expansiveness of a dream, of all ambition, the limitlessness he craved and believed in as a way of life, as a natural right at least for him, if not so it seemed for others, in view of the lives they were content to lead. He felt immediately, drunkenly, magically, whole and happy in the toplessness of flying and the endlessness of change, the constant shifts in the plane's relation to the earth, in the winds, in the layers of light, the blues and whites and silvers and grays and blacks and streaks and pillars and tremendous cloud rollers of the sky, the cottony meadows there, rain suddenly flailing across his plane like a slap, all this variation seemed fundamentally intended for him.

Spacious and stale the war spread out behind him. There had been nothing in it to stir him up except that space and sky. He remembered the war otherwise as a stale procession of cots, narrow and hard and noisy metal contraptions with their gloomy blankets; cots and splintering wood; also footlockers; the war had been beer, an ocean of beer, usually lukewarm; the war had also been noise, the bellow of bombers grinding overhead, the explosion of a fighter plane starting, the cheerless disinfected din of mess halls, the worn-out frog's-croak of drill instructors yelling, sirens which wound through the air like snakes, and then the talk, dry and flat, flat and dry, talk, the stalest talk in the history of the world, befuddling the air of the barracks; the breathy sound of soldiers sleeping; the snores, like protests from corpses; these had all been part of the stale sounds of war.

The war had been sex the American way, that is, exclusively preoccupied with germs. Cleet couldn't connect all the busy doctors and the clinical films and the kits and the prophylactic stations and the whole hospital atmosphere with which the service surrounded sex, couldn't connect all that with the joy of making love to somebody, and so he didn't pay much attention to it, assuming that they must be somehow talking about something else, not what he knew by experience: it sounded like some weather report from outer space.

But the war had been the sky also, the endless open beautiful sky. The sky, when you got up into it, was the same everywhere, over Nova Scotia and New Caledonia and Australia and Maine and San Diego and Oregon and Hawaii and Iwo Jima and Fort Lauderdale and Alaska and Amarillo and even Tokyo; over Tokyo it was just the same sky as over Washington, D.C. The whole fuss over differences on the ground confused and bored him sometimes. What the Northerners said about the Southerners during his basic training with the other Connecticut boys, in Mississippi; then what the cadets said about the enlisted men, in preflight school; then what the enlisted men said about the officers, after he was washed out of preflight school; then what they all said about the South Pacific and its natives, after he went overseas; and finally what everybody said about the Japs. He had been thunderstruck to find that the Japs were so unlike the propaganda, and after that he decided not to believe anybody's opinion about anybody else again.

He had to admit that he was prejudiced, if that was the word for it, in favor of equality, by the fact that his grandmother was a full-blooded Indian, although to be perfectly honest, he didn't think that influenced him one way or the other. His grandmother seemed like everybody else's grandmother except that her teeth were all still in her head and were very white and her eyes looked clearer than other people's her age. The only other thing about her which seemed at all Indian was something he felt rather than saw. When Cleet was six he blew open his hand with a firecracker; when he was eight he locked himself in the bathroom, couldn't get out, and had to be extricated by the fire department; at nine he was experimentally tapping a windowpane with his fist when he broke through it, the blood vessels in his wrist were slashed, and he had suffered a severe loss of blood. His grandmother had been the first to find him in all three accidents, and her eyes had not widened, the way those of other people did when they joined the scene later, her voice had not been raised, her hands had not shaken. Instead she had seemed even more than ordinarily calm, and the only different thing about her had been a kind of glow she acquired, as though radiating something. Her dark eyes seemed a little darker in those moments, and brighter, her voice sounded richer: some extra force came into her. Finally, years later, he had found the word for it: his grandmother was unshakable. He had identified it because by then he had discovered it in himself. In his own way, he was unshakable too.

Cleet had one other thing he thought he got from those Indian ancestors. He had his own theory as to why the Indians had withered and faded before the advancing whites. They had been destroyed by the firewater. The point was, Indians were drunk *already*, made so by nature at birth, created with the same pagan inner craziness he had; when this was built even higher with white man's alcohol the Indians crashed over the edge into oblivion. That's how their ruin must have happened.

This knowledge had come to him the way all knowledge came to Cleet: by personal experience. One night at the Air Force base in Kearns, Utah, the bootleggers had come through the barracks as usual with a wheelbarrow full of whiskey. Cleet had bought a bottle of something called Prince George, and he and the sergeant had proceeded to empty it slowly and methodically in the sergeant's room on the second story of the barracks. Back in Wetherford he and Neil used to drink beer some afternoons after school, and sometimes the Reardons had wine at meals when Cleet ate at their house, but since he had always been in training for some team or other, he had never before tasted hard liquor. It had quite a taste, or rather, quite an afterglow. Rather slowly the world unfolded on all sides for him and he recognized that there were, curiously enough, no problems whatever anywhere, and never had been; he was, it slowly became clear as everything else slowly blurred, perfectly competent to do anything in the world, and the only issue remaining in his life was, what should he do first? He started to consult the sergeant about this, but the sergeant would not be interrupted.

". . . any more chicken shit from anybody, and . . ."

"You know what, Sergeant. I'm goin' to fly!"

". . . you can take this man's Army Air Force and stick it up your ass. Yeah. Stick it."

"Hear me? Fly. I decided to stop being a gunner. I decided to be a pilot after all. Who do I see?"

"Me."

"You, Sergeant?"

"And just stick it all."

"Fly a P-38."

"Shitty plane."

"What?"

"And after that they can take this man's Army Air Force—"

"The *P-38?*"

"Boy is that a lousy plane."

"Who do I see, Sergeant? Stop kidding around. You see, I decided to get back in preflight school and pass that math test I didn't pass before—I wasn't paying attention the first time—and then fly a P-38."

"What an orange crate."

"So who do I see, Sarge?"

"You can take the P-38 and stick it up your ass."

"Sarge?"

"Stick it."

There was a pause, and then Cleet said, "Uh huh." This sounded deep in his throat, and was addressed not to the sergeant or to the outside world, but to himself, his inner self. Then Cleet slowly stood up, circled the table, scooped up the sergeant, crossed to the open window, and dropped the sergeant out the window.

The next day, busted to private again, he evolved his firewater theory about the destruction of the Indians, and he gave up whiskey.

One thing he had unquestionably gotten from his grandmother was the way he looked, the impassive cast to his face, the wide-set opaque green eyes, slightly longer than average straight nose, somewhat larger than average mouth, black hair—although his skin was light—and square skull. He did not turn his head much; the whole squared torso turned together. He did not face people; he confronted them. And not knowing this formidability of his, he often wondered why certain people he met seemed slightly scared by him. Because of his usual impassive expression the flash of his smile seemed to light up everything. He was five feet ten and a half inches tall and weighed a hundred and sixty-five pounds. His voice was rich, full, and level.

Hirohito's Hut turned out to be cheaper by the week: seventeen dollars. His new boss, whose name was Alex Eubanks, lent Cleet a hot plate. He bought a very small refrigerator. He got an iron, soap flakes, a coffee pot, an adjustable screen for the window, and because he thought a home should always have one work of art in it, he bought and carefully hung a large framed reproduction of "Whistler's Mother." After that he felt at home there and very content. From a magazine he cut out a large photograph of Emperor Hirohito holding what looked like crossed sticks in front of him and wearing what looked like a plate on his head. He taped that over the inside of the front door and glued his Ruptured Duck insignia above it. From the atlas he cut out the pages showing the United States, the Pacific, Japan, and pasted them side by side on the wall, and with a red line traced his four-year military route from Connecticut to Alabama to Utah and California, through the South Pacific and Iwo Jima to Japan, and then back to Wichita Falls, Texas, through Guthrie, Oklahoma, to where he was now. On that spot he pasted a school star. He fixed his discharge on the bathroom wall, at a place where he could contemplate it while sitting on the toilet. He sanded down a slab of wood, and during evenings in the cabin slowly, painfully carved a rather graceful "Home Sweet Hirohito" on it, and hung that outside over the door. At a roadhouse down the highway he got to know a waitress called Milly. He tended to like sizable women and Milly was on the small side, but in view of the dimensions of Hirohito's Hut he thought this time it was just as well.

On Sunday, his first day off, he slept until seven-thirty, got up, and looked at himself in the mirror. His atabrine-yellowed skin was turning to a bronze shade in the air and sunshine here, and he was beginning to look not so much "like a spook," as Milly had described him. At first his opaque green eyes with their level gaze, set in the impassive face of a yellow American Indian, had so startled the old lady Milly worked for that when he suddenly came through the door, she dropped a stack of dishes. Now every day he was looking less menacing and more normal, formidable but normal.

Was there actually anything menacing about him, Cleet asked himself as he left the cabin that Sunday morning and set off along the country road, its borders overflowing with wild grass and weeds and sprigs of trees and shrubbery. He had dropped the sergeant out of the window, that was true; but after all, that had been done not by him but by the primitive core of his nature he thought of as the Mad Indian. Once he broke somebody's jaw, but that had been in a fight the other one had started.

He realized that he had passions like blocks of granite inside himself, but thinking about them honestly, it didn't seem true that they menaced anybody. Most of them were *good* passions—love and sex and a sense of adventure—and only one or two were bad, such as his fear of being trapped which, as fear will, produced the passion of hate in him. That fear had driven him out into the Atlantic in the small boat, and also caused the New York business. Growing up, he had had to prove to himself from time to time that he could escape if he wanted to. As long as he was sure of that, then most of the time he was able to stay happily enough at home.

One of the few things his mother had understood about him was this fear of entrapment, and she used to say, "I don't see how he'll ever get married" and "I don't see how he'll put up with being in the Army." Marriage, a real one, was still in the future, and he didn't know how that would work out either, but the Army, the Army Air Force, hadn't been so bad. The discipline, after all, was easier than in any of the other services. The crushed garrison caps, and the fur-lined jackets, the casual sergeants and worldly majors and racy generals: well, it sure wasn't the Marines! Thank God for that. As it was, he had been just able to stand, by a tremendous act of self-control, being told when to get up and how to drill and what to wear, by people he didn't respect. He had been just able to bear that much regulating of his life by the Army Air Force because of the two freedoms it gave him in compensation: flying and travel. It had transported him across quite a bit of the world, without charge, and so when some lieutenant said to him, "Here are your orders, Sergeant" or, more often, "Here are your orders, Private," the rush of resentment he sometimes felt rise in his throat died down again because at least it was being said to him in Saipan, not in Connecticut.

The macadam of the country road under his feet had turned soft in the steady summer sunshine. There was a glow and a haze and a spell on the wide fields around him, a misty blur in the country summer air, a kind of easy scented spaciousness and laxity, as though the pollen of dozens of weedy plants were drifting at random to new connections, hanging meanwhile in the purposeless calm of the summer air. There was a heaviness about it all that was new to him, and a scintillating stillness, as though time itself were waiting in the rising heat for a convincing reason to tick on, and not finding it.

He ambled along the country road, pulling a weed up now and then and unthinkingly peeling away roots and husk to chew on its tenderest part. He veered across a meadow, took off his sneakers to wade across a chilly stream, looked around a barn. He went by a small private cemetery behind an iron grille fence, came to a dirt road and went along that for a while, past a country church and back out onto the macadam road, where after a long, thoughtful wait he was picked up by a passing truck and taken back to his cabin.

Inside he remembered that he had promised to call Milly. It was too late now; anyway it had been a good afternoon. It was rather stuffy inside and there was an antiquated fan in the corner, but he didn't turn it on because the noise would bother him. He liked to hear the buzzing and rustle from outside.

Looking across at the airfield, Cleet, suddenly tempted, reminded himself that he did not have his pilot's license, although

Alex had given him several lessons in flying the biplane. Also, the one pilot whom he had served under and liked in the Air Force had let him take the controls of the bomber several times; and of course there was the unforgettable day when he had first handled an airplane, the Reardons' family plane, when he had been fifteen.

Therefore, having a free Sunday afternoon, suddenly not able to control himself, he walked across the highway, unlocked the little hangar, lifted the tail of the tiny biplane and pulled it out onto the grass, got into the cockpit, started the engine, and began bouncing faster and faster across the field until the plane kind of jumped into the air and continued lifting, above the meadows and roads he had just been hiking along. The plane's wide expanse of wing surface sailed him up into the air in a really beautiful way; it seemed to Cleet that a biplane was less a plane than a kite, a giant box kite, and he was riding in the middle of it, sailing along not very far above the treetops, in the clean Midwestern air, the silent and empty Sunday fields stretching away close below him in all directions, and this was his idea of how to spend a Sunday afternoon.

The plane glided along over the trees like a big if not very bright bird, sending its shadow undulating swiftly across fields and hedges and haystacks. The engine clattered along in front of him—in some ways it was the funniest sensation in the world, riding this motorized kite—and he wondered just what the plane could do. He gently moved the stick over and the plane banked majestically to the right; he gently moved it the other way and it banked a little jerkily to the left; he pulled the stick back and the plane began to climb rather slowly into what the Air Force described as the Wild Blue Yonder. He pushed the stick forward and the biplane nosed over and began rapidly descending. Slowly and smoothly he leveled off at about fifty feet and swept along over the trees. Below him now he saw Milly's roadhouse; he made a pass at that, then climbed away from it and was immediately confronted by a silo which he was just able to bank around, which came and went so fast that he didn't feel the slightest apprehension, only noticing that the plane after all was moving very rapidly in relation to the ground and therefore he would have to stay alert.

He would have to stay alert, especially since he hadn't exactly asked Alex for permission to fly the plane, hadn't asked for permission at all, to be perfectly accurate, and was as a matter of fact probably breaking some kind of law—"flying without a license" seemed a peculiar law but it probably existed—and he had better be careful. Nothing as wonderful as this could be *wrong*, he understood that, but still, it might be awkward if he got into any kind of trouble. Alex might not understand, and probably the Air Police or whoever arrested someone for Flying Without a License might not understand either. He pulled back the stick a little to lift over an especially tall row of trees and noticed horses scattering in all directions as he passed over a field and a man dropped an axe he was holding to gape at him; he was probably flying a little low for complete security so he climbed a few feet higher; he passed over the macadam highway, where a car slowed down and a man stuck his head out of the window to stare at him—people didn't seem to have anything better to look at around here—and then he missed a church steeple by an adequate number of feet, it seemed to him; life was marvelous, he began to climb again, and finally he reached such a safe altitude that he asked himself whether a biplane could do a loop. There was only one way to find out and so he dived the plane and then pulled the stick back steadily and the nose went higher and higher, he was looking straight up into the deeply blue sky and then his back was pressing heavily against the seat, the plane was nearing upside-down position and he suddenly realized that he had not fastened the seat belt and was in fact about to fall out of the plane.

He was not at all frightened but instead supernaturally alert and he knew that if he let go of the stick to hold himself in the cockpit the plane might crash and as he began to slide headfirst out of the cockpit he held on to the stick and at the same time spread his legs, which were extremely strong, wide apart like an open pair of scissors and these wedged him part way out of the cockpit. He suddenly found himself shouting at the top of his lungs, a wild cry of despair or joy; his cry rang through the open empty sky and away into space, on and on further and higher, going forever; the nose of the plane slowly and deliberately began dropping back toward the farms and then Cleet abruptly slid back down into his seat and pulled back on the throttle. The biplane at last leveled off, and dizzy with conquered fear he headed back to the little airfield, thinking that this was his idea of what God intended Sundays to be: Keep holy the Sabbath Day.

The long shafts of late-afternoon sun poured horizontally across the countryside below in steady splendor; a transcendental light fixed cornfields and vegetable patches and manure piles into an aura of eternal significance; slim old trees at the borders of the fields acquired the venerable grandeur of ancient pillars and a large barn with "Chew Mail Pouch Tobacco" painted on it seemed a pleasure dome; a stream off to the left looked from above in this effulgent light as if flowing with honey and gold. Sometimes I don't see why people don't live forever, he thought to himself, and then recollecting the bottomless staleness of war he thought, but sometimes I do. He was beginning to come down toward the rich greenness of the landing field and curiously enough Alex Eubanks' prewar Nash was parked next to the hangar, or not so much parked as abandoned, since two of its doors were open. Landing was the part of flying they hadn't really gotten to in his lessons so far and as the ground came up at him he saw how fast he was going and that as a matter of fact landing a plane was like shoving a letter very fast into the letter slot since there was only a very short and narrow place at the beginning of the runway where you could touch down without overshooting and you had to get the plane exactly in there and any slight miscalculation resulted in crushing the letter against the letter box and then there was a screeching sound right under his seat and he was bouncing up and down in his seat and he realized that he was safely on the ground.

Alex Eubanks came fast across the field toward him. "Are you hurt? Is the plane?" he shouted as he ran up.

"Nope." Cleet was aware already that Alex Eubanks by asking first whether he was hurt had established himself as a rare human being, rare at least in Cleet's experience, and he vowed then and there, sitting in the plane in the twilight, to be a model employee of Alex Eubanks' from now on, if by any remote chance he still was his employee. Sitting quietly for a moment inside the biplane, he saw clearly, too late as usual, that he had just committed another of the stupidities he was famous for. He always saw them very clearly, and always too late.

He got out of the plane and Alex Eubanks settled his large frame back on his heels and said, "Well if you're not hurt you *are* the biggest goddamned fool and the nuttiest son of a bitch . . ." and Cleet closed his ears as the familiar roll call of his attributes began, his own particular styles and titles and patronymics, just as they had been recited by so many reasonable people so many times before. As this old refrain in all its richness continued his experienced ear did pick out the tone of voice and he detected that the final pitch of exasperation was missing, the B above high C was not going to be hit: Alex Eubanks in some pocket of his mind *saw* something in Cleet and in what he had done that did not totally displease him on all levels. Cleet had won a few eleventh-hour reprieves like this before and had come to understand why: a few people in this world in some mysterious way wanted him to live some outrageous part of their lives for them, some part they were too afraid or lazy or trapped to lead themselves. Alex, he sensed, belonged to this extremely limited group of people, and Cleet realized then that his job was saved. What a Sunday.

Alex Eubanks' rage ultimately ceased. They put the plane in the shed and locked the door. Cleet made a very sincere promise of reform. Night fell, and he fixed a meal in the cabin amid the shrubbery.

Later he was lying on his back on the lawn in front of the cabin, chewing on a blade of grass. The sky was very black and the stars were very numerous. The night sky had always pleased him because, as it happened, Cleet was the only human being who understood the night sky. Everyone else thought the heavens at night were black with millions of white specks scattered through them. Whereas the truth was, as he alone knew, that the heavens were a glorious blazing golden limitless cathedral of unending and eternal light, and the blackness at night was only a canopy drawn over the earth, and the "stars" were so many millions of holes punched into the canopy by the Big Ice Pick, to reveal speck by speck intimations of the limitless glory above.

In a way, that was why he was devoted to flying. If there was that unending glory above then flying was a way of reaching toward it, never attaining it of course, or probably, but at least *reaching*. That was all he asked for out of life, to be allowed to go toward those elements which gave it meaning and made it full of wonder. He knew that probably he would never arrive, any more than Columbus arrived in India, but at least he would set out, he had already set out, and many smaller and less remarkable discoveries lay ahead along the route, and even perhaps there would be, to be stumbled ignorantly upon, for Cleet Columbus Kinsolving, something someday equal to the discovery of America.

Columbus! That was rich. What he was much more like, he grumbled to himself, was one of those really stupid summer bugs which used to fly around the globe of an electric light at night on the terrace back in Wetherford, banging their tough little shells against it over and over until they fell stunned to the terrace stones, where somebody eventually stepped on them, or else they crawled over the hot globe, in ecstasy according to the amazing scientific experts who were able to announce positively how bugs felt and things like that, until they found a crack next to the socket, where they could crawl into the blinding, glorious inner core, the apotheosis and innermost transforming heart of bug paradise, where they were instantly incinerated, and dropped dead onto the bottom of the globe, forming there a small black ring of corpses, which grew larger with new seekers of paradise as the summer wore on. That, said Cleet to himself with the wave of self-scorn which sometimes overtook him, was more like what he was. Columbus!

The next morning he and Alex were checking the biplane's landing gear, working contentedly together, Alex having completely forgotten that this was the "goddamned fool" and "nuttiest son of a bitch" who never should have taken the plane up in the first place. A little later he remarked cogitatively, almost to himself, "Don't you have some kind of family somewhere?" He was examining the threads of a screw closely. "First discharged veteran I ever saw who didn't want to head straight home."

"Home? Of course I have a home, I sure do."

He certainly did have a home and a brother—both his parents were dead—and that definitely constituted a home. He had a home and of course he loved it, but the realization then dawned that it had not crossed his mind since the last time he wrote someone a letter there, which, now that he stopped to think, had been on Iwo Jima Island.

"Haven't you got a sweetheart at home, and some friends? Weirdest guy I ever met, you really are."

"Girl friend? Well there's my ex-wife but that is a different kind of category, isn't it. I haven't seen her since we got divorced, when I was seventeen, and I have one good friend, named Neil Reardon."

"Reardon, Reardon? Not the moneybags Reardons."

"Well, um, yes, he belongs to that family."

"Christ. What're you hanging around *here* for?"

Cleet drew himself up impressively, looked Alex soberly in the eye, and then said with mock authority, "I Wanted Wings."

"You never are serious, are you?"

"I want to live in fame or go down in flame."

"Should of got all that out of your system in the war."

"I want to go off with one hell of a roar."

"You've already done that."

"But I think I'll drop them a line."

"Don't they know where you are?"

"Uh, no, no, they don't."

"They probably got the FBI after you. They probably think you're dead."

"Well, no, I don't think so. See, they know me."

Cleet didn't get around to writing home to Wetherford the next day or the next, although he conscientiously thought of it and looked forward to the clearing in his schedule which would permit composition of such a letter, and then on Friday it suddenly and providentially became unnecessary because he found this surprising item in the local paper:

> Cornelius Reardon, son of multimillionaire industrialist Hugh Reardon and author of the current best seller *We're Home,* will speak at a student-faculty cultural mixer at Gifford College Tuesday at five. The young author is on a national speaking tour promoting his book, helping set up chapters of the Amvets Organization, explaining American membership in the UNO, and raising funds for Persian relief.
>
> The title of Tuesday's lecture is "Goodby, Dad." It deals, college sources pointed out, not with Reardon's father but with the "bankrupt values and flabby laissez-faire anarchy" of the pre-World War II generation in economics, politics and sex. Open to the public.

What was that saying: Everything comes to him who waits? Here he was, in the middle of the country, and Neil turns up not ten miles away. He was very curious to see Neil again and in fact he was highly embarrassed not to have gotten around to answering Neil's last letter, which he thought he remembered receiving in Japan. In general, and not for the first or second or third time, he had lost contact with home, family, friends, everything. There was probably some reason, probably a simple one, such as the fact that he had been happy, simply and entirely happy, here—had been? Not had been, he *was* and would go on being happy here. Why not? Of course he would. That was why he just hadn't happened to think of his best friend or of his home. Strangely enough he had thought of his brother, Charley, a number of times.

Now here was the first contact with his home after four years, *four years,* and he felt a kind of chill of excitement up the back of his neck to his scalp; four years when he had been so close to being killed so often that it had sometimes seemed a kind of automatic game, and life had often seemed a two-dimensional film about somebody else which he was watching, and peacetime life was nonexistent, never had existed and never would exist again, and somewhere in that fog of years, Cleet now feared, perhaps he had begun to let slip his belief, his faith, and his optimism.

And then, here, at this ridiculous airfield with this Alex Eubanks and that biplane, he had seemed to be gradually seeking out and slowly refinding all of those precious qualities of his youth which had begun to slip away in the fog of war across the world; roaming here in the middle of the continent in all of this space and openness he had been in some way regathering his used-up character. After all, he *was* part Indian. Pocahontas had died when they took her away from America, even though they treated her like a great lady in England. Cleet could feel how that must have happened. Some animals when they were sick went away from their herd and hid by themselves and just waited and either died or else finally got better, and only then did they go back to where they belonged. They waited until they were completely well and sound again.

Neil was coming on Tuesday. It seemed as though these animals sensed that they might turn rabid and do harm to others in their own pack, so they hid themselves away until they sensed that they were whole again. It was a kind of body fear, a fear of ruining themselves in their own place, of violating their own den, that drove them away. To be perfectly straight about it, Cleet was a little bit afraid of himself. Something tremendous within him was going to *have* to get out and express itself and *be,* after these four years of oppression and suppression and staleness and disappointment and frustration. For example, he had endured four years of being constantly in and around airplanes, and he had never been allowed to be a pilot. You are not good enough: that was what the Air Force had said to him all day every day of his military service. But here at Eubanks field, unlike at Chanute field and Sheppard field and Tokyo field, here at this little patch of airport he was good enough. The truth was that in the Air Force if he had taken a plane without authorization, frightened the countryside, done a loop, and then nearly wrecked it on landing, he would have been court-martialed and sentenced to approximately thirty years in prison. And here? Here his employer became angry for a little while. He could work the war-induced knots out of his character here without risk of getting thrown into prison and without risk of hurting anybody close to him. It was the first breathing-space he had ever had in his life. Milly or Alex or someone else here might suffer a few bumps and shocks, but he was not that important to them, they would not be hurt that much. His home and his own people would be safe.

Neil was coming on Tuesday. How do best friends react to each other after four years? In friendship one friend acts and the other reacts; four years ago Cleet had always acted and Neil reacted. But since those days of unquestioned following, Neil had gone into the Navy and quickly risen to the rank of officer (full lieutenant by the time he was discharged), been decorated for bravery under fire and for rescuing someone from the ocean and for an unannounced secret mission behind the lines in France. (Neil had completely mastered French since the last time Cleet had seen him.) There were also his book and his new fame. In the meantime Cleet had gone into the Air Force and quickly sunk to the rank of enlisted man, private most of the time, and had gotten through four years without being imprisoned or killed. How do friends behave after four years of such reversals? Who acted, who reacted now?

He was coming on Tuesday. That was very good news. Cracking his knuckles and squinting bleakly over this newly loved countryside, Cleet told himself again what good news that was. Seeing Neil would really mean that he was home from the wars at last. Cleet the warrior would finally be home: neither on his shield nor with it, unwreathed and with no booty, unsung and anonymous, on Tuesday the warrior would finally come trailing penniless home.

Gifford College, ruthlessly up-to-date Presbyterian, held its cultural mixers in the vestry of the campus church. Crossing the college grounds, Cleet realized that the buildings had exactly the same atmosphere as certain permanent military installations he was familiar with: featureless red-brick dormitories and heartless red-brick houses. From the outside the campus church resembled a red-brick airplane hangar, topped by a strange, shrunken, irrelevant steeple. Since he did not like or even understand most speeches, and since he remembered that Neil's graduation address had been long, earnest, and high-principled, Cleet waited outside through that part of the program.

He had been slowly getting more nervous all day, edgy in a way he hadn't been since his last mission under enemy fire. He didn't know how he felt . . . his mind roaming . . . home is the warrior . . . from the headland of Attica, the king kept watch for the sail coming homeward from Troy across the purple Aegean, standing before the columns of Poseidon's Temple emblazoned in the sun, watching for the return of his son's ship, the triumphant warrior . . . Cleet trailed up to the door of the vestry, which was all glass brick and linoleum, heard the subdued intermingling of voices inside, took a long breath—he had had his chance in the great world and wasn't bringing much back to show for it—and stepped inside. Neil, a taller, stronger, ruddier, better-dressed, and above all more serious and decisive-looking Neil, was standing in front of the glass-brick wall talking to a circle of people, and next to him was a rather tall, tanned, dark blonde girl—that would be Georgia—who, with her wide-set greenish eyes, alert, amused expression, and fresh good looks, seemed like trouble to him for some reason. She looked as though she knew a little too much.

Neil did not see Cleet coming toward him. He looked exactly the same and very different. He was reddish; his brown hair had reddish reflections, there was light reddish hair on his freckled hands, his eyes now had a more downward slope at the outer edges, his nose looked a little stronger than Cleet remembered it, his mouth a bit firmer. He was standing in a typically relaxed attitude, his hands in his pants pockets, his head cocked slightly to one side as he had held it all his life when listening closely and dubiously to somebody. Cleet was very touched to see him standing that way; he couldn't believe that four years had passed or that this encounter was happening now. He was so glad to see his oldest, closest, and best friend again. He stepped into the circle around Neil.

Neil Reardon had just thought that with no reporters here there was no point in staying any longer, trying to remember what time he had told the pilot to have the plane ready, noticing simultaneously that Georgia was getting better at talking to academic people and what bores they were one and all, and he had also been feeling slightly depressed by the smallness of the turnout and wondering who was responsible, when a movement just to his right made him glance that way into the opaque green eyes and yellowish-tan face of Cleet Kinsolving.

"Oh my Christ," he muttered shakily, almost in awe. He stared with an appalled expression on his face. Cleet smiled slowly and impassively back, and then said, "Is this the cultural mixer, or what?" Then Neil began pounding him on the back and Georgia exclaimed, "Neil, you're not running for any office, stop backslapping these nice—oh, it's, is it—not the Prodigal? My God, are you Cleet Kinsolving?" She had a wonderful, low-pitched voice, Cleet heard; I'll bet she's a bitch, he thought to himself.

"What's so amazing about it?" said Georgia in the hotel room. "You knew he'd turn up sooner or later. He always has, all his life, as you've explained to me. He's here. Fine."

"It's amazing because he's turned up at exactly the moment when I need him, very very badly."

"You?" she answered, her voice incredulous in spite of herself.

"You don't understand anything."

"Really?"

"For one thing, you don't understand money."

"I come from very poor people."

"And it shows. Look." He frowned at her. "How many friends do you think I've got?"

"I don't know. You—"

"One." He stared at her, letting that sink in. "And I'm lucky."

That night Neil, who had postponed his departure for Kansas City by twenty-four hours for this purpose, spent the evening with his old friend Cleet. They were sitting on the abbreviated front porch of Hirohito's Hut, bushes spilling over the railing toward them, crickets reverberating across the open fields, otherwise a country hush on all sides, and a bright Ice Pick firmament overhead. They were drinking an expensive bourbon Neil had provided. Cleet, knowing that the Mad Indian within him was always dangerous, sipped cautiously, but Neil drank steadily, which was surprising to Cleet. Neil had never drunk anything more than wine at his father's table in the old days and had always been swiftly scornful of people who let drinking have any appreciable effect on them. Tonight he was deliberately getting drunk. But something about the swiftness and excitability of it showed Cleet that this was not something Neil did very often; that he did it hardly ever; that, like everything Neil did, this was a calmly premeditated act.

"How is that job at that airfield? What do you do all day?"

"Answer the phone. Send out bills. Mail checks to the bank. Sometimes go up with Alex. Put gas in the planes. Call up the weather bureau. Drink coffee. Talk."

"Oh," said Neil a little defensively. "Sounds dull."

"Does it?" said Cleet in surprise.

"You don't know anybody around here."

"Sure I do. You know me. Getting to know people is one thing that comes easy."

Getting acquainted with people comes easily to you, Neil said ironically to himself in the inner contrapuntal commentary that habitually accompanied his conversations. You don't even know me, and I'm supposedly your best friend. "That's true," he said.

"I guess it is dull, though, compared to somebody with a big career started, like you."

"I don't know how big it is, or is going to be, but," he was turning his glass rapidly in his fingers, "I know it's a lot of work, a lot of details and arrangements, probably not very different from what you're doing at that airfield, when you get right down to it, except with a lot more variety." He cocked his head to glance at Cleet for a moment. "But it's so hard to find anybody to help, somebody I really know and can work with, an associate, so to speak, you know," he began stirring the ice in his drink with his finger, "not just anybody, not just some efficient stranger, but someone you know and have confidence in, and so on, it's very hard, as I said, and I don't know what to do about it and something has to be done soon. I'm paying two hundred a week, at the start. So," he leaned back and exhaled loudly, "do you want the job?"

"What do you need me for?" Cleet blurted, as though warding him off. That was why Neil had been drinking: to get the courage to make the offer. It had always been hard for Neil to offer anything, he remembered now, hard for him to issue any invitation, even to ask you to walk to the corner. That was how deep his fear and hatred of losing anything ran. "Seems like something Georgia could do," Cleet added.

"Georgia is pregnant."

"*What!*"

"I'm going to have a son." And then Neil's assumed indifference broke, and blushing to his hairline, he said hurriedly, "I can't believe it either," staring with dizzy, momentary delight at Cleet.

"Neil. Good God. Hmmm." And Cleet began cogitating on that mystery, continuation, flesh-and-blood renewal, immortality. And for one sliver of a second he resented Neil's achieving this miracle when he had not, although he had never resented Neil's officership or the medals or the book, and certainly never the Reardon money, in his life.

Neil went on. "So that's one reason Georgia can't do these functions I need you for."

"Ha! So you're offering it to Harold Phi Beta Kappa Kinsolving."

"You're no monument to literary learning, I admit. But there's one thing you have got. You're shrewd as hell." This, in a limited way, Neil believed to be true.

Cleet was pleased by this compliment because nobody had ever said it to him before and he thought that it was true; it was the one mental gift he really did have. He was thrilled to be at last recognized for what he was. To cover his pleasure he said, "Georgia isn't dumb."

"Well, no, as a matter of fact she isn't, she soaks things up like a sponge as a matter of fact. But she's too disorganized, too dreamy, too floating or something. She wouldn't work out. It has to be somebody I'm—close to, and who else is there?" Neil kind of mumbled this; if he had not been fairly drunk he never could have said anything that sentimental-sounding.

So there it was. Two hundred dollars a week instead of forty. Cleet took a deep breath and leaned his chair back on its two rear legs, his head against the front of the hut, staring at the slot of sky visible between the tops of the shrubbery and the roof of the porch. He felt deeply embarrassed and disconcerted. He did not want this position as right-hand man to his friend, and he did not know how to refuse it without mortally affronting that friend. He knew Neil.

"Boy that's quite an offer. I'm certainly going to have to think about my life and everything tonight. I sure am, what an opportunity! Whew. Uh, Neil, my God, your glass is empty, here, I'll pour in some of this twenty-year-old Bonded in Gold or whatever it is pure old Country Sour Mash Straight Mountain Tennessee Bourbon Whiskey and add one small ice cube and three eye droppers of branch water. There we are, and here's to, let's see, uh, your son and heir!"

Neil passed out at one-thirty in the morning, and Cleet carried him to bed and then went back out on the porch, sat down, and began to stare and think, hour after hour. He spent the rest of the night thinking, thinking, suffering and torn and wondering. While he was there fighting with himself the sky slowly, slowly altered from night black to a strange, haunted deep gray, and the jewel points of light gradually lost their luster, until as the generalized light in the sky came up all around them, they merged into the full fresh brightness of dawn. Nighttime wasn't any temporary black canopy pulled between the earth and the sky after all; there wasn't any endless brightness in the heavens: half of the time the sky was extinguished and dead, black as despair. The full early-morning sunshine flooded with an orange vividness all over the porch, marvelously vital and hopeful; in exhaustion Cleet blocked his eyes with his hand: half the time, as every idiot knew, the sky was as black as pitch.

At nine Neil woke up. Cleet heard a hoarse voice from inside the cabin growl, "Where is this? Who put me in this closet?" Cleet stepped into the hut and saw an uncharacteristically pale Neil looking out over the covers, baffled, blinking, stunned. Then recognition came into his expression, alarm quickly swept across it and vanished, alarm at what Georgia would say and at the disruption of his clockwork schedule, concentration appeared—searching for the quickest and most efficient way of fitting the pieces back together and salvaging the remainder of his schedule —and then his concentrated gray-brown eyes focused steadily on

Cleet as he recalled his reason for coming to the cabin, the reason he had had to get drunk. Immediately his expression cleared; he was forgiving himself for the lapse, it hadn't actually been a lapse at all. The night before, as usual, he had known what he was doing and why.

Cleet went across the highway and borrowed Alex's Nash, and drove Neil to the hotel in town. They said very little; both were thinking with all their strength. "I'll call you when I get through work, at five," Cleet said. He recognized that Neil was not leaving town, that all of Neil's plans were in suspension until he had Cleet's decision. He didn't need to be told that, and with an inner groan he recognized that it was just this instinctive understanding of Neil that made him uniquely qualified for the job.

In the hotel Neil immediately made two phone calls to Wetherford, Connecticut, and so a long-distance call from Wetherford was waiting for Cleet when he reached Alex's air-field. It was from his brother, Charley. Charley couldn't seem to get his breath during most of the conversation, so Cleet didn't find out much. "When're you getting here?" Charley just kept saying fast.

"You studying hard?" Cleet asked.

"Yeah," said Charley, "yes I am, Cleet."

"You'll graduate this year?"

"Uh-huh."

"Then . . . Mother Yale?"

"Mother herself."

"Boola."

"Cleet?"

"Um-hum?"

"When're you getting here, Cleet?"

A metallic female voice broke in. "I have an emergency call for Mr. Harold Kinsolving."

"Whew," breathed Charley. "I'm hanging up now, I'm going to hang up, will you be here tomorrow or what?"

The emergency call was from Mr. Hugh Reardon.

"Is this Mr. Kinsolving?"

"Yes, it is."

"This is Mr. Reardon's secretary?" Her voice took the Dixie

upturn; Neil's father always had charming secretaries from the South. "Can you hold on a second? Mr. Reardon's on the other phone."

There was a very long wait. Cleet was on the point of hanging up three times. If someone had walked by and accidentally nudged his elbow he would have, any tiny nudge would have been enough. But it would not have made any real difference; you did not get away from Mr. Hugh Reardon if he didn't want you to. Also, Mr. Reardon was impossible to argue against. Cleet braced himself. What had he to oppose them all with except a feeling he had about himself, a kind of dream, an aspiration, which might be just as fantastic as the glorious sky he had imagined eternally shining behind the canopy of night? What made him think that he, by staying away from home and old friends, could refind the fresh hope life used to have? What was the great attraction of forty dollars a week? Why did he have to be so obstinate? Why couldn't he just relax and let life be easy for once? Why did he always have to be rolling boulders to the top of a mountain? Who did he think he was anyway! What was all this Destiny crap! Columbus. Shit.

"Cleet, my boy, well we've got a line on you at last. Let me tell you—no, first, how are you, son? Are you all right?"

"I sure am, Mr. Reardon, and it's good to hear a voice from home." He meant that.

"I just talked to Neil and he tells me you never looked better. Except for a certain Japanese skin tone he says you picked up out there."

"Ha. Well now that's slowly fading away. I think I look more like say a Filipino right now."

"Good boy!" Mr. Reardon's clear voice semisang the words across the Eastern states. "Now, I'll tell you what, Cleet. Neil says he sensed you were a little hesitant over the job offer he made you last night—"

"Well I—it *did* come as a surprise!"

"Of course it did, of course it did. Tell you what. You and Neil and Georgia get in the plane and fly on here, and we'll get you where we can have a good look at you, and then we can talk it over rationally here and just see what would be most advantageous for everybody. How does that sound?"

"That sounds swell and I sure am looking forward to seeing you and everybody but the thing is, I've got this job here—"

"At the little airfield? Some kind of stunt flyer you're working for, isn't it?"

"No, as a matter of fact, it isn't. He does crop dusting."

"Cleet, if I'm not snooping, how much does he pay you? Don't mean to pry."

"Uh—he pays me forty dollars a week, Mr. Reardon."

An eloquently silent two seconds followed. "Cleet, I think the thing to do is to come on here with the kids. I know your father would have wanted you to do that. I'd like to go over your future with you, if that's all right with you. I feel—your dad was my good friend, and I feel I kind of owe him that."

There was a different kind of silence, and then Cleet said slowly, "I've been thinking about my future a lot. I've had a few ideas about that, or rather one main idea. It's about trying to start an airline carrying freight from Washington State to Alaska."

"That sounds like a very enterprising idea to me, Cleet, and it's the kind of thing I'd like to go over with you when you get here."

So there it was. It was settled and he knew it, and he was now afraid that if he left here he would never come back, and that once Wetherford got him he might never get away really, ever again. He feared that, and yet he had no escape route left because to evade going home now, after all this, would look completely childish or else certifiably crazy, and although he knew he was neither one, no one else would believe it, and he wouldn't be able to find words to explain why he urgently wanted to keep away from his home town, his brother, his best friend, and two hundred dollars a week. To disappear again now would mean that they probably would never trust or even respect him again, and while he couldn't bear to lose this freedom, he couldn't bear to lose their respect either. The trap was complete, the horns of dilemma were both razor-sharp, and at the end of the workday he wandered dully back to the hut. He had already called Neil. They would leave the next morning from the big airport, and he would be a passenger instead of a pilot once again.

He began to "pack." Although he had traveled halfway across the world and back, Cleet had never understood what other people meant by packing. To him it meant locating the nearest container and pitching his nearest belongings into it, hoisting the result onto his shoulder, and going. His duffel bag sagged dustily in a corner. Cleet put it in the middle of the room, opened the top, and began tossing in T-shirts, parts of Air Force uniform, the hot plate, the coffee pot, the iron, the atlas, and "Whistler's Mother." Then he sat on the sagging bed in the stuffy little room and looked around him. Small and hidden, right beside the transcontinental highway, snug and shabby and cheap, a discovery of his own, something he could afford—provided by neither the Air Force nor the Reardons—made to his own measure, very small and shabby and cheap, but still and all, an independent house, supported by him himself, right for him. He had loved it here, he realized now.

Alex came in, wiping his hands with a rag. Alex, in his shy country way, liked him, Cleet suddenly saw, which made leaving just a little harder. "Don't forget your discharge," Alex said, and Cleet remembered it and went to the bathroom, took it off the wall opposite the toilet, and tossed it into the duffel bag. "What about that map with the lines on it, showing where you've been?" Cleet silently took it off the wall. "And what about that?" He stepped back out the door and pointed to the hand-carved "Home Sweet Hirohito" plaque above it. "Oh yeah," murmured Cleet, going out, putting a chair under it, and taking it down. "Discharge insignia?" Cleet unstuck the Ruptured Duck from the wall. "Picture of the Jap emperor?"

Cleet gazed at it. "Hum-um. I think I'll just leave that there. Proves—I've been here."

Then he sat back down on the bed again and looked at his hands. Dusk gathered smokily outside in the stillness. Alex sat on the chair next to the door and said, "Why don't you write me a letter sometime?"

"Of course, sure."

"Tell us what you're doing with the millionaire crowd."

"Uh-huh." Cleet looked up. "But I'll be coming back."

Alex wiped his hands some more. "Let us know how you're making out. Well you got to get on with that fancy, careful packing of yours. So long, Cleet, you're all right," and Alex went out.

When it was completely dark Cleet went out and crossed the highway to the airfield. He stood for a while in front of the little hangar, and then, unable to stop himself, he punched the door again and again with his right fist: *I'm making a mistake!* he cried to himself. *I'm making a mistake!*

"What in the world happened to your knuckles?" Georgia said as they took off at 8:02 the next morning in the Reardons' B-18. "Did you have to *fight* your way out of the sticks?"

"That's just from a minor accident I had last night, while packing. A box fell on my hand." It was the first lie Cleet had told since leaving that compulsory and routine forum of lies, the military service.

The B-18, the only one ever made, had been bought from the government as surplus a few months before by Mr. Reardon. It looked very much like a two-engine version of the famous B-17, the *Flying Fortress,* so it had been named the *Flying Folly.* The two engines were very businesslike and powerful. Inside, the plane had been refurbished to suggest a subdued but modernistic Wall Street law office, beige and gray and mahogany, with thick, upholstered chairs, each safety-belted as unobtrusively as possible; there were two berths, a toilet, a small galley, and a seat directly behind the pilot from which Mr. Reardon customarily interfered with the piloting and navigation.

Part of Neil's success came from the exceptional concentration of energy he could assemble for a particular end. Now that he had succeeded, now that Cleet had been persuaded, Neil felt overcome with exhaustion. As soon as they were aboard, he collapsed in a berth, his face pushed into a pillow, and fell profoundly asleep. Georgia, dark blonde, more full-bodied-looking today in a yellow summer dress, turned with a shining smile to start talking to and getting to know the legendary Cleet. Instead of letting her do that, as soon as they were airborne he said "Excuse me," got up and went forward, through the cabin door, and took Mr. Reardon's thronelike seat just behind the pilot. The Reardons' prewar pilot, fat, sweaty old Arthur, whom Cleet had always liked, had been demoted to copilot of this big new plane. The pilot, named Paul, was newly hired and appeared to be about Cleet's own age. That briefly infuriated him, so he did not talk much to the pilot, and the pilot made no effort to talk to him, concentrating on the instruments and the radio with a kind of smooth professional coolness which further annoyed Cleet.

In front of Cleet's chair there was a tall, narrow table, and built into it was a map of the United States, with the flying lanes and other flight information on it. Sitting there was the next best thing to piloting the plane himself, since his seat was a little higher than the pilot's and he could see past him out into the sky, over the instrument panel and down to the map, where he followed their route.

It was a clear-blue day, although there were clouds piled up through the sky at intervals; the plane picked up the better prevailing west-to-east tail wind and began to sail across the Middle West, homeward. Homeward finally he was wending, and in style, it had to be admitted; not every dogface arrived by private plane, with two pilots manning it, and a unique, prototypical, plushy private plane at that; not every serviceman was delivered in this fashion, and wasn't it some kind of favorable omen after all that he was arriving so handsomely? Wasn't this the keynote of his future peacetime life after all, speed and style and efficiency?

Far down the sky, off to starboard, a little one-engine plane picked its lonely way between the bastions of clouds. For a second Cleet thought it was Alex's biplane, and then he saw that it had only one set of wings, and anyway it would be physically impossible for Alex's biplane to have traveled so far so fast.

The *Flying Folly* continued along the Chicago beam, then on toward Cleveland, rolling up the continent hour after hour, the big engines whipping the air past them and droning along in slightly varying pitches, the sun lighting up all the sky and clouds, and gradually the timeless feeling of long flights settled over them.

They refueled and flew on up Lake Erie toward Buffalo, the pilot detouring there to give them a good view of Niagara Falls.

"Neil, wake up!" said Georgia, shaking him. "Come and look. It's Niagara Falls down there!"

"Hm? Oh. Come here." He kissed her. "Our honeymoon at last," he said with a faint smile. They had not had time to take one. Then he went back to sleep.

The plane continued across New York State, over the Catskill Mountains, then the canyon of the Hudson River, dank and majestic, was below them, and then they began to sail down upon the valley of the Connecticut River and Cleet's stomach commenced to tingle in a disturbing way, as it used to when they had set out on certain missions in the Air Force; they came over Hartford and he looked dizzily down on it; it looked exactly the same except unbelievably smaller than he remembered; he had often seen it from the air before going away and it had looked like quite a metropolis then; now it all looked shriveled and narrow and miniature, a junior, provincial little city, which could be dropped into, for example, Tokyo and disappear without a trace; they continued down the Connecticut River, a neat, curving stream, blamelessly banal, and then there was Wetherford, a tiny swatch of a place, terribly recognizable—the Green, the Congregational steeple, the Town Hall—Good Lord, the Reardons' place, formidable and fortresslike from the air; there was the Country Day School, intact and toylike, with all the ashes of his youth in it; the football field; there were the trees and that was the lawn and those were the chimneys of his own home, miraculously preserved through four years by who knew what Act of God, there were all of the streets and all of the trees and all of the memories, as though his life were stung like pennants from tree to tree; how small it all was, he could never squeeze back into it, never; the spaciousness of the great plains he had just left recurred to him; the pilot was completing the approach pattern over the little Wetherford Airport, and then they started into the final glide, toward the runway. It was going to be all right and he was going to make all of them happy and someday, by God, there would *still* be a way of making them proud of him. He was standing just behind the pilot, trying to take it all in, pointing things out to Neil, who was standing beside him; the pilot had already said, just too laconically to suit Cleet, "Passengers will fasten seat belts for landing," just too coolly professional in tone, too chicken-shit for Cleet, who had had four years of that, under compulsion to obey; he went on standing where he was, noticing with satisfaction that Neil, in the old way, thoughtlessly went along with his action. "Don't you want to sit down and fix the safety belt—" the copilot said; Neil said at the same time, "Well, welcome home, pal!" patting Cleet cheerily on the back. Cleet had been leaning forward trying to see the field better and as Neil patted his back Cleet lurched forward against the pilot's shoulder; the plane's nose abruptly dropped, then swerved to port and the plane struck the runway at an angle, the landing gear snapped; Cleet was smashed against the instrument panel and the plane skidded crazily down the runway, the inside of the pilot's cabin filled with an immense clatter and from the rear Georgia, strapped into her seat, screamed, "The *baby!*"

Cleet was lying on the floor of an airplane. Neil was next to him, scrambling to his feet. “Whew, my head,” Cleet said. “What time is it?”

“I don’t know,” Neil snapped.

“My head,” muttered Cleet. There were two men strapped into seats above him, looking distracted. There was shattered glass on the floor and his left hand was cut. “Whew, my head,” Cleet repeated. “What time is it?”

“I don’t know,’” Neil answered, or seemed to answer.

It was very important to find out what time it was because Cleet felt disturbingly unsure of exactly what and where and how and when everything was.

“Are you hurt? Get up!” one of the men, old Art, said, and started pulling him to his feet. Cleet couldn’t think what he was doing lying on the floor of the Reardons’ plane. Not only that. The plane was definitely bigger than before, definitely bigger. Well, it was puzzling and disturbing. “Art,” he said, “will I ever make a pilot?”

“Christ,” said Art under his breath, pulling Cleet to his feet. Through the window of the plane Cleet saw the Wetherford runway; so then today really was the day Art had said he would take Cleet and Neil for a flight. Since Cleet had never been in a plane before, this was certain to be a great day.

Just below the short nose of the plane, through the invisibly whirling propeller, Cleet saw the wide lane of tarmac rolling faster and faster under them; a sense of openness spread on all sides and then the nose rose slightly and the plane laid itself on the air.

Flying; he was flying. The propeller in front of his eyes, whirling so fast he couldn't see it, was pulling them up into space. The tops of trees were just below them now; the hangar of the airport was turning into a doll's house, the town was becoming a relief map, the Connecticut River was long and thin, not short and wide, after all; the sky was—limitless, and the freest place Cleet had ever imagined. Limitless space was everywhere. Another miraculous thing was that while space was invisible, it was also solid: the plane banged along as though over mounds of rocks. Strange, marvelous flying: what could not be seen, the air, felt like rocks, and what else could not be seen, the propeller, held their lives in its invisible power: strange, marvelous flying.

Art, sweating steadily, had leveled off at about a thousand feet, and with a sidelong glance at Cleet, who after all did not yet even have his license to drive a car, and not saying anything to Neil, who was in the rear seat, reached into his pocket for his pipe and said, "Take the controls for a minute while I light this thing."

Cleet's hands sprang to the wheel. The nose of the plane, at the impact, started slowly downward.

"Pull her up a little," Art murmured, holding his pipe, and pointing with his other hand to a gauge on the instrument panel. "Keep her on that line." He turned and gazed out the window. Art had had a feeling the boy was a natural, from the way he handled himself, and was curious to see whether he was right.

Cleet vibrated with unbelievable waves of power pulsing up from the incomplete circle of the wheel, through his arms, up to his brain, where they collided like champagne. It was as though the inside of his skull had become the Sistine Chapel, for instance, indelibly set with marvelous inner masterpieces. They were traveling at one hundred and fifty miles an hour and the power of the plane's engine overwhelmed him, but only for the first minute, when he had driven the nose down. Now it did not overwhelm him; it challenged him as a bull challenges a matador, but he thought, untrained as he was, that he had a bare chance of being able to handle it, just able, by means of absolute concentration, to handle it maybe.

"We're changing course two degrees," drawled Art. "We're on eighteen now. Put her on twenty," and he waved vaguely at the compass, indicated the rudder pedals at Cleet's feet, and left the rest to him.

Changing course. Changing course. A drop of sweat ran down his side.

He then relaxed his grip on the wheel. He relaxed it because he sensed that the plane and the engine were powerful, but like certain girls he knew, they had a tendency to overreact; using only two fingers of each hand he turned to the left, to port, and the needle of the compass began to move off eighteen, but away from twenty, not toward it. The compass operated the reverse of what he would have expected. He then turned to starboard, pushing down the right pedal by instinct, and the plane curved in a, to him, extraordinarily beautiful tilting turn. Art was sucking inquiringly on his pipe. Neil could be felt holding his breath. The turn was bringing him close to twenty and he believed that he had better start to pull out now or they would go past it. But the nose: was it too far down or too far up? He began to make the plane straight and level, realizing that flying was like patting your head and rubbing your stomach at the same time, complex coordinations were required; it was three-dimensional, solid geometry.

The plane was on course at twenty degrees exactly and the nose was on the horizontal.

"Uh-huh," said Art.

Now Cleet's head was almost delirious, with millions of tingling atoms, all silently exploding, but he kept his hands lightly on the wheel and his eyes moved with steady regularity from the compass to the stabilizer to the sky ahead and around. The sky was a washed blue with ivory streaks of clouds high in it, a boring, aimless, thin sky he had always felt it to be, before now.

From the rear seat Neil at last exploded in an enormous exhale of breath, and cried, "For God sakes! You're flying this thing! *You are flying this machine!* You are—" and he went into shrieks of out-of-control laughter. "Oh my *God!*" he said helplessly, rolling around in his seat. ". . . Pilot . . . oh . . . no!"

"Yes," insisted Cleet a little thickly, "yes, I am."

"What?" said Neil irritably. He was standing in the door of the pilot's cabin with a girl—Georgia, that would be, his yes, his wife—and then he took Cleet by the arm and they started back through the main cabin of the plane, a chaos of cushions and broken cups and shattered glass all over the floor, through to the door, where Neil quickly jumped down to the ground; the plane was off the runway, on some grass; he helped Georgia jump down, and after her Cleet jumped out of the door onto the grass.

"Well, we made a shambles out of it, all right," Neil said. "The *Flying Folly*. Pretty appropriate."

"Was I flying it?" said Cleet.

"Of course you weren't flying it," said Georgia. "What's the matter with you?"

"But I didn't ask Alex for permission first. In the Air Force I'd have gotten a general court-martial for a mess like this."

"It wasn't your fault," said Neil shortly. "I must have knocked you off balance. It was an accident," he added irritably. "Here comes the fire truck or something." He put his arm around Georgia. "Thank God there wasn't any fire."

"I turned off the ignition before the crash," said Cleet.

"You *what?*" said Neil.

"Darling," put in Georgia in a private tone to Neil.

"Look at that fire truck," said Cleet. "I knew they were the ones to call, in a flood like this." He noticed Neil staring fixedly at him, so he added, "All right, freshet. But this year it looks more like a real flood."

Cleet was always pleased, every year, by the freshet. "I'm *glad* we don't have a river wall in this town," he said to Neil. Swollen by all of the snow disappearing up the valley, through Connecticut and Massachusetts, and far into Vermont, the river threatened to flood Wetherford every spring, but the placement of the town had been cannily calculated to keep it just out of reach of the highest freshet. Hooker Avenue passed along the river side of the Green and then went on to the Wetherford Cove. The last house of the street nearest the Cove known simply as the Old House, dated circa 1730, had not been touched by the annual overflow since circa 1730. In the spring the town complacently watched the waters start the seasonal rise; everyone was complacent that spring except Mr. Reardon, who got back from

Switzerland in time for Neil's fifteenth birthday and made his remark about the extra strength in the river. Neil and Cleet thoroughly enjoyed the swollen river, fished in it, and spun around in its currents in the Reardons' outboard boat. "I really like this time of year," Cleet kept saying.

The point was, Wetherford was open. Any year the river could sweep right through the whole town, round up everything, including the Reardons' court-tennis court, and leave nothing but a field of mud behind. It was the most exciting natural fact in Cleet's world, and every year he tried to urge the river on a little, refusing one spring to take baths because he assumed they lowered the level of the river. He hoped that some year all of the snow all the way up to Canada would melt at once, in half an hour, and he imagined himself on the roof of his house, being the first to sight across the treetops a cliff of gray-green water unrolling down the valley toward the town; when it slammed against his house, the house lifted and went sailing away with himself astride the roof, picking favored townspeople out of the flood as he went by.

Cleet couldn't get over the wonder of his town's lying so open to this force of nature; it almost reconciled him to the churchly veneer of the place and to some of his other antipathies, such as the prevailing bone structure of Wetherford women—Gothic—and the prevailing tone of Wetherford voices—flat. He was pretty much reconciled to it all by the river's swirling madly past every spring, flooding pastures and fields and farmland, outlying land and river-lining land, flooding up to the very step of the Old House on Hooker Avenue some years, where it always however stopped.

The Old House was a non-color, a kind of sand-mud-clay-dung color, clapboard, with pinched windows, a low door, and a short chimney, as though all squeezed up before the annual ordeal of facing down the river. Like the Wetherford Elm it was historic, ugly, and something simultaneously to be proud of and ashamed of. Someone had used it as headquarters during the Revolution, so of course it could not be torn down. No one wanted to live in it, and while the historical society dithered over the financial implications of acquiring it Mr. Reardon typically and impatiently bought it himself, and then left to settle a managerial dispute in his iron-ore holdings in Labrador, leaving the question of what was to be done with the house in suspension, as the waters rose toward it.

His son and his son's friend knew what you did with alarming old houses; you slept in them, of course. Cleet lay in the upstairs bedroom, listening to the main current of the river sliding by behind the house, and the waters of the Cove in front lapping away regularly close to the front. The house itself felt like a boat, and finally he fell into a delectable sleep of bliss at the insecurity of it all, and stayed soundly asleep all night. Neil, however, started into full wakefulness several times. In the morning the waters seemed no closer.

Two nights later they decided to stay there again. Since Neil had slept badly the first time and had studied until very late the night after that, he was exhausted and fell asleep on the couch downstairs. Cleet slept upstairs in the dusty four-poster, and he woke in the middle of the night to hear the water slowly moving the furniture around in the living room below.

Cleet hurriedly ran downstairs and woke up Neil, whom the water hadn't yet touched. The river was rising at a disappointingly slow pace, but after all, it had reached a historic new high-water mark, so it seemed to them logical to call the volunteer fire department, which anyone could do by going to the fire house and ringing the bell—which they did, and then went back to the Old House. They were vigorously defending their action against the irate words of the sleepy firemen when it became clear that the river was beginning to rise again, much more rapidly, and from being two false-alarm delinquents Cleet and Neil were quickly transformed into Paul Reveres.

Quite a few river-bordering families did in fact owe if not their lives at least the saving of many possessions to them. Five houses were destroyed that night, twenty-seven buildings were damaged, and quite a few animals drowned. The Old House, which turned out to be tougher than anyone had imagined, was flooded and filthy, but it was still there. The town decided that only a Reardon investment could possibly have turned out to be so solid.

The flood receded, leaving behind mud, silt, and a form of smalltown cosmic indignation. Wetherford was exposed, defenseless against a force of nature which, any mindless May, could eradicate it. It was an insult; it was vulgar; it had a kind of Mississippi-Missouri Valley crudity and Midwesternism which sat ill with many people. Wetherford had just not been made for such experiences. Not only that; there was nothing anyone could do because the clear logic and economics of the situation forbade building a river wall against a flood which had come only once in two hundred years. It would be extravagant, unrealistic, and showy. Probably the river would never flood again in the lifetime of any one of them. Still, the damn thing could come in the front door any springtime, and all the powers of the Wetherford Board of Selectmen, the Sovereign State of Connecticut, and the United States of America put together couldn't do anything about it.

An unsettling sense of the twilight, compromising, no-solution iron rule of life asserted itself through the town. That feeling was deeply resented.

Cleet Kinsolving alone in Wetherford liked the idea thoroughly. He was living in a life-and-death ordeal with the Connecticut River. It was the one thing he really liked about Wetherford.

The fire-truck driver and the man with him were talking to Paul and Art and examining the damage. Two other people were hurrying across the field toward them. Cleet gradually recognized Mr. Reardon and then gradually saw that the other person was his wife, wearing a white rolled scarf across the middle of her head and tied at the back of her neck, her gray-white hair hanging through it, just the way she always had. Mr. Reardon, in knee-length white shorts and a cap, looked exactly the same, tall, strong, and determined.

"Is everybody all right?" he said when he got close enough. "You are, are you? Never mind about anything else. We'll get you home. Call me this evening at six," he said to the pilot with a flat glance. "The car will be here in a minute. How are you, Cleet. Ah—welcome home," and he scowled.

"Children," Mrs. Reardon had been muttering, brushing Neil and Georgia. She turned to Cleet. "There you are. Wait till—"

"Here it comes," said Mr. Reardon, seeing the blue and gray Cadillac moving stealthily across the field.

The four Reardons and Cleet got into the car. "Now just be calm," Mrs. Reardon said with quiet tenseness. "Just stay calm, all of us calm. Thank God we're not having any hysterics. How do you feel?" she said, scanning her pregnant daughter-in-law's face.

"I'm perfectly all right," said Georgia airily. "I was strapped into my seat like any normal person would be, and so for me it was like riding a bumpy speedboat. Except for the horrible noise, that did scare me, that unbelievable racket. My God."

"Yes, thank God." Mrs. Reardon closed her eyes for a moment. "Thank God no one seems to be hurt, and there was no hysteria." She squeezed Georgia's arm for a moment. "No scenes."

"Did you ever cry, Mrs. Reardon?" Cleet asked.

"Why, not really, not since I was a little girl."

"Sometimes it's a good thing to cry. I'll tell you something. That's the trouble with Neil, he never has cried in his life. Have you? He's all dried up inside," added Cleet. "I think you dried him up. What was it you said to him?"

"We are not emotional people," Mrs. Reardon said to Neil when he burst into tears on finding his dog dead in the driveway. "Remember that."

She was disappointed to have only two children. When the first child, Geraldine, was born, she was just Mrs. Reardon on Hooker Avenue; a few years later she was hugely rich Mrs. Reardon, chatelaine of High Farms, on the outskirts of town. It was difficult to know how life should be lived during such a sudden and drastic change. At least she had not let her husband move them to Newport or Palm Beach. She had resolutely stayed in, and been the social leader of, Wetherford, Connecticut, which she understood, and which had to understand her. All her life money had been a very scarce good, to be conserved. Then suddenly there were these floods of it; she didn't understand.

"Money is an opportunity to serve," Mr. Reardon said to Neil. "And money is a temptation to other people to try and use you. What you have to learn is to use money, not let it or anybody else use you. Remember that."

Neil earned his first bicycle by working with one of the yardmen, weeding. His allowance was set by his parents on the basis of how much Cleet got from the Kinsolvings, whose annual income was on an entirely different plane from theirs. Neil went to the public schools until the ninth grade, when he entered Wetherford Country Day School.

Mr. Reardon had thought about a large preparatory school for him, but for once dutiful Neil was like stone. He declined to talk about it. He would go nowhere to school except in Wetherford. He was frightened to leave familiar surroundings, so wordlessly afraid that he defied his father. Mrs. Reardon, believing that his wish to stay in Wetherford sprang from love of home and family, took his side, and he stayed. But his father had his way in essence, as he always did. The point was that his son must have the finest education available. So he quietly arranged that the faculty salaries of Wetherford Country Day School should rise to about what an associate professor at Yale University received, and the school quickly became brilliantly staffed: the little place began to get national attention.

Neil entered Country Day School with his ideas about life fixed. He did not think people liked him for his money; he didn't think they liked him at all. He was right. But he didn't care, because he saw them all as his rivals. Life was rivalry. That belief had become as much a part of him as his skin; he seemed to have been born with it; in fact, he inherited it strongly and directly from his father. It had been in the house with him all of his life; it shot through most remarks Mr. Reardon made; it was the assumption underlying every family decision. Life was rivalry. Mr. Reardon had shown to his own satisfaction that this was true, because by acting on it as his basic assumption, he had gathered up so much wealth so quickly. Therefore it had to be true. Therefore his son Neil had to understand it as soon as he could understand anything.

But in Neil's case the principle had to be applied differently. Mr. Reardon's rivals had tried to prevent him from making his fortune; Neil's would try to take the fortune away from him. "Look for people's real motives," Mr. Reardon often counseled him. "I don't say you can't *trust* anyone. No," he repeated doubtfully, "I don't say that."

"Another thing," he told his son once, "remember that life is time."

"*Life* is *Time*?" exclaimed Neil, who at sixteen was determined to be witty. "I thought *Life* was *Fortune*."

Unblinkingly Mr. Reardon brushed that aside. "Don't waste your life, that is, don't waste time." Among the leading time-wasters, Mr. Reardon impressed upon him, were people who "aren't going anywhere." They were one reason Mr. Reardon found in the end that he preferred having Neil at Country Day instead of at one of the big, or even worse one of the small, New England private schools. Those institutions were full of fledgling time-wasters of the first magnitude, real professionals. He was pleased to have Neil educated among the simpler natures the town produced. It was like so many things in Mr. Reardon's life; even when decisions went against his will, they turned out for his benefit.

If Neil was really going to be equipped for life he could not be sheltered, not even during the wave of kidnapings of wealthy children in the 1930's. There were no private detectives, no shuttling him from place to place in closed cars, no nursemaids skilled at jujitsu, no bars on his bedroom windows. There was a burglar-alarm system, but as a boy Neil never knew it. He was allowed to hitchhike to California with Cleet. He worked in a lumber camp in Oregon; he did surveying in northern Canada. He skied and broke his leg. He hunted, and Cleet once mistook him for a deer and nearly killed him. Mr. Reardon heard about that but was undeterred. He was building a tough young man and there were bound to be risks involved; Neil was taught to box by a professional.

His outlook suddenly solidified during his late teens. People expected Neil Reardon to be a soft, spoiled little millionaire's son who didn't know anything about life; and just because of their attitude he was going to know more about life and to be tougher than most people. Not all multi-millionaires' sons were befuddled Lord Fauntleroys, as he would show the world.

By the time he was eighteen he simply assumed that all people felt as he did and were better for it: that they relished a good battle of wills or muscles or anything else. It was the healthy, American way to live. When he encountered people who had little or no sense of rivalry, he ignored them and thought them pitiable, and probably un-American as well. When he encountered people who met his rivalry with an answering rivalry, he felt sure he could defeat them and set out to prove it. So he had no friends, except his peculiar, unlettered, shrewd, erratic, dreaming, lifelong pal, Cleet.

His complexion got ruddier during these years, and his rather slight frame acquired harder and harder muscles: he was creating himself.

"You're hard as nails," Cleet said as the car neared the center of town.

"So's my old man," said Neil out of the side of his mouth.

"So that's what keeps you from getting hurt. I wish I was, then I wouldn't get hurt either."

"Did you get hurt after all?" said Neil. "Where?"

"We'll have to repair the plane," Cleet commented. "Do we practice today?"

"Practice? Repairing the plane?" Then Neil noticed that they were passing the football field of Country Day.

"Christ, I hate this town," Cleet said angrily. "Always have hated this cold, cold town. Lousy light here most of the time, and it makes everything look gray. As if all the blood was drained out. There was some Jap music I heard in Tokyo that sounded the way this town looks, tinny, no guts or anything." He talked on in his low-pitched, rich voice. "The funny thing is, I had a feeling I got *away* from Wetherford. I always did want to live someplace far away from this town. I never have liked it. And you know, I thought—it must have been a dream—that I went clear over to the other side of the world, to the *Orient,* if you can believe that, and all kinds of other places, and then I finally wound up living on the great plains and working around airplanes and learning to fly and I was going to have an airline to Alaska and," he turned on them the sudden flashing smile he used to have, "it was *paradise,* just like paradise. Boy. Well, it certainly was a great dream I had when I must have been asleep." He turned and continued staring raptly out the window. The others were looking cogitatively at him.

The big car careened onto Hooker Avenue, passed the Congregational Church, going eighty miles an hour, and shot along beside the Town Green, where a few people momentarily looked startled, then recognized it as one of the Reardon cars and looked calmer: the Reardons had their reasons.

"You'll be home in a minute," Georgia said to Cleet.

He looked at her. "Married. Hmmm. Neil is married, and what was the other news?" He frowned in puzzlement at her. "You're going to have his baby, isn't that it?"

"Why—yes, as a matter of fact, you're right. I certainly am."

"God willing," murmured Mrs. Reardon.

"Yes, sir," Cleet said, looking sharply at her. "You're going to bring Neil Reardon, Jr., into this world. I'll be damned. Who would have thought. Let's see now." He stared blindly out at his home town shooting by, leafy and crowded by nature in the fullness of summer, streets tunneled through motionless explosions of green trees, fields spilling out weeds and crops, windows wide, awnings protecting front porches like a hand shading eyes from the sun, making them secretive and shadowy retreats, pools of coolness; on a porch like that, sitting night after night on a glider which squeaked, he had courted a girl named Evelyn Hunsaker. When they were seventeen they ran away and got married. The marriage was quickly annulled by her parents on the grounds that it had never been consummated, which was, in view of his and Evelyn's honeymoon at Virginia Beach, the craziest legal fiction of the year.

The year before that in the springtime he had enlisted in the Marines, but his true age had been discovered and he had been sent home. He once puttered down the Connecticut River in a fourteen-foot outboard motorboat, crossed Long Island Sound, rounded Montauk, and been well out into the Atlantic Ocean before he was stopped by the Coast Guard. That was when he was twelve. His father had suddenly died a month before, leaving him with a stunned sense of emptiness, abandonment, and guilt. "Harold," his mother had said shakily, "why in heaven's name did you do such a thing?" He had said, "I wanted to see what was out there." At thirteen he went to New York for a month; he found a job as an usher in a movie house, and lived in a room in Brooklyn Heights, and enjoyed the swimming pool in the St. George Hotel. In all of these experiences he was helped by the fact that he had always looked a good deal older than his age. "*Why* did you run away?" his mother had demanded. "I didn't run away," he answered. "I went to New York."

"That huge city. A child alone in that huge city."

"I wasn't *alone*. There are I don't know how many million people in New York City."

"But, darling, they were all strangers to you."

"No they weren't. There was Fred, who had a motorcycle, and Preston and Harriet and the waitress—"

"But didn't you ever miss us? Darling?"

"I did miss you yesterday, so that's why I came home."

The spring he was fifteen he fell in love with a cross-eyed girl, and the following winter he plunged his mother into knots of fury, exasperation, and moral confusion by giving his sheep-lined winter coat to a tramp he saw shivering beside the Highway, near Wetherford Center. Also when he was fifteen he had the first of his many car wrecks and his first sex experience with a woman: she was a secretary at the bank, twenty-three years old. He flunked his first course, English, and his second course, mathematics. When he was sixteen he appeared in his first school play, *The Admirable Crichton,* playing the servant who emerges as a natural leader when his employer's family are trapped in a primitive land, and gave an original, convincing performance, which surprised him and everyone else. Cleet had no notion of acting technique; he simply believed every word of the play and thought it was all true and happening there on the stage. He had another car wreck, still while driving without a license, and great influence had to be brought to bear to keep him out of serious trouble. After that he promised not to borrow the family car or any of the Reardon cars until it was legal. He and Neil were members of the football team at Wetherford Country Day School. He flunked trigonometry and French. Some girls and women began acting nervous when he walked into the room. Cleet thought it over and decided he must have bad manners if he upset women that way just by walking in, so he tried to improve them. A little later at a large dance he realized his mistake by the way they danced with him. He was sexually excited throughout the dance and that embarrassed him horribly.

When Cleet was seventeen his brother, Charley, was eleven. Mrs. Kinsolving was always being surprised by Cleet, but this did not lead her to think there might be something wrong with her basic conception of him, as a mindless, troublesome boy with some nice, endearing sides to him (whom she loved as all mothers loved their children, of course). Instead she felt when he did something to surprise her, which was constantly, that was an exception.

To Mrs. Kinsolving's surprise Cleet was all patience and gentleness and affection with his noisy little brother, sometimes going to bed at nine o'clock to persuade Charley to go happily. Mrs. Kinsolving was surprised to find a kind of diary in Cleet's desk one day that year, which was full of self-doubts and big questions: "I've got this feeling I'm going to blow up if I don't find some answer." "Love has to be forever, doesn't it? I know I can love forever but can someone love me forever?" "You have to be good for something in the world and what am I good for???" "Did it ever occur to you that you don't just get everything for nothing? You don't get *anything* for nothing. What are you good for, Crazy Indian, old pal?" "There couldn't be a God because he would never allow Phyllis Morrison to be lame *and* cross-eyed, since she happens also to be very good and religious. So that's out and Who is there to talk to? Neil? Neil doesn't get excited enough about things to be able to talk to him." "I have no place to turn and just have to rely on myself and try to make it somehow." It surprised her that Cleet had ever had such thoughts. It was so surprising that she forgot it. Mrs. Kinsolving died of a brain tumor that winter, surprised right up to her last moments by this son of hers, whose grief was so much wilder than she would ever have expected. A preoccupied relative in New Haven became the two orphan boys' legal guardian and handled the dwindling inheritance, which maintained the Wetherford house for them and did very little else. In theory there was no housekeeper; in practice Miss Ethel Reardon, religiously inclined spinster-relation of Neil's, looked after the house and the Kinsolving boys as one of her Corporal Works of Mercy.

Cleet had two love affairs with older girls that winter, which he found terribly exciting at first but also terribly demanding. They seemed to think he was inexhaustible, which he seemed to be, and he didn't like their attitude toward him. He didn't feel they really appreciated him for himself. "Charley, Charley, come here, Charley," he said, lying flat on the floor in front of the little fireplace in his bedroom one afternoon that winter. "Do you think there's going to be a war?"

"Sure."

"It'll be exciting, right?"

"Yeah, very exciting, and I hope it starts soon."

"With parades and guns and uniforms and airplanes."

"Wow. I can see it's going to be *something*. When'll it start, Cleet?"

"Not too long from now. I think I'm going to try to be a pilot."

"That's *swell*, Cleet. Will you take me up in your plane?"

"Sure I would if they'd let me. And if they wouldn't let me, I'd take you up in my plane anyway, when I come home for a visit."

"Hm?"

"I'd get to come home and see you for a visit before I went to Europe to fight the war."

"Went? You mean went away?"

"Well, to the fighting, yes."

Charley twisted his shoelace around his index finger and after a while he said, "I don't think they're going to have a war." He twisted it around his little finger. "Not for a long, long time." He untied his shoe experimentally. "Maybe never."

"There's your brother in the yard," said Georgia.

"Charley," said Cleet to himself, a grin slowly widening on his face.

His brother was mowing the front lawn. He resembled a gross enlargement of the Charley whom Cleet had left, that cleverly put together little person with the big eyes and small hands, quickness and frailness; this crude parody of his little brother made his way across the lawn toward them, tanned and tall, brown-haired instead of blond. "Cleet!" it said in a startling voice, and opened the door of the car with a large hand. Cleet realized that this person incorporated his little brother in the way that the whale incorporated Jonah, and that he must act as though he were able to see Jonah still, and not show by his expression that he was staring at the face of the whale. "Hello, kid," he said, getting out of the car. "Hi."

Charley grabbed his duffel bag from the chauffeur, and Cleet stood staring at his home. "It's a small house," he murmured.

Charley stood in front of him, flushed with excitement and trying to say seven or eight things at once. Cleet continued to look at this tanned stranger, a nice-looking young man, well made, but the size of these hands and ears and nose, where the features of his little brother had been drowned, continued to disconcert him. "You're looking very well . . . Charley," he managed to say to the person, who then burst into a very wide smile, and in it, there, unmistakably and at last, his brother signaled to him. He was still there alive inside after all, and Cleet immediately caught Charley around the shoulders in relief and said, "Yeah, you look great, great, you big giant."

The Reardons were making small and hurried farewell sounds, and their car shot backward out of the driveway as Mrs. Reardon was saying to Georgia, "I realize you're perfectly all right, but I'm going to have Dr. Funston come by, just to—"

Charley said, "Cleet, what do you want—are you hungry? —what do you want to do first? Take a bath maybe?" Holding the duffel bag with one hand, his other arm around Cleet's shoulder, Charley headed them through the front door.

"Do you want a nap? Do you feel like going for a ride? I've got my license of course and I could show you what's happened around here in four years, how the town has changed. There's some alterations on the Country Day School and there's a lot of new houses out at Rocky Heights that they call a 'development,' whatever that means. A lot's happened in four years."

"Four years?" Cleet looked with a vague smile at his brother.

"A lot happens even in a little town like this in four years. You'll see—of course where you've been will make all this seem like nothing. So taking a ride is out. Dumb idea I had. Listen. You want a beer? What about—"

Cleet stood immobile and vague in the middle of the living room, clenching and unclenching his hands and looking slowly around him. "Four years?"

"I'll bet you missed it a lot, even though you didn't write very often and stopped off in Kansas or wherever it was . . ."

"What?" Cleet sat down in a rocker, next to the very large fireplace with the kettle on a movable arm inside it. This room had been the big kitchen in Colonial days. "My head."

Charley stared at him in sudden full alarm. "Cleet," he said very uncertainly, "is there—did you get wounded and not tell anybody . . ."

Holding his head in his hands, Cleet said nothing.

"I didn't have any idea the Reardons' plane would get you here so fast. It's some kind of surplus bomber, isn't it?"

"Is it? Whew. Sit down. Listen. I think I might sort of black out in a minute."

The front screen door slammed and in a moment Miss Reardon, tall, lean, aquiline, with short gray-black hair, wearing as always a colorful shawl, came briskly into the room and saw a yellowish young man clutching his head beside the fireplace. It was several seconds before he looked up and the green eyes hanging in his face finally identified him to her as Cleet. "Well, my prayers really are answered," she ejaculated with a sigh as she came toward him.

Cleet stood up and kissed her cheek. "Here I am," he said in his full voice, looking closely at her. "You look quite a bit older but I hope you're all right, Miss Reardon."

"Oh Cleet of course I'm all right and I don't care whether I look older. Maybe I'm wiser too." She looked narrowly back at him with her nervous black eyes. "Are you, I wonder."

"Me?" He nodded his head sardonically and stared at the floor. "Oh sure, of course."

"Well I wish we'd been forewarned about when you were really arriving. I would have had this house looking like something. Let me see what I can do about it now."

Miss Reardon at heart was a nun working for the welfare of others; however she felt herself too eclectic intellectually to take the veil and too closely related to Hugh Reardon to become a professional social worker. She had found a satisfactory compromise in sustaining the household of her old friend Mrs. Kinsolving, in a steady but informal way. She did not really believe in the existence of the Reardon fortune. She behaved like an impoverished schoolteacher, surrounded though she was by Cadillacs and private airplanes and privilege, and that made her seem saintly, self-abnegating, and a little mad.

Miss Reardon opened the glass side door and they went out onto a brick terrace. From it a fine lawn sloped gently down to a line of eight arching, splendid elms in full summer bloom. On the lawn a spray slowly rotated, flinging curtains of water over the shining grass. Cleet stopped in his tracks and took a deep breath. He murmured, "What a wonderful smell," and then sat down in a canvas chair. "I forgot there was a smell like that any place in the world. You know what?" He fixed his level green gaze on Miss Reardon's face. "I *am* glad to be home. Yes."

"Well," she laughed edgily, "I'm certainly glad to hear *that*."

"I'm very surprised to find it out. I don't get it. It seems like I haven't smelled that, you know, cut green grass lying around with a spray going over it, in a long time, isn't that funny, I have this funny feeling I haven't smelled that in *years*."

"I don't suppose you have. Where would you have?"

He gazed fixedly at her for a long time, and then clenching his hands in front of him he looked down at his feet, then inquiringly at her again, flushed suddenly, and finally, haltingly, he was able to say what he feared to say: "I have to tell you. I don't know where I've been." He stood up in his moccasins, suntan pants, and T-shirt, his level green eyes staring at her out of his still faintly yellowish face. "Have I been away?" Miss Reardon's hand went up to her neck. "I remember a funny thing, that I was living someplace and I didn't have a name, I had a number! I can even remember my number—11128886." A look of alarm broke over his face. "Christ, have I been in *jail?*" His widened green eyes searched hers.

"Harold—" her voice breaking.

"How old am I?" he asked, his features screwed into an intense grimace, as though from a sudden, deep physical pain. "What year is this?"

Her hand was tight on her throat, as though to choke off a cry.

"What am I doing here?" The expression of his face then opened again. "Oh yeah. Alex Eubanks. The biplane. All that sky out there. Let's see, yes," he looked grim again, "Neil, his wife, going to have a son, yes." The impassive, Indian look had come into his face.

"Stop looking like that," she said in a metallic tone. His mother had ceaselessly tried to train this Indian way of looking out of him; she felt it her duty to persist and was very disappointed that the four intervening years had not done it for her.

"My—you mean my Indian look?" he said with a little smile.

"That stupid way of looking you used to have."

"My Indian look" he repeated, and then leaning back, he shouted his Indian war cry across the manicured lawn toward the Colonial street.

"Stop it!"

Cleet suddenly looked baffled again. "This is the silliest town in the United States of America. It wins the prize. I always did know that and I don't know what the screw I'm doing here. Can anybody tell me?" He scratched his head in genuine bewilderment. "Even since I was a kid I've tried to get away. I even started in a motorboat to Europe. And I still haven't gotten away."

He stood up again and faced Miss Reardon. "Indian women are strong," he murmured, "they don't shake. Squaws don't have nerves." Then the ever-increasing lightness in his head seemed to rise higher and higher in it; there was the sense of a white and heatless flame glowing inside his head more and more brightly, so blindingly that in a few seconds the remaining ties to the outside slipped away, receded further and further until, while he could still see fairly clearly where he was, he felt that there was nothing at all holding him to it, he felt that it had no meaning and that he had no relation to it, that something was not real, the tall older woman standing, swaying in front of him was not real, and the tall tan boy standing next to her wasn't real either, and neither was the theater-set with the fake elm trees behind them, and the silvery, tinsely thing glittering on the phony grass was typical cheap theater, it was all fake and he would walk away from it except that he suspected that everything surrounding them was equally fake and that if he attempted to step off the doubtful solidity of the brick terrace under his feet the imitation grass might give under him and he would sink into it up to the knees with one step, to the hips with the next and then . . . besides the lighting was so bad and glaring and colorless, white as a shroud; it was very doubtful, the solidity of these surroundings, and because he was doubting it, it began to fade: once questioned, it began to evaporate, and it was becoming clear to him that within the next few seconds the tall woman and the tall boy were going to drift away and then the bricks under his feet would start crumbling and as he sank he would drag into the pit with him the fake grass and the house and the sets, pulled down the hole around him like a rug; it was all giving under his feet now and it was time for this to happen because he did not know who he was and neither did anyone else and in fact he was not anyone and therefore he could not think or move or exist.

"Catch him!" he heard the strange woman cry to the tall boy.

II

HIGH FARMS

Very slowly, a long time, it seemed, after that, he felt himself rising from this holocaust to the plane of things again, very very slowly and hesitantly an energy was being rekindled inside him, like the first twigs catching sparks among cold ashes in a chilled grate, until the point was reached where he had the capacity to open his eyes again and find that he was lying in a bed in a room.

The blinds were pulled down, but they were white and through them some of the daylight outside penetrated in a grayish glow, and by means of that much light he set about the laborious task of slowly separating what was real in his field of vision from the specters and shades and projections that still hovered, although more and more insubstantially, around him as he lay in the bed.

It's very still here and that's a good thing because it gives me peace to think for a minute. If nothing happens to disturb this room I'll be able to put things back in place inside my head.

Let me see: this is a large bed and there is nothing government issue about this mattress, so I'm not in any barracks any place. It could be a hotel but that's a fireplace there and I don't think I know of any hotel rooms with fireplaces. This is somebody's house somewhere. A room this size and this solid doesn't seem like a place in the Orient or the Pacific—I think I—a room this size and this solid!—there's a desk past the foot of this bed, two windows along this wall and two next to the desk—this is my bedroom.

He turned on his side to look at it in the dim light and the sheets hissed ominously at the movement, the springs creaked in a loud and sinister way, and also the walls, solid-looking though they were, seemed to threaten to fall outward and leave him dangerously and precariously exposed to whatever lay behind them. He lay motionless, breathing the bare minimum, waiting. Then he realized he had better feed his brain something before it turned on him.

When was I in this room the last time? It must have been about a year ago—1938—no, it couldn't be; let's see, the war broke out in 1939, and then there was Pearl Harbor, in 1941, and we went into the war, and so this must be about 1943 now. Christ, I can't remember. This room, this room; it's a nice, quiet good-sized room, with the little brick fireplace and that tremendous old mirror over it that never did reflect right but was always kind of misty. It's supposed to be some kind of antique. Long white curtains; all this white; you'd think I was some kind of virgin or something with all this white. Everything certainly is neat here. Of course, I used to like this room because yes this bed seemed just like a boat and a one-man airship and I could go off down the river and then sometimes take off and fly—I was really learning to fly not very long ago, that's right, not that imaginary schoolboy stuff, but really learning to fly real planes, and then—if they hadn't pulled that blind down I could see the tremendous tree outside the window there, and the hills through the other two windows. Still that same white wallpaper with the blue design. The things I saw in that design! Where's the Indian head, where is it, where? Is that it, that the forehead and those things the feathers? Yes, that must be it. Where's Mae West? Mae? Mae! Why I do believe that is your hourglass figure right there, isn't it, and not an inch thicker in the waist, and not an inch thinner in the hips! And after all these years—these—how many I don't know, years, or months. Christ. Here I am, in bed in Wetherford and going out of my mind, and I can't even remember how old I am and how I got here. Slowly going—I have to be, what else could it be—right out of my mind, around the bend over the falls to Nut Town. I've got to not shiver like this, not shiver. I'm not some little brat any more, I'm—I'm over twenty-one years old. Yes. It certainly is lonely and cold and everything here just now. Uh—sweating—hmmm—this room is uh lighted by an unpretentious but very interesting chandelier in the middle, consisting of six upside-down glass cups, frosted, with a design on them, supported by six yellow metal arms. There is a reading light just over my head, fastened to the top of the bed, and in the corner diagonally across the room from me there is an upholstered rocker covered with red and green cloth, with an upholstered footstool, and a brass floor lamp behind it. In the corner past the foot of the bed is the upright desk, with a fluorescent desk lamp. There is a wooden bench beside the far wall. And that's all, that's all, and all of the lights are out, and I'm alone in my old boat, going no place . . . Funny, I nearly landed where I wanted to go, I remember the fields and a silo and a—biplane—I nearly landed there for good, made my way by myself in the world as I wanted all my life to do. I never was any good at the Ivy League routine around here, *I* wasn't the type to go to Choate and Mother Yale, I wasn't, that's all, I'm a *slow learner* and that's the way it is and nothing can be done about it and no tutoring will help and so I knew this, I realized it without realizing I realized it when I was twelve years old, and so I started in that boat to Europe. And I've been trying ever since. The thing is, here in our great land of opportunity everybody's got it all figured out how to get *up* in the world, rags to riches and all that log-cabin-to-White-House story, Horatio Alger, but the problem for me and quite a few others who come from Real Good Families, real country-club Ivy League folks, well when you've got those fathers and brothers and uncles, then *how do you go down in the world* and not break everybody's heart and not wind up bitter and thinking what a failure and a disappointment you are, and thinking you're better than the people around you down there, *down* in the world, where you belong. Choate and Yale! There's Cow Horn O'Connor, of course, who is not Albert Einstein and *he* got through college, and there is Stud Murchison who to this day I'll bet doesn't know whether "h" comes before "j" in the alphabet and who never conquered decimals, and *he* got through. I guess I could have majored in sociology like everybody else and taken the course in Cowboys and Indians and the one in

Pots and Pans and probably gotten through, but who wanted to waste four years? Even if there hadn't been a war—a war—the war. The plane with the holes in it, like a piece of Swiss cheese, and still flying. The Japanese—u-h-h-h-h-h. Could this be—no—no of course it isn't—my legs, they're there, they're normal, I can close my eyes, yes and open them and turn my head, look I can spit, ptooui, right on the floor, real live spit. So relax, relax. Take some deep breaths slowly, easily and normally. That's right. The bed is comfortable and clean. Room's quiet. It's your own room, so just light up the pipe of peace and take it easy. You're home. Doesn't that make you feel good? Yes okay never mind, I'm sorry I asked, forget it. Still, there's no place like it: home.

Neil Reardon drifted gradually through the window toward evening. He made his way by slow stages across the room and stood finally next to the bed, contemplating Cleet. He was thinner and younger than the last time Cleet had seen him. They stood staring at each other for a while, and then Neil said slowly, "Are you going to be all right?"

"Yes," Cleet heard his own voice as though from a distance, "I think so."

"I don't want any invalids."

"What?" Again his own voice sounded muffled and vague.

"We haven't got any patience with invalids, you know that."

"I don't expect you to take care of me. I can always take care of myself."

"That's a good thing. People should be able to take care of themselves."

"I can always take care of myself," said Cleet.

"Do you trust me?"

"What?"

"Is your truss free?"

"I'm not wearing a truss."

"Oh, I thought you were. I thought you were an invalid."

"No," Cleet tried to say firmly into the funny blur and echo, "no, not at all."

"That's good. Don't be. We don't like that."

"I'm all right, I'm going to be okay, it's just that I'm tired or something and it's almost gone now and you can take it easy as far as my condition is concerned and count on me to be right there on the job and to do whatever is needed to earn the money. I want to have a place and stand on my own feet and have respect, like everybody else."

"Well, good luck," said Neil in his level voice, and then he slowly withdrew across the room and faded through the window and disappeared.

Later Cleet heard many times repeated the infernal apocalyptic clatter the plane had made skidding across the Wetherford Airport runway, Georgia shrieking and the unbelievable complex of noise, like all the world's kitchens collapsing at once, and he felt himself pitch headfirst between the pilots' seats toward the instrument panel and then there was a fundamental change in the world.

Not mad, sweet heaven, he prayed like Lear, which had been his part when they read it out loud in school; not mad, he murmured breathlessly to himself, okay, sweet heaven?

Ah—on the floor of this room there is a very interesting rug. First of all the floor itself is made of very old, hard wood and the boards are very wide because that's the way they made them in the eighteenth century, when this manse was built. We had some visitors once from out of town, and they asked who built it, and Ma answered in a sort of casual way, "Our people." I believed everything I heard then—hell, I *still* believe everything I hear—so I said, "You mean the Indians?" and I never saw Ma turn such a strange color, scarlet, I thought she was having a heart attack, but finally she recovered and just said, "Go out and play now," which I did, and I suppose she kept on giving those people the idea that our Puritan Colonial ancestors came over on the *Mayflower* and marched right from Plymouth Rock to here and started building so that there'd be a roof for the grand piano and all the hoop skirts. What crap. Some people here are trying to be so Colonial they ought to wear wigs. Wetherford did happen to be founded fourteen years after the Pilgrims landed on Plymouth Rock, and it is old; a lot of the houses are very very old, so Ma and everybody sitting around the old fireplaces and looking as the ceiling beams start growing ancestors, like potatoes, buy some old painting and put it over the mantelpiece, and right off like that they have a brand-new ancestor! What the hell, I don't care, I just felt embarrassed for her.

After all, though, everybody else in town does it and the funny thing is that I don't believe there's one family in any old Colonial house that inherited it. Things aren't like that around here: this town is full of old houses and new families. It might as well be the latest suburb of Los Angeles. Things changed, times changed, land changed, children died off, money ended, people moved to Iowa, the old shipping business died, an aircraft industry came—real Colonial—that's the way it is. All these people are like kids dressing up in costumes and playing games with each other. But I don't care. I wonder who did build this house. I wonder who made those wide floor boards. Maybe Ma was right; maybe it was one of "our people," some ugly old squaw.

I wonder if I am going a little bit nuts, lying here. I wonder. I wonder. I'm afraid to say the word "wonder" one more time because it's beginning to not have any meaning in my mind, it's starting to echo like some reverberation in it, some empty, stupid sound, a car tire blowing out, something empty, very very empty. I wonder.

Uh—yes, I have talked about the floor boards but not the rug yet. Yeah, the rug is I think what you call a Navajo rug, which I bought myself when I went out West with Neil in 1939. It's the only thing that has anything to do with Indians in this house. It's quite a few colors worked together—dark red and blue and brown—and it looks good in the middle of the dark wood floor and the white walls and the dark red-brick fireplace with the huge misty mirror over it in a gilt frame.

A plane, sounding like a single-engine fighter, a P-51 Mustang to be exact, could be heard circling widely around the house. Cleet had been hearing it for some time but had tried to ignore it, since he strongly suspected that the plane was looking for him, and his ear, attuned by four years in the Air Force, was just as nearly certain that the plane was circling in closer and closer; he could hear with exactness the radius of its pattern decreasing as it circled ever closer to the house and to his bedroom and he visualized its sharklike fuselage and the machine guns, coming in on him for some unknowable reason, bearing a charge, an indictment, against him for some act he had committed or else some crucial duty he had left undone during his four years of service, this aggressive new fighter plane carried some dangerous postscript to place at the bottom of the discharge from A.A.F. of Sergeant Harold Kinsolving 11128886, one final military penalty sent after his retreating figure, being delivered to him personally by some pilot-officer in a new, implacable fighter-pilot regiment, soulless company, arbitrary platoon, ruthless squad, grinding down on him with that strong engine and those accurate controls because of something wrong and impersonal and unforgivable which he had done or left undone during those four years.

The fighter plane got closer and closer, until the infernal rattle of its propeller just beyond the walls of this bedroom grew almost impossibly loud and he expected to see the propeller slice through the wall and start cutting giant swaths in the blue and white wallpaper.

Cleet lay back in the bed, sweating steadily, and then he knew that he had to pull together every tattered scrap of force and will power left, that in another few moments it would be too late; he assembled everything he had in him, and then he said quietly and firmly to himself, This is some kind of illusion or dream, there's no plane out there—and instantly its clattering motor grew thinner, the authority went out of its mission, it seemed to veer off over the trees, circle once or twice well away from the house, and then dwindle little by little as Cleet unwaveringly pursued it with his disbelief, renounced its reality minute by minute, until at last it faded off from himself and the house and the town, into extinction.

He shuddered, and much later on, when he had at last battled all the shadows and specters and tidal waves of feeling to a halt, he fell asleep.

Dr. Funston came early the next day, diagnosed Cleet's trouble as a mild concussion, the effects of which had now faded. He ordered him, however, to stay in bed for the time being.

Georgia came to see Cleet later that morning. She wore a summery light-yellow dress. The weather was ideal New England midsummer outside and as it drifted in through the windows its balmy air gave Cleet a sudden sense of well-being. Things were not really so bad after all. He was not going crazy. He had just banged his head somehow when the *Flying Folly* crashed, which was why it had functioned even more peculiarly than usual. Now it was as clear as it ever was, and it notified him that the accident had one meaning: he should never have come back to Wetherford, never have accepted the job, never have left the little hut he could afford and the job that was right for him. The crash had been an omen.

It sure takes a lot to get something through *my* head, he reflected as Georgia strode around the room, inspecting it and explaining that Neil and his father would arrive soon. "My sister, Lynn, is visiting us but since you've never met her, I said she couldn't see you in bed. Mother Reardon would never approve." An airplane had to crash to get something through my head, he repeated to himself ruefully. Well, it was an omen. Even he couldn't mistake it. *Don't come back to Wetherford* was its meaning.

"It's nice of you to come and see me," he said to her. It was easier to tell a woman bad news—and his immediate departure from Wetherford really was bad news for the Reardons, for some reason—because women were more elastic than men, more elastic especially than Reardon men. Maybe she would help him, maybe she would know how to break it to them. "Uh—Georgia?"

"Yes, Cleet?" She sat down next to the bed and looked smilingly, perhaps a shade mockingly, at him.

"I sure am sorry about that accident."

Why had he said that! That was for the pilot to say, not for one victim to say to another.

"That's all right," she said rather expressionlessly.

"I sure am sorry," he was furious to hear himself repeat.

Her face assumed a rather set smile and she nodded a little.

"I don't know how it happened," he added. What a stupid remark.

She looked faintly surprised and then said, "Neil says he hit you on the back or rather as he puts it, he 'tapped' you on the back and you suddenly went headfirst over the pilot's shoulder and into all the buttons and levers and things. And then we crashed. He says he was surprised you lost your balance so easily, since you seemed to be standing, you know, very solidly—"

"I didn't see him about to touch, I mean hit, me and I must have kind of jumped, you know the way you do when something startles you . . ."

"And all of a sudden you were all over the cabin and the plane of course crashed."

Cleet, to his amazement, felt his brain congealing into a state of pure rage. He looked at her with the level, unwavering, daunting glare which in his boyhood had been labeled, with a measure of uneasiness, Kinsolving Eye, that is, his Indian look, and in a constricted voice managed with difficulty to say, "What are you trying to say?"

"What would I be trying to say?" she answered in a higher, smoother, semisurprised tone, gazing it seemed to him with a kind of fake wide-eyed innocence back into his glare.

"What would I be trying to say!" he mimicked in a savage murmur.

"Yes," she said more assertively, "what would I be trying to say?"

"Get out," he rasped at her. "Get out of here! I can't stand insinuating females! Why don't you come out and accuse me!"

"Accuse you of what?"

If she gave him any more of that wide-eyed innocent act, he thought he might hit her.

"Out. Get out," his eyes shut with rage, "go on. Out."

Georgia stood uncertainly next to the bed, not nearly as furious as she thought she ought to be. Her husband's best friend had just ordered her out of his house for no reason at all, but she was far more puzzled than furious. She continued to stand next to the bed, looking closely down at this enraged man. Outside in the morning sunshine the birds had never sung more cheerily. Georgia thought her way along what had been said, and finally she found herself having to ask in a quiet tone, "Do you think you caused the plane to crash, Cleet?"

He looked up at her aghast for an instant, then fixed his opaque green eyes on the far wall in front of him, as though listening intently for a voice from anywhere to tell him the answer to her question. He began shaking his head slowly. At last he answered in a dulled voice, "I don't know. I don't really know." He stared vacantly at the sheet over his knees. "Do you? Does Neil?"

"I wasn't in the pilots' cabin, I didn't see anything. I don't have an opinion. Neil is—just, well, puzzled."

He closed his eyes. That's it, he said with quiet finality to himself and almost, strangely enough, a sense of relief; that's it. I wanted to stop myself from coming back here so much that I caused the crash. I tried to stop myself at the very last minute possible. That's what the ignorant Indian inside me did. Cleet then without a second's hesitation abandoned his plan to leave Wetherford. This was perhaps the fastest, and by far the most painful, decision of his life. But he saw no other course. The blunt force of life inside him had made a monumental mess. He could not smash so much and then walk away from it.

He decided on this severe penance; he also decided, however, that he was not going to be a martyr. He looked up at Georgia in a new way and said evenly, "It was an accident."

"Of course," she agreed immediately, smiling brightly. He didn't think she believed him; but also, perhaps irrationally, he thought that she wouldn't mention her suspicion to anyone else.

Then they began to talk rapidly about hairbrushes. There was one on the little table beside the bed. Georgia said that flexible bristles were better for the follicles, and Cleet said that firm bristles stimulated the blood circulation in the scalp. Georgia said that she liked a handle on a hairbrush, while Cleet said he liked a brush designed to be gripped on the top, like a bar of soap. Georgia complained that when she was overseas with the U.S.O. she had lost her brush and been unable to find a suitable replacement there. Cleet agreed that in foreign lands first-class hairbrushes were few and far between. "What kind of hairbrush," he at length asked in quiet desperation, "does Neil use? I can't remember."

There was some commotion downstairs, and Georgia, looking relieved, left this question unanswered. Neil and his father were coming up the creaking old stairs. Cleet smoothed the sheet over his legs several times with his hands. The two men came through the low door and began making the standard Reardon bedside jokes: hearty, denigrating the patient, and embarrassed. They acted that way because they instinctively considered any physical incapacity pure selfishness.

The two men sat down on the uncomfortable wooden bench on the far side of the room and looked expectantly across at him. Bald, firm-faced, slightly pink, broad-shouldered Mr. Reardon, in a tan summer suit, sat with his forearms on his knees and contemplated Cleet optimistically. Reddish and reserved, Neil in polo shirt and slacks looked at him more soberly. Sitting side by side, father and son for the first time appeared to Cleet to be partners. They had never been that before the war. But of course now they were no longer older man and adolescent, now they were two married adult millionaires. The distance between them had narrowed tremendously. They looked as though they understood each other and co-operated with each other, now. They made a formidable combination. "You're looking well," he said to them, idiotically.

Neil smiled very briefly.

"How are you feeling, Cleet?" Mr. Reardon asked.

"Okay, fine. They want me to stay in bed for a couple of days though, I don't know why." He rubbed the stubble of his beard. "Mr. Reardon, I want to ask you, how much is the plane damaged? Is it a wreck?"

"Not a wreck, no, not a wreck. The damage is . . . extensive, and we may have trouble getting parts for a prototype like that, but we'll work it out."

"It certainly was a freakish accident," began Cleet in a hearty voice, "and I certainly had a part in it, which was very clumsy of me."

After a short silence Mr. Reardon said, "I'm firing the pilot."

"You are!" Cleet sat straight. "I wouldn't do that, I don't see why, I mean naturally it's for you to— Oh."

"Do you think I'm doing the wrong thing?" asked Mr. Reardon in what seemed to Cleet a careful tone. It was very unlike him to consult someone else, especially someone of Cleet's humble status, about any decision of his. "Why no, I don't *think* so, not at all, it's for you to decide, Mr. Reardon."

"He should have made sure you boys were in your seats, with belts fastened. He was in command. He lacks authority. I'll find someone better."

"It was mostly . . . our fault," said Neil quietly.

"No, no," said Mr. Reardon in a judicious tone. "If he can't keep order in the plane it's his fault. He doesn't belong in the job of captain. I'll find someone better."

"How much will it cost to repair?" asked Cleet, choosing to

have all the shocks at once, in a timid voice which infuriated him.

Mr. Reardon laughed once. That laugh meant that it would cost a great deal, and Cleet's misery went even deeper. "I'll make that my first project, to help in any way, ordering the parts and things like that, for instance."

Neil was looking at him analytically; then he said,"We can talk that over when you're up in—did you say two days? Fine. Rest. You look terrible, like a Jap prisoner of war or something. Come on, Georgia, Dad," his manner becoming pleasant and superficial, "get better, boy. You look like a Jap prisoner of war. Yes, helping find repair parts for the plane might be a good way for you to start, that might be appropriate." Cleet glanced almost fiercely up at him. "Because you like working around planes, don't you," said Neil with a small smile.

That's it, said Cleet to himself as the three of them went out the door. He knows.

Two days later Neil Reardon drove in his habitual uncompromising, competitive style along the Highway, which circled through the outskirts of Wetherford, past the automobile showrooms with their multicolored pennants flapping in a summer breeze, and their salesmen, the most loathed and feared tyrants of 1946, comtemptuously baiting customers within, past the diners, the still-functioning blood bank, the gasoline stations, which had gasoline again, the drive-in movie, the drive-in hamburger stand, the drive-in ice cream stand, the Highway furniture store, the Foodarama and the A & P, the Exhibition Snake Farm, the motels, the real estate office, and the miniature golf course, past the driving range and roller-skating rink, to the traffic light at the intersection of the Highway and Broad Street, turned right into Broad Street, and in a few yards he had left the Highway, with its impersonal postwar links and relations from Maine to Florida, behind; all its thin, shiny connections up and down the Atlantic seaboard disappeared, and he entered the old part of town.

He drove rapidly down the shady street to the Green, which had once been the center of Wetherford, before the Highway took over, but was now a dreaming backwater. The Green was about four blocks long and two blocks wide, a sweep of silken grass with a small pond near the center and also an ancient graveyard, punctuated with seven stately elms. On all four sides, facing the Green, there were houses, none newer than 1800, all set well back among protective lawns and trees. The Congregational Church, immaculately white wooden Colonial with its virginal white steeple pointing simply and firmly toward heaven, also faced the Green.

At the far corner of the Green, its pride and climax, there was the Wetherford Elm. It had been planted about 1700, and while the surrounding groves and forests were cut down or killed off, this elm continuously spread more widely, its six major branches rising powerfully out of the trunk close to the ground and arching out further and further until their great shadow covered a circle with a circumference of five hundred feet. It seemed an umbrella of natural security and permanence, an elemental monument to their presence there on the Connecticut River, a presence which the tree proved—since it had been planted by an early settler of the town—had not begun yesterday and was not likely to terminate tomorrow.

Neil's car sprang impatiently around the corner next to the elm, and out of the corner of his eye he perceived something unusual about it; all of the leaves on the outer half of one of the great branches were discolored, unhealthy-looking, were, it seemed just possible, as a matter of fact, dead. Death on part of one branch of the Wetherford Elm; it meant, inevitably, that before very long the whole great tree would die.

There was a drowsiness filtering down through the high, thick motionless trees, settling around the ancient red-brick houses with extravagant doorways; there was an archaic stillness about the mummy-dry wooden houses, such as the Swayne-Strickland House, 1668, the oldest in town, mud-colored, with its overhanging second story, a last attenuated speck of medieval London architecture which had been put up in this wilderness and survived, a final faint echo of the Plantagenets on the Connecticut River; over the perfect lawns, where patches of sunlight drifted, there hovered this archaic feeling of bare survival, an antiquated hollowness and brittleness, as though only the countless coats of paint held the old wooden houses up, and simple inertia kept the brick ones together; all of them were scrupulously cared for and lovingly preserved, but as with senile people, no amount of fussing over them alleviated their distant indifference and their complaints.

Neil continued along State Street under its covering of branches and leaves, making a small detour this way so that he would go past the Webb House; the Webb House, in this town which revered the past, was the holy of holies.

George Washington slept there, for not one but five irrefutably documented nights. In his own handwriting, in his diary for May 19, 1781, he wrote the famous triptych: "Breakfasted at Litchfield, dined at Farmington, and lodged at Wetherford, at the home of Joseph Webb." The house, capacious Colonial, white and close to the road, was there, and it at least bore no sign of blight. Washington had not simply slept there for five nights during some routine week in the culminating stages of the Revolutionary War. He had held a series of conferences in the Webb House with the commander of the French troops in America, the Comte de Rochambeau, and his aide, the Chevalier de Chastellux, and they had planned then the final, victorious campaign which ended in the Battle of Yorktown, the Treaty of Paris, and the creation of the United States of America.

All the same, this town means something, Neil said to himself. There's more to it than just old dead things.

He drove on parallel to the river, to High Farms, the Reardon family estate, on a bluff above the river.

Neither Neil's mother nor his father nor Neil himself felt comfortable amid ostentation, but the property seemed to have a generative life of its own, one small new wing requiring two larger ones, a little kitchen garden needing a large flower garden to screen it, and that needed piped-in water, which logically produced a small, and then a large, fountain, the fountain compelling sculptured figures, and these had to be set off by shrubbery and trees and landscaping, and then the fountains and sculpture had to be screened from the garages, so that a gigantic privet hedge sprang into being, elaborated by the gardeners into a labyrinth.

It had all started as a big old Victorian country house with two working farms attached to it. Then the original house had been defaced and a countryside Gothic stone exterior put in place. First Mr. Reardon and then, as he grew up, Neil became obsessed with physical exercise, so that a very large addition, faced also with Gothic stone, had been added to accommodate these interests: two squash courts, a gymnasium, a golf practice room, a tennis court, and one of the six court-tennis courts in the country. There was also a pseudomedical subdivision in this part of the house, containing a solarium, heat room, massage room, and steam boxes. Outside, there were other tennis courts, a shooting range, and a stable.

Thus the property continued to generate extensions by itself; in business Mr. Reardon had seen many men ruined by allowing just this process of overextension to get out of control; here at High Farms, however, it was harmless enough, and this danger which he rigidly controlled in business he here gave its head. It even amused him, in the fleeting surface way he found things amusing, out of the corner of his eye.

Neil drove directly to the gym wing, undressed, and got into the steam box. Angelo closed it and adjusted a towel around his throat. He reflected that this old-fashioned contraption ought to have been replaced by a full-sized steam room long ago; now that the war was over they would be able to get the materials and the workmen. It would mean adding a sub-wing to the gym wing and they had all agreed the court-tennis court was positively the last addition, but then a steam room was an exception, a special situation requiring a suspension of the rules. It was not something new, since there already was a steam box here, but merely a replacement of the old model by the up-to-date one, like a new car or washing machine, and that made the difference.

"How hot am I?"

"Hundred thirty-eight."

"More."

Angelo increased the intensity of the heat, and Neil reflected that the real reason he wanted a steam room instead of this box was that taking a steam bath in this box was one of the few experiences in the world which he was very much afraid of. It was like sticking your head through the canvas at a carnival and letting people throw balls at it. He was in effect handless, armless, and bodyless; his head was there, on a platter, like John the Baptist's, for anybody to knock off. It was true that he had his teeth as a defense, but that was all, unless you could blink somebody to death.

Angelo was a nervous, self-distrustful type of Italian-American and seemed as harmless as a hen, but you never knew, you never knew. What if he had some grudge harbored against Neil, or against the Reardon family, or what if he suddenly went crazy? Things like that happened.

Neil therefore habitually kept an observant eye cocked at Angelo the entire time he was in the steam box. In addition his manner toward him became subtly more genial; a kind of flush of camaraderie came over Neil on these occasions. ("The squirt ought to spend night and day stuck in that thing," Angelo said to the other trainer, "the way it turns him almost human. You know what I think? I think he remembers there's a hell where he's going someday, and I don't mean purgatory.")

Neil kept his eye on Angelo and talked along cajolingly with him until twenty minutes passed. Angelo then unlatched the lid and opened the side, and Neil, reddish by nature, stepped out, lobster-colored. Angelo began wrapping a huge towel around him. Neil sighed a shade impatiently, which he would never have dared to do while still in the box, and Angelo worked faster. Then Neil went into a cubicle to lie down on a cot for five minutes.

Georgia came in wearing slacks, with a kerchief over her head. She was carrying a small pack on her back.

"What's that," he said, sitting up and leaning on one elbow, "a papoose?"

"You're still thinking about Cleet, aren't you. This is a pack. We're going hiking, Lynn and I. We're going hitchhiking," she added with her brightest smile.

"You're what! *Hitch*hiking! Oh come on, darling."

"Hitchhiking," she repeated, trying for an arch, playful look. "We always used to at home. I hardly went anywhere any other way. Of course the West Coast is different, I guess."

"It certainly is. You're not serious."

"Of course we are, Neil. It's something to do, Lynn's beginning to—"

"You can't *hitchhike* on these highways here."

"Just on back roads, down the river road, then take the ferry over to the other side, go on through the hills there, and back. To see if we can make it. We can always send for a car to bring us back."

"*Hitch*hike!"

"You make it sound like streetwalking or something."

"It practically is," he muttered into his towel.

"That's silly."

"I don't know what else to say."

"Then don't say anything. You're busy all day and all week and this is something original to do, for Lynn."

"Is she getting bored with us?"

"Not at all bored. She's just not comfortable, darling. It's all so enormous to her. I mean she's afraid to leave her bedroom because if she forgets to take anything it's such a long walk back."

"That's what we've got servants for."

"She doesn't like to ask them. She doesn't like to order people around. She says it makes her squirm."

"Neither do you, do you?"

"No," she said with quiet querulous sincerity, "I don't."

Proletarian mentality, Neil thought to himself, in that cool interior commentary he had carried on with himself for as long as he could remember, uncompromising observations about everyone and everything, including himself, which his inner voice made without relation to any feelings or affections or even to any self-interest. There was Georgia's proletarian mentality cropping up again. Lynn would always have it, but Georgia could get over it. She was a learner.

That was one of the principal reasons Neil had married her.

"You have to learn to order servants around. It makes them restless when you don't. That's what they're here for."

"It isn't true, is it, Neil, something I heard your mother saying on the phone the other day. There aren't seventy-three servants around here."

"Seventy-three? No, of course not, I don't know. I don't think so. That would be talking about the farm help and everybody and their number changes depending on the time of year. Why?"

"I don't know, it just sounded so unbelievable, seventy-three."

"You aren't going hitchhiking."

"We are. She wants to and I think it will be an adventure, in a way."

Angelo came in to say that the five-minute rest period was

finished, and so the discussion did not intensify into an argument. Georgia went out to find her sister, and Neil thought, Will she always be this erratic? Is it because she's pregnant?

As soon as he was dressed he hurried after her and learned that she had gone out the side gate to the river road; he went to the side of the house overlooking the river and saw Mrs. Cornelius Reardon and her sister being picked up by what looked like a delivery truck.

"Isn't this fun!" Georgia was saying. "Isn't this the way to really see things!"

"You bet," said Lynn. "You bet."

They crossed the river on the small ferry, and the truck let them off at a country crossroads. Georgia stood in her sneakers in the dust, gazing contentedly down the road. "I'll bet we don't have enough money to get back," she said with a giggle. "We're stranded!"

"I've got, let's see, a dollar and fifteen cents."

"And I've got exactly fifty cents. We *have* to get a ride or we'll spend the night sleeping on the ground."

"We could call them to come for us," said Lynn apologetically.

Georgia frowned. "We may have to walk all the way back, just like we did from Berkeley that time, remember? When nobody would give us a lift? God, that was awful," she finished enthusiastically. "My legs felt like stumps! Well, nobody's driving along here, are they? We'd better start walking. There's a highway over that hill, I think I remember, or," she laughed contagiously, "is it over another hill, fifty miles down the road?"

"Oh, Georgia. Maybe we should call them up."

"No. We can't," said Georgia shortly. "Come on, this is fun. It really is fun."

A car approached and went by, ignoring their cocked thumbs and expectant expressions. "What a louse," said Lynn. "These New England people make me sick. They've got no time for people who are down, who need help, poor people."

"They don't, do they," said Georgia.

Standing in the high dark study, a heavily paneled room in the original, Victorian part of the house, Neil irritably fumbled among some magazines, sat down in a deep, green-velvet, depressing armchair, got up, climbed up a narrow iron spiral staircase to a tiny gallery running along the four walls of the room near the ceiling, examining the spines of unread books, staring at dark portraits in insets between the bookshelves, portraits which were now faceless because the oil had darkened and because no one ever turned on the small lights to illuminate them, nameless, anonymous presences that had come with the house when his father bought it. Here, as elsewhere in Wetherford, the house and not the family had the lineage.

The room smelled of old leather, old wood, varnish, glue, old fireplace fumes; when the wind blew hard, as it often did on this promontory above the river, this part of the house slowly creaked and dully groaned, and the big bare panes of glass in the windows rattled ghostily. Neil liked it.

He looked up at the dome of the ceiling, with the circular glass "lantern" which from the outside of the house looked like a glass top hat sitting comically on the dome. The only houses he liked were Victorian. When someone said "a house" he instinctively saw three or four turrets, stained-glass windows, strange pie-shaped balconies high above the ground, oval windows, balustrades, conservatories, small closed rooms now used exclusively for the telephone, zinc pantries, lattice, enormous locked attics, basements with rooms no one had ever opened, a huge front porch, a medium-sized side porch, a small back porch, bathrooms with huge tubs and small fireplaces, mysterious maids' staircases, and questionable electricity.

He walked back along the gallery to the circular stairway and came down to the big table in front of the window. It was a baronial setting, the massive furniture, the huge room, the great perspective over the Connecticut Valley, a ponderous, powerful house built by somebody else, and now dominated by his father. Someday he, Neil, would fill it with his own drive and force and power, set his own stamp on it and on everything.

His father had just left for Chile. Someone had to take a look around the farms. He telephoned the Kinsolving residence. There was no answer.

Neil leaned back in the enormous leather swivel chair and began with grim self-mockery to twiddle his thumbs. It was time, past time, for him to take firm control of the people he had gathered around him, or else they might escape and he would be left alone in this huge room with his huge fortune. At the bottom of his mind he really wanted to be alone, just as he wanted to be a robber baron, which was why he was liberal, and possessive.

But now the idea of being alone frightened him, his fright made him angry, and he began bombarding the Kinsolving home by telephone, calling every ten minutes, his anger increasing with each unanswered ring. The ninth time he telephoned, he heard the receiver being picked up and Cleet's full level voice said, "This is the state mental hospital, do you need help?"

There was a towering silence on the line and then Neil in his most tight-throated, biting tone rasped, "I thought you were too ill to leave your house! Where have you been!"

"I was out in the back yard—"

"You're not suffering from the concussion any more, I take it. Three days have passed. If you're up and ambulatory I wish, if it's not too much trouble, you'd perform one or two small services for me in your spare time."

There was a new silence on the line. Then Cleet's voice deepened as he replied, "Is that an order? That's what we ask in the Air Force when some officer says something to us that way. Is that an order?"

"Yes, it's an order. Who cares what it is, I have my wife wandering with that idiot sister of hers on the highways alone and I want you to go and get her."

Cleet got ready to say, "Get off your ass and find her yourself."

"She's roaming all over the highways in pants and then you disappear."

Cleet felt himself losing his temper completely. He would probably wreck everything. He usually did. But then a kind of speech impediment came over him, to his amazement. He could not force the words out.

While he struggled Neil went on a little more calmly, "You'll know how I feel when you're married." For a moment Cleet thought Neil was going to apologize, but a second later he knew that he wouldn't, couldn't. "See if you can find her. Right?"

There was a final silence, both men listened to it, and at last Cleet said "Right" in an odd, hesitant tone which he didn't recognize as his.

"She and little sister left by the river road toward the ferry, in a delivery truck. That's all I know. See if you can find them." He hung up.

Cleet walked the mile to High Farms, where he borrowed the most modest Reardon car, a Ford station wagon.

Wetherford was very still in the midst of a summer afternoon. It was not entirely rational. The children who were too old to take afternoon naps, where were they? The adolescents, with their natural vocation for making noise, somehow failed to do it in this old town, didn't shiver the afternoon silence with their urgent pleasures and problems. Housewives stayed in their own back yards, husbands were quietly at work somewhere else, there was no streetcar, no bus line; the movie house was on the Highway, on the outskirts, along with the shopping center and the other stores and the bars; there was nothing here except houses and churches, the grammar school, which was not in session, the ancient houses, the great immobile trees, the burial ground founded in the 1640's, a plaque here, a marker there, memorials and evidences so old that often no one knew what they stood for any more; a sense of patient waiting, almost of hopeless waiting, hung over the town and the trees and the river.

When he got to it, the Connecticut, navigable here by good-sized ships, flowed in a wide, serene bend past the town, both banks crowded with trees, forming one of its handsomest stretches between Hartford and Long Island Sound. Here, this far along its course, it had become, in the tradition of American rivers, broad and beautiful, one of the rivers which had forever been the strength and backbone and sustenance of the continent.

A sense of patient or hopeless waiting meditated along the river too in the silent afternoon suspension, as though a stream of such depth and breadth had to be on the point of springing alive with the arrival, abruptly, thrusting around the bend all at once, of a flotilla, a crowd of masts and spars and agitated climbing seamen, furled sails and flags and shouts; it was not reasonable otherwise that the river should exist in all its expansive power, any more than Wetherford's broad and grand tree-lined avenues and courtly Colonial houses could exist always in their present passivity: they too were waiting for some event worthy of them, perhaps the arrival of General Washington again, with his suite, and Rochambeau and his lieutenants, to settle the Revolution.

Cleet Kinsolving, driving alone, had never felt the threatened waste of this power more forcibly.

Trying to calm himself, Cleet thought, first of all, he must not let this Reardon complex of power overcome him. He must fight to remain what he had always been.

Cleet also realized that he was at last beginning to understand what money was, how hard it was to earn more than a subsistence amount of it, what strength it gave those with more than they needed; he saw that money embodied, of all things, creativity. His own little freight airline hung absolutely on his obtaining a certain amount of money.

Money seemed to be crucial in everybody's life. Consider what it had brought Neil. It had even brought him Georgia.

Cleet's level green gaze had not escaped noticing that here was an attractive girl, at least to look at. He didn't like her himself; there was something too self-confident in her manner that he didn't care for, and above all a note of low-pitched, self-congratulatory pleasure in being alive that set his teeth on edge. She knew too much, or thought she did, to suit him.

Cleet knew, knew in the way that he knew in advance when

someone would and would not make love with him, that she would never have married Neil Reardon if he had not had a fortune. That was not the same thing as saying she had married him for his money. He did not think she had; she was too arrogant for that; she had too high an opinion of herself. But Neil's money had placed him in the appropriate frame from Georgia's point of view, she could get a clear look at him because of its glow. It highlighted his good points. It was like an exceptionally fine photographic study of him. She could see his character in it. It helped to clear her head. Her marriage had not been like marrying money at all; it had been being true to herself.

All of this Cleet grasped unanalytically, as he grasped everything which he could grasp, all at once, through a natural gift, like perfect pitch or an ability to play the piano by ear.

Slowly gathering in him as he drove along the still, leafy old streets, trying to like them and feel at home again, was the sense that he really was at home, after four years, and that it was in these streets that he had spent his boyhood and youth. He passed a tree with a thick low branch which he used to love to climb. Further along the street was a particular triangular flagstone he had stepped on every day of his life for good luck. In the next block he passed a hedge with a gap in it still faintly worn where they had stepped through as a short cut to school. The next corner was where they had played Watch the Moon Skip the Rocket, and there was the first street light he ever broke. Most of all, the streets were haunted and saturated and electric with all the love and the desire which he now saw, for the first time in his life, had obsessed every cell of his body and mind then, engulfing him so totally that he had not been entirely aware of it all, half dazed and hypnotized by passions which these placid streets and sedate houses reignited in his memory. Unquenchable as the sun and overpowering as a tidal wave they had inebriated his youth, leaving him sometimes half dead with desire and a typhoon of emotions, reeling from encounter to dream to party to movie to meal to ball game to picnic to work to study to class to home to a standstill. The very trees seemed laced with all he had felt. For four years, between the ages of eleven and fifteen, he had seen one particular older girl every noon hour of the school year as she went into her house for lunch. He had never missed; she had never noticed his daily vigil. She had seemed so beautiful and gentle and so magical, with some kind of cosmic connections, linked to the Southern Cross and possibly ancient history and astrology and the future, a miraculous possession who found herself by some awe-inspiring accident in the town of Wetherford, Connecticut. Her name had been Mary Carpenter and she had gone away to school and then to college and married someone else and he had lost track of her and even forgotten her, so it seemed, forgotten everything about her for many years, and yet he had only to see a tree and a flagstone and a hedge, and her reality, and all of the life he had poured into it, rose up around him and filled the streets with herself, and also with himself, as he had been and felt and dreamed.

What a waste all that had been.

Or was it a waste? How could anything like that be measured? His devotion to this mirage he had never really spoken to stretched away into his past as evidence, at least, of his power to feel and dream and *to be;* it existed there as a testament to the unquenchable force of his feelings and of his life; the energy of it could have blown up Wetherford and badly shaken Hartford. There had been something very beautiful in all of that early, very early, passion of course, and there had also been an almost volcanic eruptive force in it which, it was possible, he couldn't have controlled if for instance he had found himself alone with Mary Carpenter and she had seemed to give him the slightest encouragement; as a matter of fact, he might not be able to control such passion within himself now.

Mary Carpenter: the name itself broke upon so many stuck doors that it almost scared him. It wasn't really the kind of name he liked. "Mary" was too plain and too religious to suit him. "Carpenter" was too old-line New England for his taste. Probably she herself wouldn't have suited him either. But of course it hadn't been and it couldn't have ever been a question of getting acquainted and then adjusted and then intimate with each other; it had not been on that plane at all; his feeling for her had been linked to the Southern Cross and astrology and noontime in Connecticut and being eleven and twelve and thirteen and fourteen and fifteen years old and with a miracle that existed inside himself.

Did it still exist in its full strength? He wondered very much about that, and he did not know whether to hope that it did or that it didn't. He passionately hoped it was still there, in a way that Admiral Peary might have hoped to conquer the North Pole again, and he also hoped it wasn't, in a way that people living on a flank of Vesuvius would hope.

He reached the Cove and in the shimmering afternoon silence the circle of water, less than a mile wide, looked as domesticated as a birdbath. A rowboat, two dinghies, and one outboard motorboat were tied at moorings; there was a little wooden dock close to where he stood. That was all.

But Cleet had his own way of seeing the Cove: a grove of masts riding on the water, pinnacles and sloops and brigs and even square-riggers, back from the West Indies with molasses and sugar and rum, or outward bound to Lisbon with salted fish, or outfitted for five years of whaling in the South Seas, or loaded with flour for Bombay; the waters of the Cove bustled with the world's business, protected by the guns of the fort off to the right of where he was standing, at the entrance of the Cove, pointing down the Connecticut at the bend in the river; around it, drawn by horses, came ships from China to the fortified inland port in the middle of the Colony of Connecticut, which pirates and raiders and enemies of the king could not reach, landlocked and influential and secure, the Cove of Wetherford, which was known in India and to Jamaican pirates and at the Court of Spain.

Someone on board the motorboat, he noticed, was bailing out water from last night's shower.

Across the Cove from where he now was, there had been the busy shipyard, and the almost equally busy stake. In 1648 a woman named Rachel Withers admitted that she made a habit of "committing Uncleanness" with not only men but also devils, that she murdered a child and could change herself into a calf, that friendly devils cleaned her hearth for her every day, that they drove off the hogs of neighbors at her bidding. She was burned at the stake, to the general edification of the town because as the fire was consuming her legs she screamed, "I am unclean! I repent!" over and over again, and these shrieks one after another brightened every face and filled every bosom with joy because they proved that the townspeople had done the right thing. There was the admission of guilt and the redemption coming from her own mouth: they had saved her soul.

He had read about these early days in two huge volumes, *Chronicles of Early Wetherford,* which he had found at home. They came with the house. He had never succeeded in learning from his mother whether her family or his father's family had always lived in Wetherford. She "supposed so," that was all she would say.

He was secretly sure of it himself. He felt exactly the way they had in the old days. Most of the men in the town then, as described in the *Chronicles,* had tried to get on the first ship which would take them away from this town where the most important accomplishment was to have a more prominent pew than anybody else's in church, this woman-burning, lecture-reading, pillory-placing, Devil-fearing town.

The only people he admired from those days were the boys who almost as soon as they could stand upright toddled down to the Cove and tried to hide or hire or wheedle or argue themselves onto a ship, any ship, and sail away, out of the Cove, down the great sweep of the river, through the Sound, away to the mysterious and spice-filled, whale-seeking riches of the rest of the world. Most of them were never heard of again, except through a rumor that "he died among the whales" or "he later had land and some slaves in the Indies" or, often, "lost in a storm." One of these, however, by the name of Samuel Sillman, came back up the river one fine day aboard his own square-rigger, a captain of his own ship and at home in the world, to visit his father's and his mother's graves, and then to turn his prow back to the river and the seas and to freedom. That was the one Cleet devoutly hoped was his ancestor. In those days a man who would take a dare and had the strength and fast reflexes and inner force would carve out a life to fit himself at sea or on the frontier or in a battle; in those days, Cleet thought quietly to himself beside the little recreational Cove of 1946: Well, that's when I ought to have lived, back then.

These days, what the Air Force and the business world and commerce wanted from him was some kind of trained and faceless co-operativeness if he was going to succeed or even going to find work at all, to find any real place for himself at all. A man these days had to be trained and faceless and co-operative. Cleet recognized that he had no real training except for firing a machine gun, which had just gone out of style as a profession, that he was about as faceless as Mussolini, and that he just hadn't been made to co-operate.

Neil hadn't been made to co-operate either, but then Neil had approximately one hundred million dollars to make his unco-operativeness easier. Cleet had not quite four hundred dollars in war bonds between himself and destitution. And he had the Reardons.

In the Cove, the battles over, the ships for India gone, forgotten in Jamaica and anonymous in Madrid, the teen-ager had finished bailing out his motorboat. He started the motor; its obstreperous noise filled the air like a dozen dentists' drills; the craft made a few busy circles and then sped noisily past the site of the Wetherford fort and out into the majestic vacant waters of the river.

Caught in reverie between remembered love, when he had been an atom linked by love to the universe, and his present dangerous directionlessness, all links broken, facing that universe with an Air Force discharge, four hundred dollars, and one friendly family, Cleet drove along the streets of this town, the last place he wanted to live, and the one in which he was trapped. After a while he found himself on the dirt track that ran through the high, coarse sea of grass in the Great Meadow near the river.

Two figures were walking along the track in his direction. Although both wore pants he discerned that they were women, young women, and finally that one of them was Georgia Reardon. She looked dusty, tired, and carefree.

"Fancy meeting you here," she said. "How's your head?"

"Normal," he answered, getting out of the car.

"That seems hard to believe," she murmured, and then more clearly, "Oh, this is my sister, you haven't met her yet, have you? My sister, Lynn Sommers. This is Cleet Kinsolving."

Cleet and Lynn warily eyed each other, smiling. She was shorter and thicker than Georgia, with an expression on her face which was either sulky or puzzled.

"Are you going fishing?" said Georgia.

"Without any equipment?"

"I thought maybe you dived in and caught them with your mouth."

"Well no. I do—uh—bite sometimes."

"I'll bet," said Lynn.

"Where have you been?" said Cleet.

"We took the ferry to the other side of the river and went ten miles or so in the hills over there and then came back this way."

"Quite a walk."

"People picked us up, that is because we asked them, you know." Georgia mimed hitchhiking, cocking her thumb and smiling in a way Cleet in spite of himself found infectious.

"Well, Neil—" and then he was about to say "sent me" but caught himself, "was pretty upset about you roaming around alone so I said I'd look for you."

"Well, you found us. Neil's very busy this afternoon," said Georgia. "Why don't you—I mean, if you're his—you could do some of that work, couldn't you?" She surrounded this with a dazzling smile.

"Maybe. I hear you're pretty good in your line. You did some USO tours, I hear. Too bad you didn't come out to the Pacific. I'd have liked to see you do your juggling."

He didn't give a damn about her; to hell with her.

But Georgia burst out laughing uncontrollably. When she recovered, she said, "Juggling. That's really funny," her eyes brimming, "I love that, juggling."

"What do you do?" said Lynn.

"I fish."

"Ohhh," she said wonderingly.

"Shut up," said Georgia. "Let's go wading."

Cleet scowled. "Wading when you're pregnant . . ." he said in a low voice, giving her a sidelong glance.

"Do you have any objections?"

"It's your baby."

"I always believed in prenatal conditioning. And the baby has *already* been in an airplane crash. We're so grateful," she added sharply. "After that," she shrugged, "wading . . ."

I don't think she really is a bitch, Cleet said to himself wonderingly, but she's doing her best. "The airplane crash, if you want to call it a crash, and it wasn't, was an *accident*."

"Was it?" she said with studied absent-mindedness.

"What," he said in his low-pitched and most alertly neutral tone. She, perhaps all the Reardons, was going to hold this suspicion over his head.

"I was just joking," she tossed at him with a fleeting smile, "about going wading. We're on our way home."

Cleet's belligerence momentarily reversed itself because he suddenly noticed that she looked tired. "Get in the car and I'll drive you."

"I do feel a little tired," she conceded. "Don't you, Lynn? I have to admit it. Although Reardons are never tired," she added in a reciting tone.

"There's that," agreed Cleet.

"Never tired. But I'm only a Reardon by marriage, and you're only an Associate Reardon, so are we allowed to get tired?"

"We're allowed—I mean we can be ourselves, that's all."

"Of course. That's all anybody can be."

"Yes."

"But Neil," she began in a strained voice, as though not wanting to say this but unable to resist saying something so pressingly felt, "doesn't feel that way. He wants to construct me," she said with a nervous little giggle, "like doing over a house, like their house as a matter of fact. I never thought of that."

They were suddenly saying too much to each other too soon, criticizing the man who was her husband and his friend. Still, he said, "Neil constructed himself. He was one kind of kid and didn't like it, so he made himself into another. Hell," he added more comfortably, "I admire him for it."

"So do I!"

They drove slowly along the dirt track in the middle of the thick, coarse field of grass, their backs to the river, the low, ancient roofs of the town visible three quarters of a mile ahead. Georgia said, "I'm glad you came for us, and in the Ford. Usually when I send for a car, there I am, standing on a street corner in my slacks, and up will come the Rolls! They always send the Rolls when I'm dressed like an itinerant fruit picker. I used to be an itinerant fruit picker, did you know about that?"

Cleet shook his head noncommittally.

"It was the family profession for a short time," she went on in a humorous tone, "the way some families are always scientists, the Curie family, you know, or the Huxleys. Well we were dedicated fruit pickers. Pop was our Nobel Prize-winning picker. What was his record, baby, how many acres?"

"Who knows," said Lynn.

"Wait till you meet him. Mother Reardon's giving a party for me—have you had your invitation yet?—and she insists on sending the other Reardon *plane* for Mom and Pop. Oh my God. They aren't going to understand each other, Mother Reardon and Pop. They're both such snobs, only happy associating with their social inferiors, which means that Pop is going to devote himself to the stables, I guess." She chattered on lightly, half comprehensibly about her father—fruit picking, hopping freights, getting arrested—and Cleet, since he couldn't believe all of it, didn't believe any of it.

Still, he was beginning to like listening to her, first of all because she had a voice he could listen to for a long time. It was somewhat low-pitched and it sounded always close to the edge of laughing with amusement at what she was saying, whatever she was saying, at the comedy in the world. Happiness always sounded on the point of breaking out of this voice. Her accent was neither Eastern nor Western nor Midwestern nor Southern; he thought Neil had said she was from California originally, but her voice just sounded like good, educated, unaffected American. It didn't screech or purr or snap or drawl; it expressed her, good-naturedly and directly.

As they drove along talking Georgia glanced over at him with a quick smile now and then. He realized that she was flirting with him in an abstract way, not because he attracted her or she wanted to cause any trouble or for any other reason except that that was the way she understood dealing with men. That was the only reason for it and there was no trouble possible, he recognized with a sweeping sense of relief, deeper than he had thought possible.

He was not attracted in that way to Georgia Reardon. He had never been wrong about the women who did and did not attract him, and he knew he was not wrong now. He *liked* her. From the moment she burst into spontaneous laughter when he mentioned her "juggling," Cleet had started to like her. Liking and loving were totally incompatible in his nature; he liked dogs and the outdoors and President Roosevelt and Spencer Tracy and football; he had loved and managed certain girls; he had never liked them, and with a huge wave of relief at the disappearance of a fear he had not known he possessed until it evaporated, he saw clearly that he was going to like Georgia.

He had not expected this at all; it was in fact the last thing he had expected. And yet here it was: she was likable. His suspicions of her were groundless, he concluded as they drove through the vast sunny field of high grass. Whatever picture he had at first framed of her, an adventuress—whatever that was, he had never met an adventuress as far as he knew—or a gold digger or a slut or a schemer, had been dissolved by her infectious, genuine burst of laughter—"I love that, juggling"—by something unguarded and aspiring that he suddenly saw in her, something brave and a little vulnerable, gaiety and strength.

And since he liked her he could never love her, and so that menace between himself and Neil faded away like the phantom P-51, which vanished as soon as he ceased to believe in it.

They continued in silence up the dusty road. A wind had risen from the south and came sweeping over the grass at them, making a strange, distant hissing noise, and the old oaks beside the road groaned slowly. Something wild skittered excitedly among the high grass to their left.

Cleet now felt so relieved and comfortable with her that he told her about the airline to Alaska. "I knew you must have some dream like that," she said enthusiastically. "You would have to."

Georgia came into the dark, paneled old library. Neil was making notes on a yellow pad at the heavy old table, with the river visible through the bay window behind him. In this light she could see only his dark, square-shouldered silhouette, faceless and judicial-looking. He had apparently looked up, but he did not move as she spoke.

"Well that gave Lynn something new in the way of experience in Connecticut. The natives were friendly. Not one improper advance."

"Stop trying to sound daring."

"Don't you think I am? Hitchhiking?"

"You're doing your best."

"We ran into Cleet down by the river. He drove us home. I didn't know about his airline to Alaska."

"Did he talk about that?"

"Talk about it! He practically sang a song about it." Georgia could see nothing of the expression on his face, hear nothing in the tone of his voice, but there was something in the silence.

Mr. Reardon, back from Chile and about to leave for South Africa, met his daughter-in-law by the goldfish pond, where she was feeding the fish.

"They don't seem hungry," she said.

"They're overfed," he commented. "Maybe they don't get enough exercise, like the rest of us."

"Not enough exercise? You and Neil get more exercise even than these fish, and they never stand still. But then they never get anywhere. Do they ever sleep?"

"I suppose they must sleep."

"I wonder how. Probably they just hang in the water. They're beautiful with those wonderful wavy fins."

"Mmmmm."

"I wonder how they make love."

"Hm?"

"Make love. I mean, have sexual intercourse." Georgia was still struggling, but more hopelessly every day, against the Irish Catholic puritanism of life at High Farms. "I think they do it side by side."

"I'm told you had some exercise today yourself."

"Yes, Lynn and I went for a walk. We ran into Cleet Kinsolving.

"How is he?"

"He seems fine now. Evidently it was only a minor concussion." She scattered more food above the goldfish. "I liked him, I never expected to, because before, he seemed so—implacable, I don't know, as though he was the only thing that mattered."

"We've all always been very fond of Cleet."

"I didn't know until today about his ambition."

"When you're young, ambitions are simple."

"He *is* a very single-minded person."

"Oh I wouldn't call him simple-minded. Certainly he's a little slow mentally."

"I—ah—my word was *single*-minded."

"Yes, I suppose he does have the kind of mind that can only handle one thing at a time."

"Is that a good trait?"

"It can be, it can be. I can remember when he was determined to get to Europe in an outboard motorboat."

"That was when he was a little boy, wasn't it?"

"Yes," said Mr. Reardon a little sardonically, "that was when he was a little boy."

"And you mean, now he's—what?" she said faintly and querulously.

"As you get to know him better . . ."

"Then you don't have too much confidence in him?"

"We all like Cleet very much. I've known him all of his life. I see him as he is. He has some fine, solid qualities. He always has had them, and he is never going to change. He is always going to be a fine, solid, loyal person who lives in a world of his own. Maybe that's where his strength comes from, or what you might call his capacity to be consistent, solidly consistent. We're using that quality to help Neil by putting Cleet next to him as a kind of confidant and assistant. Neil," he finished quietly, "needs him."

"I can see," she said uncertainly, "that he's useful to Neil, yes."

"I wonder if he'll stay with us?" Mr. Reardon murmured in a suddenly confidential tone. Georgia felt he was fishing for information about Cleet's feelings, and also that she should use any influence she had to see that he did stay.

"I wonder," she said.

"People at that age like to think they should be what they call 'independent.' Nobody is in this world, damn it. Am I, for instance? The answer is no. I'm dependent on the institutions which lend me money, to open up the iron ore in Labrador, for instance, and for the mining in Chile and South Africa. I'm dependent on labor, on contracts with labor unions, on the bureaus in Washington that make these goddamned regulations and restrictions. Every time they let more Venezuelan oil into this country to compete with American oil and American coal, I'm in trouble."

"Coal," she said, "oil, that's where the—money comes from. Neil has never really explained to me."

After a short pause he said, "That's right. Anthracite coal, of course, not that money-losing bituminous. Yes, we have gone into oil extensively too. And the iron ore in Labrador is going to be our biggest interest for the next ten years at least. That is a really major project we have going now. And then," he added, pulling on his cigar, "there's the real estate." He was silent for a moment, and then continued to speak because, she saw, he took her seriously. "They've been saying for years now that large fortunes are disappearing in this country, that the old ones will dwindle and there won't be any new ones. I don't believe," he concluded with deliberation, "that that's going to prove true, in spite of everything those college professors running the government in Washington can do. There's too much potential in America, and there're comparatively few people who know how to make it work. Those people will continue to make fortunes."

"I see what you mean," she said, convinced.

"I'm dependent on others, you are, Cleet is, everybody is."

"I have the impression that if—when Cleet gets his little airline he will have the kind of independence he wants."

"He's worried about the plane crash the other day."

"Yes."

"It was a very unusual accident."

Georgia was silent.

"The pilot accused Cleet to me of full responsibility for it. In fact he got so mad when I fired him he made a few what you might almost call threats against first Cleet and finally me, all of us. The funny thing is, I was considering rehiring him after I heard his version of the accident, but then he made these threats, semithreats. People defeat themselves all the time, don't they, trying too hard. And then," he added vaguely, "firing him helped impress the seriousness of it on Cleet's mind. It's not always easy to make an impression on that particular mind."

Georgia glanced quickly at him. ". . . Impression on Cleet's mind?"

"You noticed how he reacted when I said I was firing the pilot, didn't you?"

"It upset him."

"Why?" he asked like a teacher hearing a student's lesson.

"I don't know. He's good-natured, he felt sorry—"

"In my opinion, he feels responsible for the crash," Mr. Reardon cut in evenly. "He thinks he caused it. That guilty feeling is there. Strange boy. You know he's part Indian. Now he feels he has to stay and help out Neil, which is a very good thing for Neil. And a very good thing for Cleet too. You know we always try to help those who are . . . close to the family." Georgia translated this last phrase as "dependent on us" and she had to agree that it was true, impressively true. There were literally dozens of people who owed their educations, careers, businesses, or health to the fact that they were close to the Reardons. And now there was Cleet.

After a silence Georgia asked quietly, "Do *you* think he caused it?"

"Of course not! What motive could he have? It's just Cleet's peculiar imagination."

She was slowly coming to realize that the Reardon family lived in, and she was having to learn to live in, a world where the dimensions were broader than any she had imagined, financially and geographically. They also used for their own ends emotions and deception and generosity and bribery and loyalty and ambition and philanthropy and willfulness, on vaster planes of operation, where they moved with a startling daring and coolness, with charts and by means of instruments she had never heard of, never suspected existed, passed on from fortune to fortune as though these very rich families all belonged to some secret confraternity, with special totems and rituals and, above all, special rights.

But slowly she had understood that there was no conspiracy, there was not even any discussion, and perhaps not even any comprehension, among these families: there was only the same rarefied experience acting on all of them alike. They were like mountain climbers, and the Reardons had reached a beautiful but in some ways also a bleak altitude of power-charged money, and in the thinness of that spotless air a kind of euphoria seized their brains, a rapture of the heights, and in such an effervescent atmosphere their doubts evaporated and their timidities disappeared; limits had been left down below, out of their range of vision, and the sole goals which could challenge them now were the final, highest peaks, where their apotheosis awaited them; there and only there could they have the transforming experience which alone was worthy of them. To help them get there, anything and anyone who was useful was used.

Mr. Reardon was a part-time mind reader. It was one reason for his success. He began to think out loud. "Cleet has never been better off than he is right now. Still, we're going to do our best for him. After all, he's almost one of the family. I'll make this prediction: he'll never find a better place in life than he has right now, working for us. He's a very peculiar boy, Cleet. Every year it's going to get harder for someone like him to find a place in American life. If he were wise he would stay with us." He looked silently at the fish.

"But if he were wise," Georgia said suddenly, "he wouldn't be Cleet."

Cleet is something like Pop, she recognized at that moment, very much like Pop. *That's* why I liked him so suddenly and felt so—concerned about him; of course, that's what it was. Then she thought of what her father's life had been like, and with a clear chill the recognition that Mr. Reardon was right seized her, and the recognition that Cleet was in danger, and that he didn't know it and might be too stubborn to avoid it, too stubborn to accept life as it found him, to be reasonable, the way all normal people were, to settle for the lesser of two evils, to look out for himself sensibly, to grow up in a certain sense, if that was what it was; to abandon part of his nature in exchange for safety. That was what was meant by "growing up," by "acting your age," that was what these reproving orders by the older generations really meant: abandon an irreplaceable part of yourself in exchange for safety.

Her father had never learned how; gloriously and hopelessly

he had lurched from disaster to disaster, clutching every last one of his unrealized gifts and dreams through every last disaster: nothing ever abandoned, and nothing ever gained.

Intimidated, she glanced up at her father-in-law. He knew how to "succeed." Pop and Cleet didn't know, and so they were victims of their own marvelous imaginations, of their towering sense of what they and what life could be, possessed by glorious visions which had for them the awful additional power that somewhere, once, they had come true for others, and that somewhere else, sometime, they would come true again.

There beside the goldfish Georgia Sommers Reardon glanced at the well-organized profile of her father-in-law and almost wept with relief at finding herself in the hands of the realists at last, feet on solid, cold money, saved from those marvelous men who were born two hundred or two thousand years too late, or too early.

Mrs. Reardon was going to give a real party. The war was over. A week after the hike she was sitting with Georgia in her "office," a small room with low windows opening on rosebushes. The room contained a very large, old-fashioned, painstakingly neat desk, filing cabinets, a great many books, and three telephones. She was wearing a sleeveless white dress, and with her tanned golfer's arms, her tallness and air of competence, her hair, gray-white but short and smart, she looked as though she were forty, instead of fifty-five, and always would be.

"Let's schedule the party about a month from now. That would be—let's see, around the end of the summer. I believe it'll be the first sit-down dinner for fifty people this part of Connecticut has seen," she observed in her well-modulated, rather high, slightly girls'-school voice. She gave parties the way nations launched attacks: they were rare, and they were all-out.

Georgia huddled in a chair and imagined that the sit-down dinner for fifty people would go away. There was no sign of her pregnancy yet, so she could wear a wonderful dress and her new jewelry and she knew she would look wonderful. She knew that objectively. But what would she do, what would she find of interest to say to anyone, how would they like her, what would Neil think of her? She visualized this party as a "ball," a starchy period fete from the 1890's—Many a heart is aching,

After the ball—a fluttering, lacy occasion where ladies developed the vapors and gentlemen sought to compromise a lady's honor amid the potted palms, where the guests conversed in epigrams and the air was filled with the awful danger of committing something called a *faux pas*. That was her vision of this party, and she might as well be asked to enjoy herself and feel comfortable at a circumcision ceremony in the Congo. The parties she knew and enjoyed had been the kind where people brought their own liquor, or beer.

"I'm going to have to do something to control the drinking," Mrs. Reardon went on. "I do *not* want anybody under twenty-five getting drunk."

Georgia's spirits momentarily lifted. "I'm sure they won't," she said dutifully.

Mrs. Reardon gave her a worldly glance but said nothing. So people did get drunk at balls. Georgia felt slightly better.

Then she remembered that not only would she have to be present, but so would Lynn and so would her mother and father: four itinerant workers at the ball in the mansion. They would all look like waifs, she saw it clearly—she would look like a waif in emeralds.

Cleet was perusing Neil's manuscript of *We're Not Satisfied* and thinking about grasshoppers. They could jump approximately eight times the length of their own bodies, he estimated. Now if he could do that, he would jump right out the window and halfway to the tennis court.

"What are you thinking about?" said Neil from the other side of the big table.

"Me? Grasshoppers."

"What part is that you're reading?"

"About how machines are going to replace men more and more and increase unemployment."

"Doesn't that interest you at all?"

"I guess it will interest a lot of people. But the truth is, I'm only usually interested in things that apply to me personally."

Christ, thought Neil. He's blind as a bat. Opaque. Aloud he said, "How did you like my article in yesterday's *Times*?"

"What article was that?"

"I told you. About the death of rugged individualism. Didn't you read it?"

"Not yet. But I will! You sure do write a lot," he added in what was meant to be an admiring tone.

"Have you ever read anything I ever wrote?"

After a second's hesitation he said, "To be perfectly honest, not usually all the way through." He took a good look at Neil. "But I *liked* the parts I did read."

"Thank you."

"I'm not much of a reader."

"Oh."

"Do you feel like going bowling?"

"I'm on the radio at eight o'clock."

"Again?"

"You certainly are a fan of mine."

"When you start talking about something that applies to me, well then I'll listen."

Blind as a bat, Neil repeated to himself, opaque. Aloud he said, "Such as what?"

"Oh," his face assumed the almost stern dignity that came over it when he was trying to concentrate, "making something of yourself, not getting in a trap, doing what you were made for, making the best of yourself. Things like that. You know the words better than I do." At an earlier time in their friendship, before he was working for Neil, he would have blithely added, "Anyway, you don't believe what you're writing yourself. It's what you think people want you to say. If you said what you really feel, I'd read all of that. That would be something. Of course it would scare the hell out of everybody and they'd probably lock you up. But at least it would be the truth." This impulse to say this, however, never quite became clear in his mind. Today, as an employee, he did not clearly become conscious of these words.

So now there was no one to say these things to Neil.

"You're not used to dealing with ideas enough to grasp my message," Neil commented.

"I guess that's it," said Cleet cheerfully.

"You're my pal all the same," said Neil with a surprising show of sincere feeling. Like all Neil's attempts to show warm emotion it was boyish and awkward and embarrassing.

Cleet continued to smile.

"In fact, you're the only one I've got."

Cleet's smile persisted. At last he found this to say: "That's right. And we're going to stand by each other."

"Right," said Neil almost solemnly. He meant it; he could be counted on to stand by Cleet. He had given himself his word on that, and he never had broken and never would break his word on anything. He realized that with most people he was often intolerant, irritable, short-tempered, arrogant, ambitious and chilly. Know Thyself was his philosophy and he knew and accepted these things about himself and they did not disturb him. But no matter how uncompromising he was with people in general, he was resolved that to this one person, outside his immediate family, he would be tolerant; he would put up with all of Cleet's vagaries and obtuseness and lack of consideration. It was just these failings that made his boyhood friend need him.

Cleet and Charley were discussing the airline. "It's a great idea," Charley kept repeating, looking at him without blinking, as though the split-second when blinking shut out Cleet would be time for study and admiration irretrievably lost. At the same time Charley was furiously wondering how he could lead the conversation to a point where he could hint, not ask certainly but just hint, that he would like to apply for a job, any job, with that airline. Finally he just blurted it out.

"After you've had four years of college, maybe," said Cleet.

Cleet was becoming nervously aware for the first time that his brother thought of him as some kind of god. Now there are two people I can't let down, he thought, Charley and me.

Charley admired him so much not because of anything Cleet had done; after all, what *had* he done? He had served for four years without any official distinction in the Army Air Force, where his only important decoration had been the Purple Heart, won for getting in the way of a piece of flying shrapnel.

So far in his life he had not done one thing of any importance. But Charley loved him not because of anything he had done, but because he was Cleet. That was fortunate because he did not really know how to do anything; he only knew how to be Cleet.

And he sensed, more and more every day that he spent among those archdoers, the Reardons, that being yourself was not enough. Nobody gave you anything in exchange for that; you couldn't get anything for it. Nobody wanted it. It was the thing he valued most in himself, but life was exchange. You had to be very good at doing something, whether it was splitting the atom or crooning. What a strange world, where no one paid any attention if you said, "I am"; they only listened if you said, "I do." The first question new acquaintances asked him was invariably, "What do you do?" always with a winning smile, since for all they knew he might answer, "I am a violin virtuoso earning two hundred and eighty thousand dollars a year." They wanted to know first and foremost what he did. And the next thing they wanted to know was how well he did it.

As Cleet mulled over this necessity to do something, anything, sex thrust itself into his mind. So that was why they called prostitution the world's oldest profession. He could see why that was now: you didn't have to go to an accredited college to learn how, no degree was required, the classes were impromptu, and they met anywhere.

Somebody, he said to himself, God or somebody, or that old Indian squaw who saved other people's children, not just her own, had put a sense of life and how completely beautiful it was inside him. He was not going to let that glorious forecast prove wrong. Clattering still in the back of his mind there was the engine of the P-51, over the rim of the horizon, circling steadily and calmly, as though on patrol duty, as though it might come at him again someday with its indictment and guns if he did not live up to that image of life.

His deepest ambition was not merely to operate an airline to Alaska; that was just the means of reaching his goal. The goal itself was simply to be a full human man, making the best of himself.

He was disgusted and fearful of what failure to do that had done to many people, to most people he knew. He did not want to be like some of them, twisted by subservience; he did not want to be like some others, ground down by poverty; he did not want to be like people he knew who were slowly poisoned by contempt for themselves. (That eliminated prostitution as a field for him, if there was such a thing for males, which his experience in the world, as a matter of fact, had shown there was.) Most of all, he did not want to be defeated as most people in the world were, that is, simply by not really living, eaten by the termites of a half life semilived.

All the same there was one wonderfully encouraging fact, which he kept the firmest possible grip on at all times. He actually knew one or two people who had broken past all these blocks and became real, true, full human beings. But it was going to be harder for him than it had been for them for two reasons. First of all, he was not very intelligent in the way intelligence was officially measured, and that certainly was a handicap. For example, Neil seemed to be able to sort of *file* information in his mind automatically. Who the hell else knew that Constantinople fell in 1453! Who except Neil knew that Cleet's present job made him an amanuensis! *How* could Neil predict the way people were going to react to a speech of his, and always be right, and even predict opposite reactions to the same speech in towns a few miles apart! He not only knew facts, he understood situations, which was much more important in the long run. Cleet realized that he himself did not know many facts, and he only understood one person at a time.

But the second reason it was going to be so hard for him to become a full human male was even worse: there was too much to him. He was *too* healthy. His eyesight, he had discovered in the Air Force, wasn't normal: it was better than normal. So were his hearing and his taste buds and his sex organ; they were all installed in the appropriate places in his body, working away as though the fate of the world depended on them! Not only that; his feelings were so enormous that it took a deep intensity of experience for him to feel alive at all. If Neil's work was going well and he was getting his way professionally and Georgia was co-operating sexually, then he gave every indication of feeling fully and contentedly alive. That was what Neil thought of as a full life, and these days he was leading it. The fact that he was also in the process of becoming a father was giving Neil a huge excess of happiness and fulfillment.

But Cleet had to be closer to the pulse of life, to feel it pound, to be scared and ecstatic and despairing and triumphant by turns. Otherwise, he believed, his adrenalin gland would clog up and his blood thin out and his veins harden and his liver slacken, because there was no urgency challenging them to their peak performance. Like a muscle never exercised, they would turn bad and useless.

That was why cramped old Wetherford oppressed him; when the last privateer's ship in the Cove fell to pieces from disuse, living at that height drained unstoppably out of this brittle town. He had always sensed that, dimly, and now he plainly knew it.

He and Charley were walking past the Green and there was the ancient burial ground where the witch and the pirates and the founder and the old flame-tongued preachers had left what remained of themselves when life frittered away. "Why don't you go someplace this summer?" he said to his brother. "Hitchhike to South America, for instance?"

"Hitchhike to South America? I don't think there's a road all the way down there. What made you say that? Still," Charley couldn't really bring himself to be negative to any suggestion of Cleet's, "do you want to go with me? I mean if you'd like—"

Cleet frowned and shook his head. "I'm past that. I'm busy here. But it would be a good experience for you."

"You get the funniest ideas."

"I agree with you there," he said quietly.

They walked along in silence for a while, and then Cleet remarked, "They're giving a party at High Farms."

"Am I invited?"

"Sure, I suppose so. I don't know. I don't even know if *I'm* invited."

"Well of course you are."

"I don't know if I am." He glanced at Charley, who no longer looked so large, and was in fact not quite as tall or as heavy as Cleet was.

"Of *course* you are."

"Do they invite the help to parties?" he said with a grin.

"*What!*"

"I might have to get used to thinking of myself that way."

"What are you talking about?"

"After all, the Reardons are a very important family and I can be—uh—one of the assistants."

"Assistant *what?*"

"Just an assistant. They're very important. It might not be bad at all, like being Lafayette to General Washington. *Everybody* can't be a leader."

"You can."

Cleet stopped to inspect the decaying bark of the ancient elm, frowning, rubbing it with his thumb as though it were a personal sore. "What kind of a leader can I be?"

"You can be, well, a lot of things, for instance—" and then Charley got lost among his contradictory thoughts.

"I'm beginning to wonder," said Cleet, half to himself, "what I can ever be."

"Are you going to let them take you over?" said Charley edgily, shocked at talking that way to his brother, but even more shocked at Cleet's talking that way about himself.

"Listen, Charley, I've got to be more responsible," said Cleet with an attempt at sternness, "I've got to have a bank balance and insurance and join the Junior Chamber of Commerce and—fit in, someplace. Well where? I think I'm stuck, I'm stuck in Wetherford, for a while, anyway. I just hope, well, I just hope I don't *explode.* I aim to fit in, I aim to *reform.*"

"Reform? Why should you? What's there to reform?"

"I'm going to be organized, like everybody else."

"Swell," said Charley with a sour smile.

"Cleet can help with the parking," said Mrs. Reardon. "We're going to use that field next to the stables and it'll be a mess if nobody is supervising."

Georgia gazed at her but didn't say anything.

Mrs. Reardon, although she did not look at Georgia, felt called on to modify this plan by a grim silence emanating from her daughter-in-law.

"But of course he'll be in his dinner jacket, so that wouldn't be suitable. I thought that before the party really started he might just see that it's being done right. When the guests were just starting to arrive."

Cleet did not own a dinner jacket. It was one of the order of possessions he never got around to acquiring. A dinner jacket was in the same category as life insurance, which he had resented having to carry in the Air Force and had dropped the instant he was discharged. How could life be insured except by whoever was God?

How could money replace life? It was the same thing as trying to compare a sixty-watt light bulb and dawn. He regularly lost wrist watches. In the first place, they wouldn't work on his wrist; he had been told they stopped because he had an excess of static electricity in his body, which didn't surprise him in the least. It was as if that had always been his central problem. He had always given away clothes, relieved to find someone to take responsibility for them. He misplaced address books, letters to be answered, and bills; he could never remember who owed him money and vice versa. All his life he had been like this.

Now, though, he began to remember. Although he never said anything directly, Neil did not like Cleet to be late, so he needed a watch. If Neil advanced him money he liked to be repaid. If Neil saw him every day of the week he was pleased if Cleet wore different clothes from time to time. And the addresses of his friends in Kansas, these Cleet learned to keep. He realized that he was growing up—or was it old?—finally; he realized in any case that he was growing more like other people. The Reardons, whom he worked for from day to day, were perhaps finally giving him a sense of responsibility and teaching him to fit in to life as normal, successful people lived it.

After all, he was twenty-three years old. It depressed him sometimes to think how far people like Benjamin Franklin and Lou Gehrig and Michelangelo and Napoleon had gotten at that age. It was probably his irresponsibility that had been holding him back. So now he scrupulously wound his wrist watch every night before going to bed and set his new alarm clock for seven forty-five; and often he heard it when it went off in the morning.

One special morning it woke him on schedule. He slowly opened his eyes in the white bedroom with the huge old mirror and the little fireplace, and began to recollect steadily his place in life: I. Now I'm a civilian, the job two hundred dollars a week, Neil and his writing, MY airline, Wetherford late summer, hungry, muscles contracted, so I'll stretch, coffee, ORANGE JUICE, sex feeling, why am I always ALONE in this bed? Routine day ahead. Then he recalled that this was to be a critical day in his march toward being more like other people. His stomach began to tighten at that thought. It was not unlike the feeling of stale and numbing tension and vague fear he used to experience before bombing missions.

As on those mornings, there was nothing to do this morning except force himself to the confrontation. He got out of bed slowly but firmly and stood naked on the Indian rug in the middle of the floor. In the old mirror he saw that physically he had not started to deteriorate in this sedentary new life. His shoulders were still wide and full, chest well developed, stomach flat, legs and arms muscular. One of these days, one of these years, if he allowed himself to be caught and held by a chair and desk and four walls, his stomach would start to sag, the muscles everywhere would loosen, shrink, and his physique would begin the slow corrupting process of falling away from his frame toward the graveyard.

He took a long breath, of determination and boredom and perseverance, and then stomped into the bathroom, and then dressed.

Downstairs he found the sunny dining room, with its black Colonial-style table and chairs, empty. Breakfast was waiting on the stove in the kitchen where Charley had left it. Before the war they had at intervals been able to afford a maid, but now wages and employment were different and they would probably never be able to afford one again. The house was very heavily mortgaged. He reheated the coffee, made some toast, ate the cool bacon and then, pausing very uncharacteristically to straighten his tie in the hall mirror, he went out into the bright Connecticut morning and down the street to the little business section at the corner.

It was exactly nine-fifteen when he steeled himself for the final, decisive act, and then stepped defensively into the Security National Bank of Wetherford to open a savings account.

Cleet started across the marble floor, railed-off desks on the left and people in cages on the right, and at the end of the room a terrible, round, intricately equipped door which suggested the entrance to a penitentiary death house, feeling suddenly as though he was about to be operated on, gelded, feeling as though he was taking the decisive step toward the trap of a business life, and into his mind sprang a picture of himself as Uriah Heep, standing for the rest of his life in front of a high counting-house desk, slowly growing a hunchback, losing his teeth, and talking to himself. At the same time he felt buoyed up by an opposite feeling, a sense of achievement at facing up to this unnatural institution and so acquiring a certain weight in the community.

As he continued toward the row of cages he remained, all the same, fundamentally alarmed at finding himself inside this institution. It was a place concerned entirely with rows of numbers, percentages, formulas, calculations, slips, passbooks, checks, and balances. The meaning of simple English words was clear and obvious to Cleet, and he regarded the vocabulary of banks as deeply suspicious. When they lent someone money the usury they extracted was called "interest," of all things, and the individual behind bars he was approaching, who never revealed anything, was called a "teller."

He did not want this robot to notice his nervousness and incredulity at what went on inside a bank, and so he cast his face in its most emotionless river-Indian expression and tonelessly asked how he opened a savings account. The face said to go into the restricted area behind the railing and speak to one of the seated effigies at a desk there. Cleet made his way across the marble floor, through the swinging gate, onto the carpet within. He approached a desk and was asked to sit down. Information was exchanged. He signed his name several times, thinking that executions probably had equally routine preliminaries. The man administering these steps was a Mr. Vining, whom Cleet dimly remembered from before the war. He did not look a day older, but then, he had always looked stoically ageless.

Mr. Vining had what Cleet thought of as a Monumental Nose. It began between his eyes, where all noses began, and then as it descended and broadened it seemed to lose contact with his facial nerves and blood vessels and tissues and to become an autonomous entity, lifeless but imposing, immovably attached to the center of the face and giving it added significance, like the steeple of a church. People with this rocklike, unfeeling kind of nose were always at cross-purposes with everything Cleet wanted and felt and believed in; he had only to glimpse a Monumental Nose to know that trouble, or at least total incomprehension of him, lay behind it. The voice, which was low, clogged, and expressionless, asked the routine questions. Squirming nervously but gazing with his levelest green stare past the nose into the glazed eyes, Cleet responded as though under oath. Eventually the transaction was finished, and turning, executing virtually a military about-face, Cleet crossed to the entrance of the building, looking neither to right nor left, experiencing some of the emotions a youth leaving a whorehouse for the first time might feel: relief, revelation, shame, discomfort, deflation, impatience, and a battered sense of new maturity.

Out in the open air again he felt that he had done the right thing. As Georgia had pointed out several weeks back, he was an Associate Reardon now and had to become much more responsible. Even more to the point, when he had his own business he might well have to deal often with these specters. He certainly didn't expect the Reardons to continue financing his company once it was, so to speak, off the ground. The understanding was that they were to help start the operation, and he was so grateful for that, he doubted whether he could ever bring himself to ask for anything more from them. On the contrary, he would have to look for ways to show his gratitude, after he had paid them back their money.

"Well here it is," said Mrs. Reardon, waving the guest list. "All my blood, sweat, and tears went into it. I think everybody's there."

Georgia listened nervously while she read and commented on it.

There were Mr. and Mrs. Hugh G. Harvey and their daughter Cassie; Charles Crownover, whose play *Maxine* had been a Broadway success during the wartime season when any theater which opened its doors had been assaulted by people desperate for a means to spend their money and forget the war; Mrs. Morgan Seelinger; Parker Evans Sharp, the retired radio singer; Fred Hatch, soccer coach at Country Day, and his wife, the librarian; the Craft girls, Ginny and Mary Eleanor; Gloria Garrison, who was very good fun and always had been; Mrs. Van Revellon; Cynthia Manning and her half brother, Clay Gingel, who always entertained at parties, she by singing "Deep Purple" and he by doing tricks; Pauline Frey; Fred and Kitty Winkler; the Jesse Gerkinses; "Red" and Phyllis McKecknie; the news commentator Greg Zahl and his girl friend; Mrs. Margaret Bitting and her daughter Ula; Georgia's mother and father; Lynn; business associates of Mr. Reardon, and so on. Georgia had met very few of them, but enough to know that they were a random selection of people with nothing in common except their business connection with Mr. Reardon or else that someone in the family happened to like them. Suddenly rich but living in the wrong section of Connecticut, the Reardons had not become a part of fashionable society. Mr. Reardon considered the subject too irrelevant to think about, and Mrs. Reardon was not impressed by it. Neil wasn't attracted to it either; his clear mind was annoyed by the bad grammar used at the best parties, and he hated girls with nicknames like "Hopsie." The family was too arrogant, too busy, and too involved in other things to qualify socially. Mrs. Reardon sometimes realized that their fortune plus persistence and good nature would have carried them to virtually any social level, and she was also aware that the most unassailable families in society were laden with skeletons in the closet, unmentionable close relatives, chilling sex habits, and other scandals which made their own qualifications look sterling by comparison, but that was all the more reason for not going through the trouble. The Reardons were too important to be snobbish; they entertained people they liked or wanted to help or found amusing or felt sorry for or wanted something specific from or through force of habit. They knew that where they lived in the Connecticut Valley was Siberia socially, and they preferred it that way.

Georgia sighed to herself with relief. In this hodgepodge of guests perhaps her family would pass unnoticed. But there was one harbinger of disaster she vowed to herself to avert; her father had to be prevented at any cost from doing his soft-shoe number. She looked up from the list. "You forgot Cleet Kinsolving's name," she said.

"Oh did I? Well put it down. I didn't think of it. He's practically family."

After completing the ordeal at the bank, Cleet walked the mile to High Farms, arriving late. Neil was at the big table in front of the bay window in the library, reading *The New York Times*. The moose heads of an earlier owner of the house reared out from between the shelves. The old floor creaked underfoot. Neil said "Hi," and Cleet told him about the new savings account, and Neil looked amused. Cleet picked up the *Herald Tribune*. They rattled the papers in silence for a while.

Then Cleet took the new chapters of Neil's book and went up the spiral iron stairway, along the catwalk under the domed ceiling, to his own workplace in the library, an alcove in the far corner with a circular window overlooking some meadows and the distant river. Neil did not ask for any criticism or editorial advice from him; he was merely supposed to catch any obvious errors the typist had made. In the afternoon he was to telephone for hotel reservations and other arrangements of Neil's next trip. Yesterday he had negotiated subletting one of the farms. The day before that had been spent for the most part taking calls Neil had not wanted to take himself. All of the preceding week had been spent keeping a persistent former girl friend of Neil's away from High Farms, taking her to roadhouses for long talks, reasoning with her, threatening her, and finally paying her off. The work certainly had variety.

After Cleet went to his alcove silence resumed control of the big old room. Neil preferred almost unbroken silence until after lunch.

Cleet started reading the chapter called "A Hand to the Helpless," and almost immediately the picture which Neil's views-for-publication always produced sprang into his mind: Neil moving his all-too-capable hands into various shapes which, projected on a screen, looked like a duck or a bear or a donkey or anything else he happened to want to pretend that they were.

Drawing, as he did when convenient, on his Catholicism, Neil began this chapter with the papal encyclicals advocating social justice, and went on from there through Abraham Lincoln to Theodore Roosevelt, the graduated income tax, Social Security, labor unions, minimum wages, and finally a limited advocacy of the new British Labour Party plan of cradle-to-grave security. Neil's writing was in favor of all these principles and programs, including such details as free reading glasses and false teeth. "Should only those who can afford it read and chew?" he ended one section indignantly, catching Cleet somewhere in his solar plexus, where he instantly tightened all the muscles in an effort to keep from exploding with laughter. The chapter was unrelievedly serious and if he laughed Neil would be offended. Cleet did not think that only those who could afford it should read and chew; surely those were inalienable rights just like habeas corpus and freedom from bills of attainder, but he couldn't take Neil's indignation seriously.

The next chapter was called "Who Is Our Neighbor?" and advocated "friendly American trust to melt the Tartar fears of Soviet Russia. Let us, in the most mature sense of the word, love them." Cleet desperately fought for control: Neil's embracing with Christian love some rampaging Siberian, turning the other cheek, giving the soft answer, persisting despite every rebuff in loving them, Neil's pursuing sweet reasonableness, it was—

"How's it going?" Neil suddenly called out.

Just like his old man, Cleet thought; damn these mind readers. Burying himself in the furthest corner of the huge room wasn't getting far enough away.

"It certainly is well written!" he called out. "I think it's convincing, a lot of it is, I'd say. You're making some interesting points."

"I see," Neil replied quietly in his level, carrying voice, "you don't like it."

"I didn't say I didn't like it!" cried Cleet, getting up and stepping out onto the catwalk to look down at the boyish figure at the huge table. "I—I like it."

The possessing silence of the library closed over the hesitation between them.

"Well," Neil said inside the silence, "you don't sound very enthusiastic."

"I *like* it," insisted Cleet, and he heard a note in his voice he had never heard there before and felt an expression on his face he had never felt there before. The note in the voice was pleading, and the expression on his face was twisted.

"Oh, good," said Neil expressionlessly.

Silence closed over the room once again. The incident was past almost before it happened, and Cleet went clumsily back to his place.

At twelve-thirty lunch arrived on trays. It was beef consommé, two ham sandwiches, two Coca-Colas, and two apples. This was typical of many meals at the Reardons'. Mrs. Reardon, Sr., wasn't interested in food. Also, she had learned to spend money in major ways, such as buying the Mexican chapel and having it shipped in segments to Wetherford, but she had not ever learned to spend it continuously, instead reverting to her early days of modest living except when she pulled herself together, concentrated, and remembered that the family no longer had to live on ten thousand dollars a year.

Georgia, who sometimes decided the menu of the day, provided nothing better. Simple meals seemed more youthful to her. Elaborate menus made her feel artificial and pretentious, and fundamentally a ham sandwich and an apple brought her intense relief; I'm just me, the same as always, this nourishment made her feel, nothing has changed, I'm not in an unreal world, I'm not losing my real identity. *Nothing has changed.*

By three-thirty Cleet could endure no more. "I'm hungry," he said loudly.

"What?"

"Aren't *you* hungry?"

"I don't think about food when I'm working."

"Well, I'm hungry."

"Ring the bell for somebody, then, and see if there's anything. Or go look in the kitchen. I'm not hungry."

But now, feeling challenged to some kind of endurance contest, Cleet turned back to the reading. This chapter was called "Forgive." Suddenly the writing seemed all right to him, and he actually believed what he was reading. Neil here was continuing his high-mindedness but not the currently fashionable kind; suddenly he wasn't saying what everyone else was saying, wasn't being another Eastern enlightened millionaire liberal. He urged that Germany and Japan be forgiven, he pleaded for remembering the common humanity of all people, he said it was inconsistent to give all compassion to the Jews and none to the Germans, everything to the Chinese and nothing to the Japanese; America, Britain, and France had all been expansionist and aggressive once, had provoked fights with weaker neighbors.

This chapter would be very unpopular. Cleet soundlessly cheered. Neil had finally taken an unpopular position and stood up for something he apparently sincerely believed in. It did follow logically from all the earlier compassion in the book. It was daring and defiant and probably, when you got right down to it, right.

"I *like* this part about forgiving the Germans and Japs."

"I'm glad you do."

"That shows a lot of guts."

"I guess maybe it does."

"A lot of people are going to hate it though. The war's hardly over, all the Americans that got killed, all the mothers, the Polish people and the Jewish people and all the other people, well, practically everybody." Cleet was definitely impressed. Neil had a scope he hadn't realized; it seemed that he was almost a philosopher.

"The German people and the Japanese people have a lot of good qualities."

Some off-key overtone echoed in that and Cleet cogitated over it for a minute. There was, after all, only one quality universally known in the Germans and Japs at this particular time: violent aggression. It was strange that Neil should have departed from fashionable opinion just there.

Hunger overcame Cleet. He had to eat, now. Like Georgia, he did not like to ring for a servant, for the simple reason that he would resent anybody's ringing for him. If he could yell for one to come it would have been all right, because there was a good informal all-men-are-created-equal camaraderie in a yell, but yelling into the corridors and halls and wings and additions and subdivisions and subbasements and turrets of High Farms would be futile, so he got up, went along the catwalk, down the circular stairway, said "Hungry" with a grin to Neil, who looked at him thoughtfully over his reading glasses, and went squeaking over the old floor, and out through the sliding double doors.

Outside the library was the Main Hall, a large, gloomy room paneled in dark oak, with a massive, balustraded staircase hulking on the left, two long stained-glass windows, predominantly green, on the right, what had once been the front door of the house straight ahead surrounded by frosted glass, a cutglass chandelier, potted plants, two high-backed formal chairs, one Persian rug. Cleet plunged into a small black corridor under the stairs and felt his way along to a swinging door, went through it into a dining room, very dim, with a vast stone fireplace, a sideboard dimly shining with silver, a high cabinet with ornamented glass doors, enormous candlesticks. Over the fireplace was a large painting which Cleet, despite the thousands of meals he had eaten in this room, had never really seen. There was a tiny light beneath it, but this illumination merely brought out a glaze in the pigment, which blinded the eye.

High Farms was a house of unseen paintings, unopened sets of books, stuffed animals shot by strangers, a church built for the peasants of a foreign country, carpets from the Middle East, and furniture from Europe, surrounded by farms leased out to professionals, horses ridden by hired hands, owned and occupied but not really possessed by a family. The Reardons had always been in too much of a hurry for it; it was home and they were forever away from home, Mr. Reardon on business trips, Mrs. Reardon going South in the winter and to the shore in the summer, Geraldine away at school from the age of thirteen. They had not even built this house, but only defaced and elaborated what someone else had built.

Cleet opened the sliding doors at the end of the dining room and went into a square room full of Victorian sofas and chairs upholstered in light green, with heavy dark green draperies, a small white fireplace, a harp, a low, box-shaped old piano which played by itself when perforated metal disks were put inside it; one wall was covered with a tapestry so old as to be indecipherable, and there was an adjustable reading chair copied from Jefferson's at Monticello. Through a door on the right he reached a long corridor with many small rooms opening off it on the right, and a door leading to a kitchen garden on the left. The little rooms had been kitchens in the nineteenth century. At the end of the corridor he went down a stairway to the present kitchen, spacious and modern, found a peach and a tomato and some celery and chocolate milk and peanut butter, and after that felt better.

Neil is not a liar, he said to himself several times, chewing. He is not a liar. He is just very ambitious, and what's the matter with that? Isn't every young American supposed to be ambitious? And tremendous additional credit was due Neil for being so ambitious and hard-working when he had the money to be able to do absolutely nothing all of his life. He deserved to be deeply admired for that, and the fact that what he wrote in books and said in speeches had nothing to do with the way he truly felt was, well that was just because he was *complicated.* That was it. He had a very complex mind and saw many sides to problems. Cleet bit into the peanut butter sandwich with renewed gusto, very relieved to have understood that Neil was not really a lying hypocrite at all. He was Cleet's closest friend from the past, his employer at present, and his future benefactor, future founder of Cleet's success, and it would have been deeply disturbing, nauseating in fact, if this foundation stone of Cleet's life had turned out to be a lying hypocrite. Cleet spread himself another peanut butter sandwich. The trouble with me is, he grumbled to himself, I'm starting to *think* too much. What good is that? He had never been much good at it, as school and the Air Force had made clear to him, not much good at it, according to them. But privately, strictly to himself, he expressed the opinion that when it came to understanding people he had a peculiar kind of talent. It came and went. He could not depend on it, but very often it gave him something.

The source of this gift was clear: his own feelings flowed in so many directions and reached such deep, artesian levels and shot up in such unpredictable geysers that he could understand many, many kinds of feelings because he once had them or had them now or could have them at any time; he could feel the way most people he encountered felt, and so understand them. The difficulty he had in understanding Neil was that Neil's actions were not much governed by feelings.

He remembered one dinner years ago in the dining room upstairs. He had been about fourteen years old, and had been sitting at the dinner table next to Neil, their backs to the fireplace and the painting over it. Mr. and Mrs. Reardon were at the two ends of the table, and some other people must have been sitting around it somewhere. Directly across from him had been a man Mr. Reardon had described as "one of the original Brain Trusters."

Cleet had been set on fire by this description: a brain truster, somebody who had the profession of trusting brains. He didn't have a chance to ask more about this phenomenon before the brain truster arrived, coming into the green Victorian parlor, where the piano and harp were, where the family always gathered before going in to dinner. The man was old with gray hair which grew in clumps on his head, a long, lined face, and a clear, certain voice. Cleet pictured him as having either a safe or an engine inside his head, calculating, sorting, classifying, dividing everybody up and putting their parts in neat piles, legs here, religions there, sins somewhere else, educations in the middle, a group of hands, a pyramid of incomes. The man talked carefully and listened carefully, as any brain truster would, and after they went in to dinner, Cleet, directly across the table, never took his wide, level Indian gaze off him and never said a word.

"People never catch up with themselves," the man announced to the table.

There were hesitant mutterings of assent from the other adults.

"That's our hardest problem as human beings."

"Mm," Mrs. Reardon hummed.

"Hum," said Mr. Reardon thoughtfully.

"Take yourselves," the brain truster continued.

Everyone waited silently.

"Here you sit in this immense house with your immense fortune and all the immense power that goes with it. And how do you live?"

Mrs. Reardon tittered lightly and Mr. Reardon cleared his throat.

"Like *bourgeois*."

Cleet instantly apprehended that this word was highly uncomplimentary; he understood it to be "bore-joy" and assumed it meant the same thing as "kill-joy" and he thought that, applied to the Reardons, it was perfectly true. They themselves did not comment; the brain truster was apparently a figure of such greatness that he could insult them at their own table.

"Take these boys," he said in his confidential voice, suddenly turning on Cleet and Neil. "How old are you?"

"Fourteen," Cleet shot back instantly, as though to fend him off.

"What are you mainly interested in these days?"

"Uh well studying and learning to—"

"I'm not the traunt officer. What are you interested in these days? What page do you read first in the newspaper?"

"Well I usually read the sports page first."

"And then?"

"After that I read I guess the funnies."

"You see? In two years he'll be ripe to reproduce and two years after that he'll probably be a soldier fighting for civilization, and he's exclusively preoccupied with games and jokes. By the time he concentrates on girls he'll be past his reproductive peak and by the time he shows any interest in world affairs he may be dead because of them." He threw himself back in the big armchair. "We never catch up, we never catch up! The phase of life we're ready for is always the one just past."

Cleet was transfixed by this man.

During dessert he noticed that the brain truster kept shifting uneasily in his chair, and then rearranging his table silver and placing his glass geometrically in relation to his knife, all the while talking, until finally he became openly nervous and knocked over his water glass. This incident remained in Cleet's mind, awaiting an explanation patiently year after year, until suddenly one day he realized that his own unwavering green stare had totally unnerved even someone as crustily self-confident as the brain truster.

That evening's dinner eventually ended and the party went back to the Green Parlor, where Mrs. Reardon put a metal disk of "The Lost Chord" into the antique player piano, and seated in the Jefferson chair, with a pipe now, no longer disconcerted by Indian Eye, the brain truster said again, "We never catch up in life. We are always behaving in a way very appropriate for the phase which has just ended. We are like actors in a repertory company, all our lives performing last week's play in front of this week's sets."

Cleet finished the peanut butter sandwich. Last week's play in front of this week's sets: that too had remained in his mind year after year, waiting to be understood.

He left the kitchen, and going along the basement hallway, heard shouts coming through a tunnel opening off it and sloping downward. People were in the pool. He thought it sounded as though they were having fun, so he decided to join them, his mind immediately blotting Neil, Neil's writing, and the library from his consciousness.

The tunnel sloped gloomily further into the depths of the house and Cleet trotted down it and came out onto the deck of the pool; there were five people, a usual number for any afternoon, playing High Farms Tag. This game had been invented years before by Geraldine; its chief innovation was that to cease being "It" a player had not merely to touch but to kick another player, which caused many falls, sprains, and abrasions.

As it had happened, Cleet hadn't seen the pool since his return to Wetherford and now its archaic peculiarities struck him. It had been installed here in the bowels of the house by a previous owner, at the turn of the century, and was what at the time had been called a "plunge," twenty yards long, seven yards wide, shaped like a coffin, fed sporatically by water pouring from the bronze head of a sea lion, with huge bronze rings at intervals along the sides of the pool; along one side there extended a row of pillars freely adapted from the Stoa of Athens. Overhead eerie Pre-Raphaelite illumination filtered down through a skylight of very dark green and blue glass. Large naked lamps hanging by cords from the vaulted ceiling also supplied a form of illumination. Because of this light the water looked unnaturally green and rather stagnant. The deck and walls and pillars and the long, shallow steps leading from the pillars into the water were made of grayish-brown stone, and the pool itself was of small tile octagonals. The air was suffused with an atmosphere of fungus, dampness, flu, and leaks.

"Cleet!" called out Geraldine in her hoarse voice. "Get into your bathing suit immediately!" Looking as usual rangy and a little disheveled, she was sitting on the deck, wearing a green two-piece bathing suit, eating grapes. Her ten-year-old son, Hugh Blanchard, was thrashing in the pool. "We want to have another game of tag. Hurry up!" Looking at the water she said, "Hugh, stop splashing and get more pull with the arms. Can't you show him more how it's done, Grace?" Grace Hartshorne had been her roommate years before at college and was now her private secretary. Standing at the shallow end of the pool on either side of the sea lion were Martin Brewer, one of Mr. Reardon's senior aides, and Barbara Armstrong, a family friend, who had shot her husband in a hunting accident six weeks before. Geraldine had flown to South Carolina to bring her back to High Farms to recover from the shock. The Reardons were always inviting family associates and stricken friends and unlucky relatives to stay at High Farms.

Cleet went into a cell used as a dressing room, undressed, and put on a pair of trunks from a pile in the corner. He took care to choose trunks which suited him well because he wanted to see if he could make an impression on Barbara Armstrong.

When he came out the game of High Farms Tag started immediately. Geraldine announced that she was It. She chased Mr. Brewer, who was forty-seven, to a corner of the deck and kicked him on the thigh. He laughed, brushed the remaining hairs of his head out of his eyes, and dived into the pool near Barbara Armstrong but couldn't catch her. Finally he caught Hugh and touched him gently with his foot. Cleet let Hugh catch him. Then Cleet caught and insinuatingly pushed Barbara Armstrong with his foot against her buttocks. She did not look very amused. Barbara got out of the pool and ran along the deck after Geraldine, who yelled out, "Oh no you don't, I'm not going to be caught by *you,* oh no you don't," slipped, fell, scrambled up, and dived into the pool, narrowly missing Mr. Brewer, who was floating on his back breathing deeply. Barbara followed her into the water and caught Mr. Brewer on the shoulder with her foot. Cleet now let Mr. Brewer, who was badly winded, catch him. Then he set off after Barbara again, swimming the length of the pool with his very good crawl stroke, catching her at the shallow end, and pretending that she was drowning, picking her up in his arms for a moment. She looked a little more pleased. No one had chased Grace Hartshorne, in her black bathing suit, so now Barbara did, catching her on the deck and kicking her with a force which Grace clearly thought was a little too much.

"Come on, Gracie," cried Geraldine, pushing her disorderly hair out of her eyes, "if you try hard enough, you might catch Hugh, but I doubt it!" Grace then changed the expression on her face and laughed. The others all laughed at what Geraldine had said except Cleet, who was absorbed in a study of Barbara's body. Grace walked up behind him and gave him a swift kick.

"Damn!" he exploded, then recollecting himself, grinned, and reluctantly chased Geraldine, who did not like to be left unchased.

When she saw he was following her she stopped swimming, saying, "It's hopeless. Nobody can get away from you. Go on, kick me." He touched her on the leg with his foot. "Good," said Geraldine, seeing someone coming down the tunnel, "we need more people," and then recognizing the tall man as he came onto the deck, added under her breath, "but not that, no, not that." It was Buddy Ashcraft, a Hartford lawyer to whom she had once been engaged.

"Hi there, how are you!" he said energetically.

"*We're* fine," muttered Geraldine to Cleet, then to Buddy, "Come in for a swim, do you want to?"

"Fine, I'd like to, fine."

"I thought his mother was keeping him at home," said Geraldine when he went into the dressing room to change. "Isn't she?"

"Guess not," said Cleet.

"Can't you, can't somebody? This is—we can't go through last year again."

"I wasn't here, remember, but I heard something about it."

"Be glad you weren't here," she continued in the same undertone. They stood motionlessly, waist-deep in the water. Buddy's appearance had acted on the game of tag like a paralysis. "When we had the gardeners keeping him from coming through the gate he hired a rowboat and went up and down the river, staring up here at the house with binoculars. He wrote us ten letters a day. He kept saying, 'When can I come home?' He called up, I don't know, twenty times one Sunday. It was awful. He began to think he was Daddy's illegitimate son, he even started to threaten us, he was going to sue because Neil and I were stealing his inheritance! Oh God, if he hadn't finally been put in the Hartford Retreat he might have murdered us all."

"He's out, so he must be better."

"Is he? When they're that crazy do they ever get better?" She shook her damp hair. "I don't know what our family does to cause . . . fixations like that."

Buddy came out of the dressing room, tall, slim, black-haired, pale, and knelt beside the pool to feel the water with his hand. "Isn't it too cold?" he asked.

"No," answered Geraldine, trying to smile, "it's fine. Come on in."

"Shouldn't I speak to the caretaker about heating it up? I might just do that."

"Please don't," said Geraldine. "Anyway, there's no heating system in this old tank. Just come in, if you want to swim. We all have to leave in a few minutes so you'd better hurry."

Buddy dived in and swam theatrically up to them. "You're right, it feels just great, just great. Certainly does me good."

"We have to leave practically right away, Buddy," said Geraldine, "so swim a few lengths and then we all have to go. Did you walk all the way out here from your house? Someone will drive you home, Cleet will." She began side-stroking away. "But let me call you and ask you to come over again someday when we're swimming and you can have a longer time."

"I don't mind staying here, if you don't. I like to swim alone sometimes."

"I'm so sorry, Daddy won't allow it. He thinks it's dangerous for even the best swimmers, even in a little tank like this. I'll call you someday though." Everyone began to swim separately and rather aimlessly, and after five minutes Geraldine called, "Come on, Hugh, out, no, right away, out. Grace, Barbara."

They all climbed out of the pool, Hugh, Cleet, Mr. Brewer, and Buddy dressing in one cell, the women in the other, and then Geraldine maneuvered Buddy out a basement door near the garage and Cleet drove him home. "What a wonderful family," Buddy said twice on the way. "I never knew people like them before, and you know, I don't think I ever will again. They can't do enough for people."

"No."

"They really can't do enough, can they? Geraldine, or Neil, or their parents, takes an interest in you and . . . they can't do enough."

What a weak sister, Cleet thought to himself, driving back to the Farms. At the same time something about meeting Buddy Ashcraft made him feel obscurely shaken, and he had an impulse to take a very long detour, for example by way of Boston, back to High Farms.

Then he remembered that he was supposed to be working with Neil in the library.

"Where the hell have you been!" Neil demanded when Cleet got back.

"Buddy Ashcraft turned up."

"Oh," said Neil in a hollow tone.

"I had to get rid of him."

"Oh," he repeated. "Not that again." He brushed some papers across his desk with a disgusted gesture. "Why do we keep getting involved with people like that?"

That evening Mr. and Mrs. Reardon, Neil, Georgia, Geraldine, Hugh, Cleet, Barbara, Grace, and Mr. Brewer had dinner outdoors. Lynn Sommers sent word that her face had broken out again, and stayed in her rooms.

The table had been set on the Sunken Lawn, which was enclosed by a low brick wall with four huge amphoras at the corners. Cleet had driven past this spot on his way to the garage not long before and there had not been a sign of preparations then. Now a beautifully set dinner table for ten had been whisked into place, with a long floral centerpiece, three wineglasses at each place, damask tablecloth and napkins, serving tables, wine buckets, chafing dishes: obviously this was going to be one of the infrequent good-menu nights at High Farms.

Mrs. Reardon was just as efficient at training and directing servants as Mr. Reardon was with executive assistants. They moved soundlessly around and through the house, sometimes it seemed passing through stone walls and rising like smoke up chimneys, so that their services appeared performed by ghosts. There was a whole labyrinth of back stairs and corridors burrowing through the heavy structure, but that could not entirely explain why a cold living room Cleet left for five minutes had a fire crackling in the grate when he returned, why when he went to the bathroom to brush his teeth his pajamas draped themselves over the bed, why magazines formed lines on tables, flowers fell into arrangements in bowls, and whole dining rooms sprang into being on the Sunken Lawn. Sometimes he caught a maid or houseman in the act of straightening up his room or dusting the library and then he felt reassured. But for the most part his movements and habits, and those of the family and other guests, were studied by the servants so that almost everything they did for him could be done behind his back. That was the way of good servants as it was understood at High Farms.

Mrs. Reardon specified black ties and white jackets for dinner. Cleet borrowed one of the latter, faintly yellowed by age, from Neil.

"What's the occasion anyway?" he asked. "Dinner jackets, black ties? Whose birthday is it?"

Neil smiled but said nothing.

As evening settled slowly over the Connecticut Valley the family and their guests began drifting across the lawn, under the great trees, the women in light evening dresses, all of them passing into an atmosphere of well-being which sprang from the sun and shade intermingling on the close-cropped grass, and the stillness surrounding them, from the vast solidity of the great gray slab of house rising behind, from the certainty of a fine dinner ahead, from the security of the fortune and the good humor evident in Mr. Reardon's pink face, and from Mrs. Reardon's golf score that afternoon, from the elimination of the great war from their preoccupations, from Neil's holding Georgia around the waist and Hugh's behaving himself, from Barbara Armstrong's choosing to wear not black but white, from Mr. Brewer's two martinis in his room while dressing, from Grace Hartshorne's flushed efforts to flirt with Cleet, and from Cleet's stimulating sense that both Barbara and Grace were attracted to him and his determined thought that the Reardons must always value him, employee or not, for himself.

"We'll go over next to the Goat for cocktails," Mrs. Reardon called out in her clear, youthful voice. She had on a flowered evening dress and was very tan. "There are daiquiris and nothing else," she added. "I hope that suits everyone."

"Excellent," said Mr. Brewer.

A small bar had materialized under a huge oak next to the Goat, which was a life-sized bronze figure placed there many years before for some forgotten reason. Cleet had once dug beneath it, thinking it marked the grave of a pet, but found nothing.

Hugh now climbed onto the Goat's back and drank a glass of tomato juice. The two Irish setters sniffed the figure hopefully for the hundredth time.

"God, I'm bored with that beast," said Geraldine to Grace. "I'm tired of being trapped here in this place, aren't you? It's not *still* unpatriotic to travel, is it? What are we all doing here in the middle of summer?"

"Yes, Geraldine," said Neil drily, "it still is unpatriotic to travel."

"I don't believe it. Now that they've delivered *Cleet* home, there can't be any soldiers slower than he was. They're all bound to be home. Why shouldn't we travel?"

"Where is there to go?" said Neil. "The Coast Guard haven't turned the *Maureen* back to us yet, so we can't sail anywhere." The *Maureen* was the family's two-hundred-ton motor yacht, which had been lent to the Coast Guard and used for submarine-patrol duty. A smaller family ship, also used by the Coast Guard, the hundred-ten-foot schooner *Chatwood,* had been sunk during a storm off Novia Scotia in 1943. The Reardon summer home at York Point, Maine, had been turned over to the Red Cross and was not yet ready for reoccupancy.

"We're trapped," sighed Geraldine.

Neil moved off to join Georgia and his father.

"There's plenty to do here, dear girl," said Mrs. Reardon. "If you'd condescend to serve on any one of my committees—"

"Valley Beautification!" said Geraldine with an incredulous smirk.

"Rural libraries," asserted Mrs. Reardon.

"The Webb House Foundation!"

"The chest-x-ray mobile."

"Not me!"

Mrs. Reardon looked irked, and then lowering her voice, said, "At least you could think about your brother's interests, his writing and his speeches and above all, Georgia with a baby on the way. You should spend more time with Georgia, make her feel more at home. Show her more about clothes, now that there are decent clothes to buy again, get her interested in new things. Take her riding. Why don't you ever ask her to go riding with you?"

"She doesn't like horses. She'd rather hitchhike."

"Really, Geraldine."

"Rather what?" said Hugh.

"Nothing, dear, nothing," said Mrs. Reardon.

"*I* like horses."

The others drifted up and congregated under the old tree, around the bar and the Goat.

"I have one further question," said Geraldine. "What's this all about tonight? Dinner jackets, long dresses, dinner on the Sunken Lawn. What is it? The reading of the will?"

"It's a surprise of Neil's," said Mrs. Reardon. "He asked for all this. Even I don't know. Now you can tell us. Neil? What are we celebrating? Is it Cleet's return?"

"Are you joking? Celebrate getting the old pain in the neck back?" Some people smiled, some chuckled; Cleet tried to beam. "Of course not. Don't you know what day this is?" Everyone was silent, thinking. Then Geraldine erupted.

"Oh no, oh Neil, oh really!" It was her wedding anniversary. She had been estranged from her husband since 1942. Then she burst out laughing. Everyone else laughed except Georgia, who looked alarmed.

"Here's to absent friends," continued Neil, raising his glass.

"Damn you," said Geraldine with a smirk.

"You're terrible, Neil," murmured Grace.

"What taste!" exclaimed Barbara.

"It's your *what?*" demanded Hugh.

"The children I'm raising," sighed Mrs. Reardon. "Well, we know where you get your sense of humor. And to think we're having shad roe and lobster for that!"

Mr. Reardon said nothing but he was plainly amused. He admired audacity, from risk investments to practical jokes. Georgia was speechless and turned the stem of her glass around and around in her fingers. Cleet saw that a typical Reardon evening at home in the style of the old days seemed to be developing. It was just possible that Neil would find Geraldine's horse in his bedroom later tonight.

"Don't be embarrassed," Geraldine said to Georgia. "You'll get used to us some year."

"I'm not embarrassed."

"It was a funny idea, a really funny idea. Crude, maybe, but I don't think so, and if *I* don't, who should?"

"Of course," said Georgia as confidently as she could.

"I wish I was still married, in a way. I mean, look at our family. This big house, and Ma having just *two* kids. It's pathetic. An Irish-Catholic family like ours and only two children, and me with only *one!* It's always been a disappointment to Daddy. He's never breathed a word but he doesn't have to. Do you know why Neil and I, and he and Ma too as a matter of fact, fill the house with friends and relatives and strays, I mean acquaintances, and anybody? We're trying to make it feel like a big family. That's what Daddy's always really wanted, and Ma too, that's what the *house* wants. Sometimes naturally we get a Buddy Ashcraft instead of someone we like, but that's life. You have lots of kids and make everybody happy." She squeezed Georgia's arm, the first affectionate gesture she had ever made to her sister-in-law aside from formal pecks on the cheek.

They moved across the lawn and sat down to dinner, torches on poles burning behind them and hurricane lamps on the table augmenting the fading glow of the summer sky. Mrs. Reardon asked Hugh to say grace: "Bless us, O Lord, and these Thy gifts, which we are about to receive from Thy bounty, through Christ Our Lord. Amen." Cleet had managed without trouble to sit next to Barbara and now started to move his left leg exploratorily in her direction. He was fairly certain he was about to feel her leg against his when he decided furtiveness was the wrong approach. He had never used it before and didn't see why he should start now, even if she was the first rich beautiful young widow he had met. He was pre-eminently of the "Do you want to or don't you?" school, and it had worked very well so far. Creeping up on a girl gave him a grimy feeling somehow.

"How was the hunting trip?" he asked in order to start conversation, remembering a second too late what had happened.

She blinked and then stared starkly at him for what seemed several minutes.

"I'm sorry," he finally said in a low voice, "I just forgot. I'm very sorry."

Turning back to her plate she said with a heavy sigh, "I wish I could forget, just a little. That may be wrong, but I wish I could. I can't help it. Don't listen, I can't go on rambling about it to everyone. You—"

"You'll get over it someday."

There was another long silence and then she said, "I wonder if I will. It's the sound I think I may never get over, the sound of my shotgun going off. I can hear it terribly clearly every time I let myself, now, for instance, goddamn it." She put her fist to her forehead. "It's not even seeing Billy—after, it's that *sound*. I don't think I can ever lose that—*awful* sound in my head."

That seemed so serious and sad that it cooled Cleet's thoughts about her temporarily and he decided just to talk to her. She told him that she was leaving to visit Billy's parents the following day. "They can't make out why I've been here all this time instead of with them, or with my own family. I can't explain to them what it is about the Reardons that makes this seem the best—well, the least bad—place to come after the accident. How can I explain it?"

"Maybe it's because it isn't yours."

"Not my what?"

"Not your family, or your in-laws. So you don't have all those old feelings from years ago here."

"Maybe that's it."

The cold lobster was being passed a second time, and Cleet helped himself to more. Georgia was on his left, and she said with a little laugh, "Can I hide some in my napkin and take it up to Lynn?"

"They're not letting her starve."

"That's what I used to do, when I was first going out to dinner with boys. They always took me to the most wonderful places. One reason was that the boys who took me out were always more or less well-off, it's just, well, that's just the way it was. When I brought food back to Lynn, it wasn't for fun, it was for nutrition! Those were the days. Damn. I'm getting this lobster all over me."

"You have to break in, like a robber. Here, use this." Cleet handed her a shellcracker.

"When I use that the lobster explodes."

"Haven't they got lobsters in California?"

"Of course they do. *They* do," she added in a murmur, "we didn't."

"Georgia is certainly going to let *Vogue* take her picture,"

Mrs. Reardon was heard to say. "She doesn't look the slightest bit pregnant."

"*Vogue,*" she breathed into her glass of wine. "Next they'll have me looking at everybody through a lorgnette. Did you see my bracelet?" she suddenly said, changing moods. Cleet gazed down at her wrist at a blinding arrangement of large emeralds and small diamonds, which looked ruinously expensive. "It's the most beautiful thing I've ever seen. I literally almost fainted when Neil gave it to me."

"That was because you were pregnant."

"I wasn't pregnant then. Geraldine had one something like it once. She lost it, *lost* it! I could as easily lose Lynn, or my, my baby. I never heard of anybody losing emeralds and diamonds."

"She does things like that. Besides, they were insured, everything's insured." And at that instant he suddenly realized something that neither Neil nor Mr. Reardon had mentioned to him although there had been several crucial conversations between them on this subject: the *Flying Folly* must have been fully insured. He put this revelation into the back of his head for study later.

"That's true," Georgia was saying. "I'll never be able to act that way though."

Dessert was strawberries *chantilly,* and champagne was served with it. Neil rose and said, "To Geraldine and Nick Blanchard, and may they always be as happy as they are tonight."

After the sharp laughter Geraldine, in her red dress, slightly intoxicated, got up and responded. "I just want to tell all of you well-wishers that what happened between Nick and I wouldn't have been possible without your help. Thank you."

"It's all right, dear, a little joke," Mrs. Reardon murmured to Hugh, who was looking uneasy.

Suddenly soured, the dinner party looked hurriedly for some diversion and settled on Cleet. He was ordered to toast somebody. "I want to give a toast to the Reardon family," he said. "There aren't any other friends like you."

That night Cleet stayed at High Farms because early the next morning he had to drive Neil to Bridgeport for a breakfast lecture for the St. Theresa Sodality.

He was given a more impressive bedroom than he had had before he went away. This room had a four-poster bed, fireplace, bathroom, telephone, balcony, and a circular iron stairway leading down to the South Lawn. Here he fell asleep at eleven-thirty and woke promptly, for no apparent cause, at three A.M. Through the glass doors opening on the balcony he saw that moonlight was spread all over the grass below and that it was a night of rare, clear, still and meditating enchantment. He felt that he had to have some way of participating in such a night, so without hesitation he got out of bed, as usual not wearing pajamas or anything else, and went out to the balcony, and down the stairs, to the empty lawn.

The grass was moist under his feet, which felt very good, so good that he decided to lie down on it, for refreshment. That felt even better, so just for the hell of it he decided to roll across the grass. The light was soft and unchanging and bore messages which someone could decipher, somewhere. He had what he felt was a ridiculous urge to get as close to as possible, even inside, anything so beautiful, and he expressed it now. No one would ever know; it was ridiculous; it made him happy.

At least this magical night was not going to get away from him, as so many magical things, from Mary Carpenter to piloting a plane in the war, had done.

A light snapped on in a turret window and the window started to be raised and Cleet abruptly recognized his situation, rolling naked on wet grass at three o'clock in the morning. It would not be possible to explain why he was doing that. He stepped quickly behind some bushes, alarmed but at the same time almost convulsed by the outrageousness of his situation, circled around the edge of the lawn, regained the stairway, and sprinted back into his room.

"I must be going crazy," Georgia said the next day. "I thought I saw a nun all in white out on the lawn last night."

"Probably a ghost," said Cleet, fixing her with Indian Eye.

The members of the St. Theresa Sodality sat at their U-shaped breakfast table, listening with semireverential attention as Neil addressed them on the subject, "Are the Vatican and the United Nations Organization Natural Enemies?" Cleet did not pretend to understand a word. They did not discuss it during the drive back to High Farms. But it was going to be a Catholic day.

That was unusual at High Farms. Normally Catholicism occupied no more, and usually less, time than golf in the lives of the Reardon family, but Neil's marriage, Georgia's religious instruction, the coming birth of the heir, had turned their attention for the time being to marriage and baptism, to sacraments and dogma and shrines, to grace and plenary indulgences, to the Stations of the Cross and novenae and scapular medals; Mrs. Reardon took to wearing the Miraculous Medal and murmuring ejaculations at odd moments; she had a tiny shrine with a statue of the Virgin in her dressing room and a small Renaissance Madonna over her bed; she now unfailingly murmured grace not only before but also after every meal; devotional books replaced the works of Daphne du Maurier in her rooms. Her son had recently been married; her daughter-in-law was going to be received into the Church; another grandchild was going to enter the world; finally, she herself was not getting any younger: birth, marriage, conversion, death; who but God encompassed all of these fundamentals? Mrs. Reardon began going to Mass every morning.

Mr. Reardon had never been noticeably devout. His relations with the Church were almost purely financial. As he saw it, earning money was what he did best, and he offered it, hoping that, like the Juggler of Notre Dame's, his particular tribute would be acceptable. He privately and secretly admired the inventive convolutions and ramifications of churchly undertakings requiring the financial support of the laity, the genius somewhere in the diocesan chambers and behind him, buried in the Roman Curia, some wizard who produced so multifarious a list of indispensable, poverty-stricken, high-principled causes requiring help. From starving Asians to deserving seminarians, from incipient hospitals to illiterate Africans, from the basketball team to Christmas flowers, from the nuns to the Pope, all gently and deservingly and undeviatingly extended a hand, palm upward, in the direction of Mr. Reardon. He responded with controlled generosity and expected that God therefore absolved him from doing very much else about religion.

He did instinctively believe there was a God, and that being so, certainly the Catholic Church was the one true path to heaven; he could not imagine a Supreme Creator manifesting Himself through the Congregationalists, for instance, and not the Unitarians, and not even the Lutherans he saw around him.

Neil's interest in religion deepened when Georgia told him that she was pregnant. Suddenly provision had to be made for this heir materially, politically, and also spiritually. With any kind of luck at all the Reardon fortune would last through his lifetime, the American governmental system probably would hold together, and the United Nations Organization had at least a Chinaman's chance of keeping world peace. But his heir had to be taught how to behave and how to live and what to believe in, so Neil began to take Catholicism very seriously, and he persuaded Georgia to begin instructions in it.

Until then he had thought of the Catholic Church as the squat white wooden building on State Street, with the stained-glass windows and the terrible choir, the breathy organ and the plaster statues, the exceedingly uncomfortable kneeling benches which adapted themselves neither to kneeling straight nor to leaning back against the seat, the ranting voice of Father Tobin belaboring the congregation for their frivolity and the scandalousness of the women's way of dressing ("If only priests were allowed to marry," Georgia now commented about these sermons, "perhaps he could talk about something else") and about how much money they spent on Occasions of Sin and how little on Christ's work on earth, sermons in which virtue was equated with suffering, plainness, deprivation, and ugliness, and sin with beauty, relaxation, warmth, and spontaneity; as the grinding, exasperated voice ranted on, Neil would stare at the colored-glass picture of some out-of-proportion cherubs and think about himself as a great sports leader, later a great political leader, sometimes even a great religious leader, often a great military leader, not merely winning battles and the war but administering a great foreign country afterward, a proconsul, feared but respected, enforcing his will impartially for the welfare of his subject people. That got him through Father Tobin's sermons.

The Catholic Church had been those Sunday mornings. It had also existed in his mind as a series of numbers: the Seven Capital Sins and the Five Last Things and the Three Persons in God and the Six Corporal Works of Mercy and the Five Loaves and Three Fishes and the Twelve Stations of the Cross and the Seven Sacraments.

Most of all, the Catholic Church was hell's fire and a wordless, transcendent fixation on sex as the root of all evil. Morals, strangely enough, meant purely and simply sex and nothing else in the Catholic vocabulary: cheating, lying, stealing, and murder were not the same thing as "morals."

And search as desperately as he did, Neil could find no Catholic route to sexual fulfillment. There was, it was true, marriage, where, if he was still alive and sane, he would at last be permitted to have sexual experiences, but only within stringently limited confines.

As the long, twisted road to such a circumscribed target became clear to him, when he was about fifteen years old, Neil felt entering into his bones and blood vessels a fatalistic sense that life really was not going to be possible. The discovery of this contradiction in himself before life stunned him. Thereafter the possibilities of life became more trivial and more unreal, and at the same time he began to feel himself becoming rather irrelevant.

When he was twenty-one years old and on leave from the Navy he spent a week at High Farms. The family had few full-time servants then, and so Mrs. Reardon sometimes cooked. One evening as she was inexpertly preparing an omelet for him and Geraldine in the basement kitchen, they began discussing the desirability of not having a large family and the unreliability of the "rhythm system" in preventing it. This was the most daring conversation Neil had ever had at High Farms; his uniform seemed to have induced some reduction in the level of prudery at home. Mrs. Reardon and Geraldine agreed that the "rhythm system" could not really be trusted, that birth-control "contrivances" were forbidden by the Church, but still, a limited number of children was desirable.

"So what do you do?" Neil inquired in his politest tone.

"Why," his mother answered drily, "practice continence."

"*Continence!*" he shouted in a rasping voice, feeling a kind of explosion taking place inside his head. He had not suspected he possessed such rage; neither had they. The two women looked at his distorted face a shade timidly. "You're both crazy," he managed to say.

"That's what the Church teaches," his mother said somewhat hesitantly.

He could hardly speak from fury. "If any wife of mine tried that on me I'd throw her naked out on the street and her clothes after her. I'd kick her all the way down the front stairs."

Mrs. Reardon turned back to the frying pan and shook it uncertainly and Geraldine took a long, wide look at him for the first time in many years. Finally his mother cleared her throat and said, "Well then, what would you do? Disobey the Church?" And then the flames of hell rose up to confront the flames of desire within him and he felt that his innermost nature was about to be incinerated; he had to turn like a pillager, and at once, either upon the Church or upon his own passions and wreck one or the other in order to exist.

The idea that after enduring the staggering hardships of adolescence with no sexual satisfaction of any kind except at the risk of hell's fire forever if he happened to die in such a state of mortal sin, suffering at the very least the gnawing teeth of guilt and of self-disgust, and after enduring a thousand false starts with the wrong girls, the aborted courtships and mutual disillusionments, then finding at last a girl who was not wrong, getting through somehow the endless alarms and bottomless suspense and fatal menaces of falling in love, at last, getting married, with then, supremely, sexual love sanctified by her, himself, Father Tobin, his mother and the Vatican, that after all that his found wife should propose that they practice *continence!* His mind turned opaque at the word. He then easily and simply and completely comprehended how a man could strangle a woman; nothing in those circumstances would seem more natural to him. Continence: that any human being, let alone his "own flesh and blood," could suggest that the end of this appalling struggle upstream to the spawning ground should be continence filled him with a kind of terror of incomprehension and a sense of outrage beyond anger itself, a becalmed black rejection which existed on the far side of outrage and removed him from any emotional contact with his mother for the rest of her life.

The shuttered sex of his youth had, however, receded with the advent of Georgia and he began to forget what he had known, blur what he had understood, gloss over what had been glaring. He imagined that his sexual conflict had, by the act of marriage, solved itself. He also began putting on weight. The hungry-hound appearance he had had since the age of thirteen began to blur around the edges, now that he was kenneled and leashed and properly and punctually fed; like all young American men he had been homeless and roaming, underfed and hunting and doubt-filled and violent, until now; having a hundred million dollars and belonging to a family possessing four houses made no difference; he had been spiritually as homeless and roaming as any orphan.

After he had gotten married the Catholic Church was still there, as it always was and had been and doubtless would ever be, and his profound resentment and disgust with it blurred with his jawline; it was as much a part of his life as Wetherford itself, he had no alternative religious convictions, and so he merged with it again. Father Tobin ranted on about morals but Neil let the issue pass him by. After all, Georgia showed not the faintest sign of suggesting anything like continence ever.

Neil and Cleet had lunch in the glass-walled conservatory overlooking the river with a family friend, Monsignor Monroney, who had stopped at High Farms on his way from Hollywood to Bar Harbor. It was a typical High Farms lunch: tuna fish and potato chips. The monsignor, who looked like a very well established movie star, sat swiveled in his chair, ankle on knee, smoking and discussing recent developments in Hollywood, and then some of the least-known struggles among factions at the Vatican. He gave Neil a rosary made from Palestine olive wood, which had been blessed on the Holy Sepulcher itself.

"What happens when it's blessed?" asked Cleet afterward.

"It makes it official," said Neil shortly.

"Oh."

Neil was very ill informed about his religion; his father had been determined that his family was not going to be forced into any minority group and so had not sent his children to Catholic schools. Neil was trained to be a good, private, open-minded, unobtrusive Catholic on the side; in the center he was trained to be a vigorous, representative, patriotic American.

"That's not what worries me," Neil added as a non sequitur, which however Cleet followed without difficulty.

"What does worry you?"

"Oh—let's go have a steam."

When they had both been enclosed side by side in steam boxes, staring straight ahead, which was the positioning Neil wanted, since he could not have looked at Cleet during this disclosure, he said quickly, "What worries me is sex."

"It does? Why?"

"It's not the birth-control part, it's the part about it being a sin to enjoy it—"

"A sin to—!"

"Well that's the impression I get. You're only supposed to do it when, you know, you're trying to make her pregnant, that's what I understand. You're not supposed to . . ." Neil could almost be heard forcing his throat to form the next words, "vary—the—position . . . for instance." There was a long pause; then he said, "Now, for instance, when she's pregnant, you see I don't—uh—do it, and I think—I don't think Georgia understands. There are a lot of things about religion Georgia doesn't understand. So that's what worries me. How can you be doing it for reproduction when she's already pregnant? I almost asked Monsignor Monroney that, if we could have gotten him off the subject of Metro-Goldwyn-Mayer."

Cleet shook his head slowly. "You're not supposed to do it for pleasure," he repeated in slow wonderment to himself, as though it were a phrase in Arabic.

"That's what worries me and I don't think Georgia understands."

"What I'd do if I were you is forget about it."

"Forget about doing it?"

"Forget about what you think that they think you're not supposed to do."

"Oh." After a pause he continued in his flattish, swift way of speaking, "That's easy for a Red Indian to say. *You're* not going to burn in hell forever if you die in a state of mortal sin. I am. You're just going to the Happy Hunting Grounds. You would." Neil felt that religion was almost the only crack in his armor. He uneasily suspected that there just might be a great deal to it; he had always feared power; there might be a God who just might be what He was claimed to be, the Supreme Power; and power was the only thing in the world he really respected.

He felt quite depressed, but Cleet on the other hand was

very cheerful, especially at the mention of the Happy Hunting Grounds. It accorded with his own view of the nature of things to anticipate some such afterlife, the natural result and climax of what he sensed in himself and around him on earth and embedded in the philosophy of the universe. All day, since the drive to the Sodality breakfast, he had been vaguely and steadily oppressed by the encroachments of institutionalized religion; the statue of Christ in the Sodality breakfast room with brambles around the head and the heart shockingly exposed to the air, and the terrible holes in the hands; the bleakness and grayness, the varnish and hush, the rattle and incense and tinkle and damp of churchliness had clung to him all morning, the scrubbed, unadorned, whispering decrepitude of systematic Christianity had slowly encroached on him like a clammy shirt which however much he squirmed and pulled at he could not take off.

"I've got something for you to think about," Neil said. "How do you feel in that steam box?"

"I feel hot."

"How would you feel if it was twice as hot as it is?"

"Terrible."

"You couldn't stand it."

"You're right."

"Well that's what hell is, only it's a thousand times hotter than that and it goes on forever."

More irritated even than incredulous, Cleet finally managed to say, "Do you really believe that?"

"I think I do," said Neil. "I think I'm supposed to, and I think I do."

"Well I'll be damned," muttered Cleet without any intention of making a pun. Neil noticed it. After meditating a few moments Cleet added, "If that much heat didn't kill you, then you'd be some kind of superman, right?"

"I know what you're–"

"And if you're superman you can't feel pain, so why worry?"

"Go to hell."

"Well, isn't it logical?"

"Um–hum."

"So why worry?"

"It gives me something to do," said Neil sourly. After a pause he suddenly said with deep intensity, "The Catholic Church is a real pain in the neck, I can tell you that."

"I always did think so, from watching you. Why don't you just leave it? You're over twenty-one."

"My mother and father and the whole family and the scandal and the shock, that's why. And also people would think I'm trying to conform. I'm not going to let it look like public pressure or some such thing forced me to do anything to appease it. The hell with that. They would say I wanted to be more upper-class. Besides, I *believe* it, damn it. If they excommunicated me for some reason, it would shake me right to the core, I don't really know why."

"Fear," Cleet murmured in spite of himself.

"If they excommunicated me," Neil went on with increased volume, to drown that word, "it would have this effect. Perhaps it is childish but I can't shake it off. Everything I know about religion I learned when I *was* a child, so that's all I know."

"It's pretty spooky if you ask me, blood and wounds and bodies and spirits and torture and sin and penance, that's what it seems like to me. It's a very strange religion. Of course I'm just telling you what I picked up around you and around here. What do I know about it?"

"It's very complicated," said Neil abstractly.

"It sure is. I don't think it makes much sense."

"Well it's not supposed to make sense! It's supernatural."

After a thoughtful pause Cleet said heavily, "Oh."

"Of course if I had a vocation to be a priest or even a monk it would have been simple. Since celibacy is the best way of life—"

"What!"

"That's what they teach."

"Are you serious?"

"Of course I'm serious."

"And you're supposed to be intelligent!"

"Intelligence has nothing to do with it. It's faith and it's a miracle and it's just as embedded in me as, well, as for instance patriotism, and after all we all just risked our lives for that. It's even deeper, much deeper."

"It's childish," said Cleet suddenly.

"Maybe that's it. I wish Monsignor Monroney weren't so fashionable. Maybe he could help."

"What about the priest here, in the church in Wetherford?"

"Are you kidding? Father Tobin?"

"Well then forget about it, about hell, and especially stop thinking about *celibacy*. How can you believe that?"

"That's what my Creator teaches. Intelligence has not a thing to do with it."

"Listen," said Cleet, frowning over his effort to think clearly. "You say you have a deep faith, very very deep. Well, haven't you got any faith in your own guts, in how they feel? Don't you have any faith in that—that *heat* in your head when you love somebody and want somebody, in your body, in the wonderful feeling in the way—in all the tremendous power when you're in love? Didn't whoever created you make that, make it stronger than anything else in you? *Why* did he! Didn't he want you to use it! Don't you have faith in that!"

Neil, after a long pause, answered quietly and sadly, "No, that isn't what they taught me."

Cleet was incredulous about these sexual scruples at first, recalling Neil's several intense affairs before he was married. But he realized that at that time it had been a question of temporary situations absolvable in Confession, passing errors. Marriage and his relations with Georgia were permanent.

That afternoon, religion reappeared—for it was a God-haunted day, God hung like funeral drapery over them that day; like a tail of incense drifting through draughtless halls, the lifeless Odor of Sanctity pervaded High Farms and all of Wetherford, imbuing the day, which happened to be a Thursday, with the starched artificiality of a Sunday, the party manners and flowered hats and strained meals and dusty afternoons of Sunday, endless and drained and purposeless; religion encircled them as though for a second St. Bartholomew's Day, hovered overhead in dank transept stillness, unchanging and unbudging and unadaptable and irrelevant and remorseless and irritating and unconquerable and inconvenient and a bore: that afternoon Georgia was receiving instruction in the Catholic faith from Father Tobin, and Cleet called at the rectory afterward to drive her back to the Farms.

She came hurrying out the door as soon as he pulled up; she was wearing a dark blue dress with a high neckline and sleeves to the wrist, and a hat with a little veil. Dropping onto the seat beside him with a sigh changing to a groan, Georgia snatched off the hat.

"That man!" she groaned. "Now I know what being killed with kindness means."

"I thought you liked him."

"Like him? Oh yes," she sighed, "I like him."

"What's he teaching you about now?"

"About marital duties and related fields." She turned on him a look of wonder. "I didn't know my body was the Temple of the Holy Ghost."

"Well I hear there are a lot of mysteries in religion."

"Yes, I'll say there are."

"Do you think you're going to be a good Catholic?"

"I don't think I'm going to be a real Catholic at all," she murmured in spite of herself. "For instance, I just don't see how the Virgin Mary went bodily to heaven. And I can't picture the Virgin Birth either. How does the wine turn into the blood of Jesus at Mass every day?"

"There are a lot of mysteries in religion."

"On the other hand it's easy to believe in heaven and hell and purgatory and even limbo. I've been in all of them myself, right here."

"Have you confessed all your sins to Father Tobin yet?"

She breathed sharply through her teeth. "Not yet! I'm scared to death of that. Telling an older man all my sins! And I'm not even sure what things I've ever done *are* sins. And *fish* every Friday. Church *every* Sunday. Rosaries. Madonnas. Fasts. And I have to promise to raise my children as Catholics. I hate doing that. Why can't they be exposed to religion and decide what they want when they're old enough to? Why do I have to force this on them when they aren't even born yet? It doesn't seem fair. Oh Cleet," she turned to look at him, "I've married an Irish Catholic."

"Georgia?" When he had something he felt was important to say, Cleet always summoned attention first this way.

"Yes, Cleet?"

"Listen. How can you turn into a Catholic if you don't believe in it?"

"Because my husband's a Catholic, it's as simple as that."

"But you're supposed to have the true faith, to join the Catholic Church."

"Neil is a Catholic. He wants it. That's all there is to it. I'm not going to stand on principle and say my conscience prevents me from embracing the Catholic faith. Men who stand on principle are marvelous, like Patrick Henry. Women who stand on principle are awful, like Carry Nation. Women aren't meant to stand on principle. They're supposed to *be,* just to be."

"Like vegetables?"

"No, like trees."

"That priest'll see you aren't really serious and he won't let you in."

"I'm an actress."

"Well then, you know what'll happen? You'll burn in hell forever, what do you think of that?"

"If I believed that, I'd be a real Catholic and I wouldn't go to hell, I'd go to heaven. If I don't believe it, God wouldn't be unjust enough to send me to hell, would he, just because I was so ignorant? So all I have to do to keep from going to hell is not to admit there is such a place. If it exists, I can't go there."

"Poor old Father Tobin. I hope he's a Jesuit."

They encountered Neil on the South Lawn. "How's it going?" he asked Georgia.

"Fine. Clearer and clearer. I think Father Tobin is pleased with me."

"Good."

Miss Ethel Reardon came to dinner. She arrived in a flurry of beads and tassels and good spirits and plans. She dominated conversation at the dinner table and afterward thought this might be a good time to broach one of her long-contemplated projects: the conversion to Catholicism of Cleet Kinsolving.

A half hour after dinner was finished he found that he had been maneuvered into the Mexican chapel by Miss Reardon. They stood amid the blood-red walls with bulbous Indian baroque ornamentation and she pointed out to him an ugly, black, wood statue of the Virgin which Mrs. Reardon had recently acquired.

"Why do Catholics worship statues?" Cleet wondered aloud.

Aunt Ethel retained her composure. She offered a quick prayer to St. Sylvanus, asking for more self-control, and then said carefully, "Catholics do not worship statues, Cleet. That was a pagan custom which Christianity, that is, Catholicism, which is the same thing, rejected and replaced. A figure such as this one is merely an aid to the Catholic in his prayer, a means of focusing his devotion on the Virgin visually. No one supposes that Mary or any other holy person is present in any statue. A statue is merely a—well, this is a very crude comparison—merely like an advertisement, to remind you of the real thing. There are a couple of books I would be very glad to let you have which explain that and many other things about Catholicism very clearly."

"Well," he said, wishing to get the basic questions settled first, "what about priests taking money for forgiving sins?"

She composed herself by a second monumental effort, invoking St. Anastasios to strengthen her endurance of ignorant malice. "Sins are never forgiven for money," she then said musically. "They are forgiven only by God and the priest acts as intermediary, and there is no money in any form whatever involved. You certainly do have some—mistaken notions about the Church, haven't you?"

"Well, I don't know. There are just some things I heard somewhere, like the—uh—sex between priests and nuns in the convents," and he looked at her to see whether she would confirm or deny this.

Aunt Ethel's arms were straight down and her hands were clasped together in front of her; her only visible reaction now was a certain tightening of this grasp. She prayed to Blessed Theodore of Cyprus for fortitude, and then clearing her throat, succeeded in enunciating almost cheerfully these words: "My, my, Cleet. Your head's just stuffed with wrong notions! How did you ever hear such incredible fables, such complete fabrications," here Blessed Theodore seemed to be deserting her, "such outrageous lies as those! Great heavens, my dear man!" Then she stopped herself, called urgently upon St. Philomela of Fiume, and finally said, "There is of course not a grain of truth to that sinful accusation. Frankly I never heard it before and," she added more drily, "I hope I never do again. I really must give you some literature so that at least the worst misconceptions will be cleared up for you."

Cleet sat down in a gold-colored pew and contemplated the brilliant altar flashing back at him. The sacrament was not present, and so the altar light was unlit, but although he was perfectly comfortable he could see that Aunt Ethel was uneasy talking in church.

"I couldn't believe in the Catholic Church anyway," he resumed.

"No one could expect you to believe until you know something about it, something more than all those silly myths."

"I didn't *think* any of that was true at all but I just thought I'd ask. Aunt Ethel? I'll tell you. The Catholic Church *does* believe it's the true church and the only real one and the only way to heaven, doesn't it?"

"Yes, although you somewhat oversimplify it all. In essence that of course is the Catholic position and has been ever since Our Lord said, 'Thou art Peter, and upon this rock I shall build my church.'"

"I would've joined it right then."

She gazed wide-eyed with mock wonder at him. "Would you? And who wouldn't?"

"But later on, no. Not now anyway. I don't believe it now. It can't be the only right church." He shifted his position to study her face, and she stood in the aisle beside his pew, smiling her best charitable smile. "How can all those millions of Japs be wrong, for instance, every one of them? They've *got something,* I saw it, they feel something, they're praying and somebody's hearing, and it's Buddha! Ma was a Congregationalist and she *had something,* I saw it. How could she be wrong? What about all the millions of people before Christ was even born, what about the Jews and the Moslems and the Hindus and all those, what about all those ancient Greeks who were so smart, Socrates and those people. Just because they were born before Christ do they have to burn in hell forever? It wasn't *their* fault!"

She had been shaking her head with a neat, set smile on her lips and now she said, "Oversimplifying, oversimplifying. I've just got to give you one or two basic books and then you'll at least be clear about some of these points."

But Cleet had no intention of reading any books because the one thing he was clear about was that the Catholic Church was not in very close touch with God.

Cleet knew there was God as surely as he knew there was sky. God was not only up above, he surrounded the world on all sides, everywhere, contemplating and cherishing what he had created. Cleet had thought and read a lot about it during all the empty hours in the Air Force. God was there when needed and many people had gotten into contact with him, establishing a connection very much like a long-distance telephone call used to be, brief, tenuous, full of extraneous noises, and subject to interruption at any time, the frailest, fleetest link between God and some overwhelmingly aspiring person, a person willing to wait and wait and wait, to humor and cajole all the vague, temperamental operators who had to relay the call from point to point if it was ever to get through, an undiscourageable person such as Buddha, Abraham, Christ, St. Theresa of Avila, Moses, Mohammed. Such people who managed so briefly to achieve this direct link with God were instantly transfigured and inspired; sometimes a religion quickly formed around such an obviously God-touched person. The words he had heard from God became the basis of the religion, the divine, garbled message that had been half heard through the blur. Cleet saw that in Wetherford and Kyoto and here and there buildings had been erected and religious services fabricated based on what the person had heard; later the first gestures of faith became a habit and then a practice and then a tradition and then a dogma, and anything else became heresy; finally, as the centuries dried the freshness out of the religion, the buildings and practices became old and stylized and brittle and strange, like the shrines of Kyoto, or the Congregational Church of Wetherford or, although he had never seen it, St. Peter's in Rome, and the few half-understood words from God Himself became finally buried and crushed and almost indecipherable beneath all the weight of long habit and success. He thought it was very strange, all the *reasoning* that tore the original message to shreds and left the darkness almost as complete as before it had come through; night closed in again, and then suddenly on the other side of the earth some businessman or farmer or maiden established the stunning, direct connection with the voice of God once again, and a few more sublime words came indistinctly through.

That was how he interpreted, in a fashion which made sense, what he himself had seen and experienced: his mother's calmly balanced certainty in her Congregational God, his Indian grandmother's seemingly serene reassurance springing from the seasons and the fields and the river, the mellifluous dialogues in chapel between the headmaster at Country Day and his moderate Episcopalian God, the spiritually listening Japanese at Buddhist shrines, Aunt Ethel Reardon's convinced, armored Catholicism. To Cleet their different beliefs were all vestiges of fragments of messages once received from the same God.

Georgia came into the chapel to say that the game of charades was about to start. Cleet immediately got up and he and Aunt Ethel filed rapidly out of the chapel, following Georgia. The game was about to start; at High Farms that meant unhesitating compliance. Occasionally a visitor arrived who innocently announced that he did not enjoy games. If he had said that he thought all millionaires should be shot he could not have made himself more unpopular.

The Reardons played games morning, noon, and night. Mr. Reardon thought certain kinds of games built character, Mrs. Reardon found they reduced what she called "bickering," and Neil took grim joy in anything competitive and Geraldine found games full of rich opportunities for arguing. At High Farms they played word games at breakfast, Identities at lunch, and Essences at dinner. They played croquet, softball, football, badminton, tennis, bowls, tag, red rover, chess, bridge, poker, checkers, and when all else failed, a lone Reardon played solitaire. They were never unoccupied. They felt that in being unoccupied they were not being true to their money, they were insulting its creativity. *No one* who was rich had a right to be bored. They read only in impatient snatches, reading being too passive. Neil was once described by Geraldine as the only writer in history who had written more words than he had read. They did not sit still or mope or contemplate or waste time or fidget or vegetate or mull; when Neil had twiddled his thumbs after both Georgia and Cleet eluded him it had been the burlesque of an action he could never have performed naturally. Mr. Reardon could not have recalled spending one unoccupied afternoon in his life. Mrs. Reardon was the high priestess of the telephone, maintaining a network of communications with friends and interests from coast to coast, with deep penetrations into Mexico and active bureaus in Europe. Except during the wartime restrictions on travel, Geraldine's social calendar left her little time for High Farms. She used it principally for changing clothes.

It was as though the energy which created the fortune burned as fiercely in the new generation as ever, but with no goal now, and where it had before pursued the next deal, it pursued a fox or a stag, the genius for investment gambling was turned to poker, the family tenacity transferred from commerce to tennis, the gift for grasping the moment's opportunity shifted from finance to tourism, the ability to organize complex situations quickly and efficiently passed from the world of business into the world of friends and picnics. All of the Reardons had excellent minds, and often the sense of waste was glaring, as these sharp intelligences focused all of their acumen on badminton strategy, or on how to lay out the new garden. They were beautifully equipped to earn a fortune, now that the fortune had been already earned.

Cleet took the dogs for their nightly walk. He had begun asking himself what exactly he was becoming around High Farms. He concluded that he was becoming a chauffeur and a dog-walker at this time. Soon he would become a hedge-clipper and a lawn-mower and a manure-spreader, and finally a garbage-emptier and a toilet-cleaner. Very soon now he was going to have to put a stop to this downward path he had let himself be persuaded to set out upon; he was going to have to halt this descent very soon or else, he sensed, it would be too late because he would have lost the power to escape, based on his own self-confidence and his own respect. If he took one gram too much of humiliation here then the fuel of self-liking necessary to carry him away might be gone, and like so many men he had seen in their dismalness, he would turn from a venturer into a clinger, caution would move one degree higher on the scale than ambition and so dominate it and finally crush it, doubt would inch ahead of certainty, fear would crowd out confidence, and his life would in all essentials be finished and its great issue lost.

Striding over the sloping, damp hill above the river, he made himself a promise in the dark: as soon as Georgia had her baby and fatherhood had happened to Neil and he had presumably survived it, Cleet would depart to find his own life and fate. Now he was not really living. It was true that he was being well paid, but he felt that in exchange for his salary he was slowly giving up his life's blood.

It was a shining night and the wide, empty waters of the Connecticut shone expectantly below him, as though awaiting some major deployment of ships, some important convoy, some crucial disembarkation. Behind him the turrets of the old house rose formidably against the night sky; the dogs, the two Irish setters named Pat and Mike, picked up exciting scents in the grass, and with all this significance around him, all the beauty of the night, the splendor of the river, and the vastness of the house, even the vitality of the dogs, surrounded by all this, Cleet had never felt flimsier, never seemed less important to himself, nor more out of place, than here in his home town at the house of his best friend. Shit, even the dogs weren't his.

He came back toward the house; he had taken a much longer walk than he realized and the old mansion was almost totally dark. Cleet let himself in by the door next to the library, and as he closed and locked it behind him the burglar alarm under the stairs tingled inquiringly: the Wetherford police were asking whether he was a housebreaker. Cleet went to the alarm box and pushed the button one long and two short, holding the handle to the left, and the tingling subsided into contented silence.

A pale shaft of light was coming out of the library through the slit between the two sliding doors. Cleet slid them apart and looked in; Neil was seated at his huge table with only a colored-glass-shaded desk lamp for illumination, and from the pool of light this cast on the papers in front of him shadows clung and reached up into the big, vague dome above, sloped strangely along the catwalk, and hovered among the banks of books, while behind Neil's seated figure the great bay window stared blindly at the blackness outside.

"Georgia's mother and father are getting in at the airport at eight-thirty in the morning," the figure said. "She can't meet them but Lynn will go with you." He looked across at Cleet and inquired, "Don't those dogs need a bath? Where did you take them? I don't know who's supposed to wash the dogs around here," the figure added, musing aloud.

Cleet stared unblinkingly at it for a moment more, and then without saying anything he went out and up to the bedroom which he used.

At four o'clock in the morning he sprang out of bed from a deep sleep, panting and sweating. He had been dreaming that a fighter plane was about to crash at him through the balcony doors.

The second Reardon plane, a DC-3, landed on the Wetherford airstrip at eight-forty-five. Feeling a little light-headed, Cleet was there with Lynn to meet it. As soon as the cabin door opened a middle-aged couple, looking surprised, stepped out. She wore a blue coat and a black straw hat with berries; he was wearing wide white flannel trousers and a navy-blue yachting blazer. "Don't they look stupid," Lynn muttered.

Cleet didn't agree; he felt drawn to both of them as soon as he saw them, to her because of the way she planted her hand decidedly on the crown of her hat to keep from losing it in the wind, to him because of the way his eyebrows went up in the middle in an expression of inquiring amusement. Cleet could detect this expression across all the intervening field because of his exceptional vision.

"Did you ever see two stupider-looking people?" Lynn went on without moving her lips and she and Cleet walked toward the plane. He didn't reply, and she added, "Look at them," in a scornful mutter, "just like Mr. and Mrs. Astor." Cleet finally said through his teeth, "They look like real nice people to me," and then they were shaking hands.

Mrs. Sommers, saying, "I'm Genevieve Sommers," in quite a loud and low-pitched voice, seized his hand. She was almost ugly, with her wide nose and rolled brown curls and large mouth, but still Cleet could sense some peculiar magnetism which made her attractive.

"Ken Sommers," murmured her husband, slowly and very winningly smiling. He had a used version of an exceptionally handsome face, with a straight nose, rather large blue eyes full of humor and sympathy, fine mouth and chin, wide forehead, graying black hair. All of it was overcast with expressions and markings produced, Cleet learned much later, by many joyous and many sad whiskeys, many packs of cigarettes smoked each day, a stream of unpaid bills harrying his conscience and his pride, firings from jobs, evictions, kited checks and rubber checks and postdated checks and worthless checks, third-hand automobiles bought on the installment plan, wonderfully moving reunions with old bosom friends where his inability to buy even one round of drinks slowly and surely, drink by drink, as though plotted on a chart, turned rancid and humiliating and wounding, a taste for classical music stunted because he could afford neither concerts nor recordings and could hear only what his radio offered through the static, trips around the world never taken, clubs full of charming people who suited him never joined, lovely dresses his daughters never had, the Steinway grand piano deeply and proudly and gloriously promised to Genevieve the night she said she would marry him never, twenty-seven years later, bought, his own graceful manners and considerate ways continually and irritably brushed aside by countermen and doormen and bus drivers and tavern bartenders and barbers and shoeshine boys, a careful feeling for himself and his own ways and how fine life should be and an appreciation of it and of human beings and of colors and daylight and beautiful young and old people and of consideration and dreams, these times and trials accumulating all his life had marked his handsome face as it was now marked.

"Hello, Dad," said Lynn, kissing his cheek, "we're over this way," motioning, "with the Cadillac."

"My God," said Mrs. Sommers loudly, surveying her, "what kind of clothes are you getting yourself into?"

"It's the style," said Lynn shortly.

"My God, you look like one of those *French* girls nobody has any respect for."

Lynn was wearing a very short sleeveless pink dress and sandals, like the very young society girls she had been noticing on this visit to the East. She now conformed to their taste in clothes: the brief swaths and swatches of dress worn out of doors only by American society girls and prostitutes.

Mrs. Sommers hurried on to another subject. "That plane is sheer heaven on earth, or else in the sky. What upholstery! Ken, wasn't it wonderful? Get the bags, where are they, we didn't bring anything, just ourselves and one outfit for the party because we just are going to talk to our girls and not go any place or accept any invitations for anything and that's that, isn't it, Ken, my God you look awful."

"A very beautiful plane," he said in a low-pitched and musical voice in which Cleet heard the source of Georgia's, "a beautiful plane and it flies very well."

"It cost enough, it ought to," said Lynn.

"The clothes you're putting on your back," Mrs. Sommers intoned, "what next?"

"We better get going," said Cleet in his level tone.

"You bet," Mrs. Sommers said, "and you just take us around to some side door of the mansion of our in-laws and let us get up to our room and freshen up and take it easy for a little while before we have to meet anybody."

"You can't creep in like servants," said Lynn in an exasperated undertone.

"Ken's tired, don't tell your mother how to behave, Ken's tired and I don't need your advice on what to do and how or whatever. I'm going to get a decent dress back on you before anything. You look like one of those French girls nobody has any respect for. Are we ready to go?"

They walked to the car, and Cleet and the pilot carried the two small suitcases. He drove them rapidly through Old Wetherford—"It's like some old exhibit at a fair!" Mrs. Sommers remarked in a startled voice. "It's just terrible, isn't it, I wouldn't even want to *retire* here"—and up the hill to the great black and gold main gate to High Farms. "That looks more like the Gate of Hell than the Gate of Heaven," she said with a laugh, and continued commenting as they went along the curving drive, the tires purring expensively on the gravel, passing between the gymnasium wing and the tennis courts, to the granite porte-cochere. A thick mantle of deep green ivy lay over much of the house like a cloak partially thrown over it. Above the third story High Farms broke into slabs of chimney and turrets and strange obtrusions and hooded porches, great sloping sides of roof, a delicate crest fence ornamenting the apex, and the whole gray-granite bulk of the house, unbeautiful as it was, conveyed with great fidelity the domineering power and the vast capacity to resist implicit in Victorian industrial wealth. They continued through the porte-cochere, which shielded what was now the principal entrance, and on to the earlier entrance, next to the library, since the rooms for Mr. and Mrs. Sommers were in that part of the house. Driven past in this way at a certain speed, the house gave the impression of being a successful private school which had been suddenly and erratically expanded, a building where class bells were about to sound shrilly along the corridors; the restlessness of school buildings pervaded all of it. The Reardon brand of restlessness had indeed a private-school panache about it, as though field-hockey sticks and bulletin boards were about to sprout everywhere.

As Cleet stopped at the door he noticed that Geraldine's Buick convertible had been driven onto the lawn and left under a tree, both doors open. Beside it on the grass was a red coat, which apparently had slipped from the seat. "What's that car doing there?" said Mrs. Sommers suspiciously. "Whose is it, why's it there like that?"

"Quite a place," observed Mr. Sommers in his melodic voice. "Lots of peace and quiet in a place like this, off by itself with all your own land around you, protected."

Mr. and Mrs. Sommers were installed in the Rochambeau Suite, so named because the reputed saddlebags of the general were displayed on the wall there behind glass, and the furnishings were Louis XVI. There were four maids and two men servants to help them, all imported from Ireland, who worked with a devoted, wordless speed which left Mrs. Sommers speechless for a minute. "I never knew anybody had help like that," she said resentfully to Cleet. "Where did they get people like that?" He started to say something, but the answers to her questions didn't interest Mrs. Sommers, so she never waited to hear them, preferring always to be querulous, interrogative, in the dark, constantly confronting an inexplicable world which her mind could forever test, speculate upon, and be astonished by. She did not really know where she now was and she didn't want to know; to her, the private airplane had whisked her to Atlantis, and these Irish servants might be leprechauns. "Where are you from?" she said to one maid and then walked away into the bathroom. "My God! Sunk!" she said loudly over the bathtub.

Mrs. Sommers wanted three things. One was to be left to herself for the rest of the day "to get my ears back to normal" after the air flight, the second was a quart of cold beer, and the third was any kind of small piano. She played popular music continually, by ear, and very well; she had to have some kind of piano. Cleet remembered the little Chickering in the gym and with the two men servants succeeded in hoisting it up into the Rochambeau Suite ("Now," he growled to himself, "I'm a piano mover"). Once she had the piano, Mrs. Sommers sat down and swept up and down the keyboard with "You're the Top" and "Mine" and "There's a Train That's Leaving Soon for New York" and "Dinner for One, Please, James" and "These Foolish Things," and she was alone, a little high, and happy. The Reardons appreciated people who knew what they wanted and so were not at all displeased with her demands. After seeing her Georgia said, "Hasn't changed an iota and never will," with a trace of a dubious smile.

Mr. Sommers was assigned to Cleet, who began dutifully taking him on the standard High Farms tour. They visited first of all the pool. Most visitors were amused or fascinated or repelled by this relic, but Mr. Sommers just smiled abstractly and waited to be led elsewhere. The Mexican chapel never failed to stun or shock or amaze visitors: "Lots of color," he remarked. He thought the great domed Victorian library had "a nice view from the window"; the grounds, landscaping, fountains, and statuary were "peaceful"; the farms, model operations studied by agricultural colleges, seemed "fine." As they drove near the river, along a dirt road leading into the Great Meadow, Cleet finally realized that Mr. Sommers had not really been seeing anything or listening to anything he was told. Some inner story or drama had occupied all his attention since he stepped off the plane, and now he related it for the first time to what was going on around him by turning to Cleet and saying, "Do you think we could get a drink somewhere?"

"Sure," said Cleet heartily, "they've got everything back at the Farms—"

"No, I mean out somewhere, a tavern or bar, just some little place where we can sit down."

They drove to a roadhouse on the Highway, where Mr. Sommers ordered rye and Cleet a small beer. "You don't drink," said Mr. Sommers, not asking but stating a fact.

Cleet shrugged. "Can't. I—" He started to tell an interesting lie he sometimes used to explain his abstention, describing how he had nearly died of alcohol poisoning when he was seventeen and thereafter had to give up drinking, the doctor having told him that two consecutive shots of eighty-six-proof whiskey would kill him instantly; he thought of telling that story, or else the one about the fortune he would inherit from his great-aunt if he refrained from drinking hard liquor until he was twenty-five. But looking into the light blue eyes of the man opposite him, with their tolerant and humorous and curious expression, Cleet felt that this man already knew the true reason for his not drinking, already knew that Cleet was subject to mental blackouts, and so he didn't finish what he started to say.

"Where are we?" said Mr. Sommers.

"On the Highway, between Hartford and New Haven."

"Oh. It's a nice road, very good." He scratched the back of his neck. "But why do they ever build roads like this?"

"Excuse me."

"What did they build it for? I don't understand why."

"Well, they built it for, you know, traffic."

"I wonder why. Why didn't they build a, well, for example, a ski lift?"

After a pause Cleet replied carefully, "I don't think I follow what you mean, Mr. Sommers," wondering whether just one shot of whiskey always had this effect on him.

"Well now, a road is built because people want to get from one place to another, am I right?"

Watching him with his levelest gaze, as a large cat would watch a small dog, Cleet nodded.

"You drive your car on it because you want to go somewhere, or maybe only *part way* there, you want to turn off perhaps on some side road. People drive along the road for different reasons, to different destinations, so there has to be the road. But if *everybody* is going exactly the same way, to the same place, why do you need a road? You could just as easily build a string of towers with a cable and hang the cars on it, like chairs on a ski lift, and then switch them off at these 'exits' you have on these parkways. You don't have individual drivers doing different things, in other words, and so you don't need a road. Think of the wear and tear on the tires you would save, and the gas, and the strain of driving. People could play cards, for instance, right as they're driving from Hartford to New Haven. Do you see the advantage?"

Cleet's gaze remained fixed on the bright, inquiring expression on Mr. Sommers' face and his head moved slowly up and down.

"Then they wouldn't have to spend millions of dollars clearing the land and grading and laying down the surface. They haven't thought enough about it, that's what's wrong, they haven't really stepped back and thought about it from the beginning. Now take airplanes, for instance, why don't they take off straight up? Um-hum, one more rye. The thing is, they ought to. Practically all the accidents are taking off or landing, because they come in and take off *at an angle*. But if they did it straight up and down, there'd be nothing to hit or anything like that. Don't tell me they couldn't build a plane like that. They can do anything. They don't want to because it would cost too much and reduce their profits," adding with a resigned intake of breath, "so people get killed."

Cleet studied Mr. Sommers more intensely than ever because this last idea happened to be one Cleet himself had often entertained but never uttered, thinking people would laugh at it. Hearing it from someone else was for him like having someone else confess to a crime of his. Cleet's expression and mind had been continually on the point of mocking these high-flying theories, but something had held him back from giving in to that attitude.

The second shot of rye disappeared and then Mr. Sommers, looking thoughtfully at the ceiling, said in his low and musical voice, "I wonder why anybody ever commits suicide."

Falling into rhythm with the flow of his speculations now, Cleet immediately answered, "Things just get hopeless, I guess."

Mr. Sommers shook his head with a little smile. "Things are always hopeless," he muttered hurriedly. "No, but I mean if you want to die why not do something good with it, volunteer for a very dangerous mission or for some medical experiment or, you know, try to kill Hitler—"

"He's dead."

"Of course he's dead," he said a little irritably, "but I mean before." He ordered a third shot but when it came he began merely to sip it a little at long intervals. "Do you think," said Mr. Sommers, "fish feel the cold?"

Cleet started and blinked. It was one of the questions he had often asked himself. So his attitude toward Mr. Sommers teetered once more, higher and more precariously, and at last fell heavily on the side of comradeship, away from mockery. "You know what. I think they probably do. That's why they migrate, isn't it."

"Maybe they just migrate for food or to go to favorable spawning grounds, and not because of the cold at all."

"What about birds?"

"It's warm in the Gulf Stream, of course."

"Birds shed sometimes, I believe."

"The fish of course in California," Mr. Sommers went on in his growing personal reverie, "are really exceptional, they grow so big. I think probably the earth is going to be farmed out, you know, turn into a dust bowl one of these days. But there'll still be a tremendous amount of nourishment in the sea."

"Human beings were originally fish."

"Did you ever notice how people you meet today resemble their animal ancestors? Some people have a lot of fish in them, some have eagles, a few are obviously descended from frogs."

After a dignified, impressive pause, moved, Cleet answered, "Yes, I have thought about that."

Unsurprised, Mr. Sommers went on, "And did you ever think that everybody is made to be one certain age, lasting a year or at the most three or four years, an age when they're just right, just what nature intended them to be, just what they ought to be, when their faces are fulfilled and match their personalities very closely? With some people it's three years old, for instance, beautiful little children. With many, many people it's sixteen. But did you ever meet anyone sixteen years old you knew was just waiting to be forty-two, who already *was* forty-two inside? Sometimes it's sixty-five or even ninety—"

"What is it with you?"

"Nineteen," he answered immediately.

"What is it with Emperor Hirohito of Japan?"

After a discerning pause he said, "Twelve."

"What about Greta Garbo?"

"Seventy-five."

"Hmm."

"My girl Georgia was perfect when she was seventeen. I can still see that perfect seventeen-year-old in her signaling out to me, signaling a little more faintly," he added slowly, "every year." Then instantly cheering up, "When she was seventeen she was pretty, so pretty, and like a flower in the morning, and her eyes were so wide open and so shining, and her body was like the stem of a flower, and she felt everything and she had everything and loved everything, and everybody loved her."

"Do you know something?" said Cleet. "Do you know what happens after we die?"

"As a matter of fact I think–"

"Let me tell you what *I* think, and see if it's the same. We lie around and watch the life story of every person who ever lived, acted out–after all, we've got eternity to do it in–and then everybody understands everything."

"I never thought of that exactly. I always thought that as you die you pass through a kind of cave or tunnel, really a dark place of your mind, I guess, and then you come into a marvelous brightness at the other end and in that light it's all clear, it's all clear," more than ever to himself, "it's all clear. It's all behind everything somewhere, behind this shot glass and your fingernail and this table, back just behind it all is the pattern, and when you die I think–I like to think it all becomes beautifully clear at last."

"How do elephants mate?"

"More or less like dogs, I think."

After a thoughtful silence, Cleet resumed. "What's behind my thumbnail? Besides my thumb, I mean."

"The pattern, the purpose, sort of like a deep underseas current running through everything, even this table, that carries the meaning and is what everything is about."

"Do you think electricity has anything to do with it?"

"It's possible. There's something very strange about electricity, isn't there?"

"There sure is."

"I don't know how electricity works or even what electricity is, to be honest with you."

Cleet just glanced in his eyes and nodded.

"Do you know what I would like to see?" said Cleet, studying his thumbnail.

"What's that?"

"I'd like to see a new kind of tournament, the kind they used to have in the Middle Ages, with jousts and things like that, only brought up-to-date, and entered by every man in the world. For instance, first there'd be one gigantic free-for-all, which would eliminate an awful lot of people. Then there'd be races, and tests of guts, and then co-ordination, and then will power, and I guess leadership. And the people who won would be the leaders."

"What about brains?"

"That would be part of the tournament too, of course. But only part, not all of it, the way it's getting to be now. I don't think things are normal any more, I think the world is unbalanced."

Mr. Sommers gazed at him in his humorous and resigned way and said, "Well, someone's unbalanced. Hmm. Maybe it's you and I."

Cleet nervously turned his beer glass. "Did you—uh—have a nice flight?"

Mr. Sommers nodded.

After a pause Cleet said, "I think it's too bad to waste all the fresh air there is up in space when the air down here, especially in the cities, is so bad and polluted. Why couldn't they make a huge suction machine and attach a hose to it and then tie a huge balloon to it and raise that up into space and get some really good air down here?"

"They probably will someday."

Suddenly, clenching his hands in front of him and frowning furiously at this stranger who nevertheless spoke the language, heretofore unintelligible to any other person, of Cleet's own heart, he said demandingly, "What if you don't use yourself up? What if you don't use it all? Do you walk at night like a zombi or a vampire for the next two hundred years, trying to work off all the life you didn't live? Or like a leper with a bell, like a corpse with chains, what if *that's* what happens when you die! I'm—I'm—well, it's a dumb and conceited thing to say and you'll think I'm the biggest jerk in the world, but—I'm," he swallowed, pulled his thoughts together, and then with a settled, straight look at Mr. Sommers and a serious, quiet, almost stern expression, Cleet said, "I'm immortal." He waited quietly for this outrageous and ridiculous statement to sink in, waited for Mr. Sommers to laugh in his face, waited for the explosion of mockery he had always been sure this statement, if he ever dared utter it, would pull down on his head.

But instead Mr. Sommers just looked back at him with waiting interest, calmly, and after combing this face with his closest attention, Cleet leaned back, took a breath, and risked going on. How strange to be about to say this!

"What I mean is, I don't think I can be killed right now. I can't be killed. I used to be scared during missions in the Air Force, as scared as anybody, not because I could be killed but because I might get hurt. I did get hurt. But I knew I couldn't die and I still can't. Nothing can put me out, not now, not yet. It's too strong. It's too *unused,* I haven't used up hardly any of it yet. Did you ever just want to walk for about a month? There's something the matter with me. Listen. I don't know, you're like me, in a way." Cleet inserted this quickly and apologetically. "So do you mind listening?"

Mr. Sommers shook his head and smiled a little.

"I can't get on a train without walking from the last car as far forward as they'll let me go, through the baggage cars sometimes to the engine, just because I've got to see it all, everything there is there. Do you know something?"

The waiter came up. "Is your name Solvent?" he said to them both.

"My name's Kinsolving."

"Maybe that was it. There's a telephone call."

Cleet looked at him, and then shook his head. "No, I forgot. My name isn't Kinsolving, it's Plaster, Mike Plaster. Excuse me." The waiter made an exasperated face and left, and Cleet said, "It was bound to be Neil. Nobody else could have located me here. He called the police or Taxi Service or the telephone operator or somebody. He had to know. That's Neil for you."

"You ought to take the call then, especially from your—"

"My boss? I suppose you're right. But would *he* take a call from *me* if he was having the most interesting conversation ever? No. *N-O.* Why should the Reardon family run me? I don't *like* being a hanger-on to millionaires! I never realized that until this minute. I think it was talking to you about the air and the atmosphere and the habits of fish and eternity and all that that brought it out. I don't *like* being a hanger-on to millionaires," he repeated, testing it, and finding that the statement rang true.

Mr. Sommers gazed at him a little sadly. "I guess that's the tragedy of being rich. The people they try to help, sooner or later don't *like* them for it. Do you know why? Because our self-respect is hurt. And self-respect is all we've got. Do you know what the opposite of self-respect and self-confidence is?"

"Hating yourself . . . and—"

"No. It's insanity."

"Insanity!"

"Yes. Self-confidence and self-respect are what keep people from going crazy."

"My God," breathed Cleet to himself, thinking about his own present position and opinion of himself.

They reached High Farms forty-five minutes later, and Cleet told Neil that he was going to have to resign from the job. That was when Neil told Cleet he was going to be given flying lessons by Arthur. So that resignation was withdrawn.

Mrs. Sommers accumulated her own kind of party in her rooms that evening. She had never given a real party—although there had been times in her marriage when she could have afforded to—because the idea of being a hostess, of playing any sort of "great lady" role, made her feel foolish, uneasy, and suspicious of herself. She knew she didn't look the part, with her horizontal curls, her broad nose and big mouth, her ranginess and loudness, most of all her total lack of artificiality.

Handsome and gentlemanly Mr. Sommers was entranced by her. He thought of her as a phenomenon of nature, a waterfall or a geyser; she could therefore not be criticized but only wondered at and sometimes endured, and most often deeply appreciated. He knew that beneath her loud and confident manner was another person, unendingly shy. But that shy person still controlling her, from the days when she was the plainest girl in her grade-school class, had been muted by these rooms, the piano, and the beer, and Mrs. Sommers was now entertaining all who came.

"Sit over there, Neil, no, next to Georgia, on that settee thing, my God the furniture you've put around here, I don't see how it holds up, with those spindly little legs on it, like a child with rickets, Georgia, when are you going to start looking pregnant, you're not kidding everybody, are you? You're going to get the whipping of your life if you are, and I don't care how high-class you're supposed to be these days. Ken, give your famous son-in-law a drink out of that cabinet thing over there, it's got everything in it except mother's milk, what a display."

"Oh." As she turned to contemplate Cleet, sitting in a window seat, this startled "Oh" escaped her. "You really are spooky-looking, it's those weird green eyes, very strange, don't you ever blink or anything? Where're your people from anyway?"

"If you're wondering where I got my eyes, I got them from my grandmother, and her people are from right here."

"How do you mean? I'm talking about what country did they come from originally."

"They came from this country originally and only this country. My grandmother's a full-blooded Indian."

"Aho!" exclaimed Mrs. Sommers very cheerfully, surprised to discover a squaw so close to the drawing rooms of High Farms. This pleased her very much, linking this pompous, starchy Eastern manor house to the huts and adobes she knew in the Southwest. "Well," she went on, "what do you want to hear?"

"What do I want to hear? Well, I want to hear that I just inherited an air—"

"No," she interrupted in a disgusted tone, "what do you want to hear on the piano? This is a musical tea party and I'm going to play," and swiveling around to face the piano, she swept into "I Feel Like a Feather in the Breeze," using almost the whole keyboard; inventive, carefree, she grasped rich chords with her big hands and sang along in her full, low-pitched voice, singing strictly for the hell of it, not caring whether it was good or not and not entirely aware that anyone was listening.

"That was pretty *good,*" said Cleet, staring at her.

"Thanks, honey. Ken, give him something to drink."

"I—uh—don't. I'll have ginger ale."

"Georgia, where are your in-laws? I hope they don't think it's too rude of me, just meeting them like that and then hiding up here, but you know how I feel in strange places until they get used to me. You explain to them, your mother's peculiar, all right? Did she explain that to you, Neil?"

"She sort of hinted," he answered quietly with a little smile. "As a matter of fact," he added, "they'd all like to come up here, but they don't think they're invited."

"Well of course they're invited! In their own house! Oh my God. Ken—do something."

He nodded pleasantly and then said, "Play that number about love, you know—"

"About *love!* That number about *love!* They're all about love!"

"The peculiar one about you know the . . . prostitute."

Her face lighting up, Mrs. Sommers swung back to the keyboard and began playing "Love for Sale" and then singing it. That reminded her of "Ten Cents a Dance," which she played and sang also. "It seems funny to me," Mrs. Sommers began talking the instant she finished the song because her conversation had by necessity ceased while she sang someone else's words and her mind had gone on manufacturing a steady flow of sentences, "that song 'Ten Cents a Dance' reminded me with that line 'Pansies and tough guys, rough guys who tear my gown' about you, Georgia, having to be in those USO dances and overseas and places, and well here you are, married, and I'll say it right in front of Neil, you've married a millionaire and you don't even have a home! You can't call this place a home! It's a hotel and a country club. Who could have a real family life in it?"

"I don't know, Mother, I like it. Things are different. This is home to me." Then she added, "The first one I've ever really had, as long as this is Truth Night."

Mr. Sommers glanced at the floor and then at his knuckles. Mrs. Sommers said several things at once about "silly—not true—your father—plenty" and Georgia looked downcast at what she had said.

"Hell," said Cleet quietly, "I hardly ever had a home either."

"You're right," Neil's clear voice cut in, "High Farms isn't a home, not for us either. The Reardons don't have a home."

They glanced around in silence for a moment, and then Mrs. Sommers, unfailingly reviving, played and sang "Dinner for One, Please, James." "This house reminds me of that song. 'Dinner for One, Please, James.' Sophisticated."

That evening Cleet encountered Georgia. "I like your father a lot. He's a very fine person. We have a lot in common. I never met anyone who thought so much like me. He's like a—double of me."

Georgia was chilled by these words of Cleet's, but she had expected them. "Pop's always had a lot of charm."

"It's not that. I know he's got that. But it's his, I don't know, *spirit* I'm talking about."

"Oh." She continued along the parapet in the dark. The glass doors leading to her and Neil's bedroom were at the end of it. They were waiting for him to finish dressing for his first television appearance.

"I think your father's got just about everything, everything that counts."

There was a long silence and then Georgia, in her lovely voice, forced herself to say slowly and as kindly as possible, "Cleet, Pop's a failure, a disappointed man, Pop doesn't have any hope."

Cleet stopped in his tracks. "I don't believe it. He's not a failure in the ways that count."

Looking down at the stone floor as they walked back and forth on the parapet, Georgia repeated, "Pop is a failure, he's bitterly disappointed in himself." Then she added, "Don't take after my father."

"What?" Cleet said dully.

"He broke his heart."

Cleet caught hold of her arm and turned her. "What do you mean? How did he?"

"He was too wonderful, Cleet, too dreaming, with lots of ideals. Too wonderful, that's all. I can't explain."

And then as they continued pacing back and forth on the parapet looking down on the lawn and the hillside and the river, she continued talking about her father and trying to explain what had happened to him. He had started as a newspaper copy boy and then reporter and was doing quite well at that when he met and married Genevieve, who had been working as a telephone operator. That had been in Montana. After that they had lived in California and then New Mexico and after that Wyoming and Nebraska and then back to California and to Salt Lake City and to Washington State and then once more to Santa Ana, California. Her father worked at many things but it was as a salesman that he did best, with his charm and his sincerity. But he could not continue, even when he was doing well and everyone approved of him and encouraged him, because he did not see himself as a salesman, so that one day he would lose all his orders and get very drunk and even beat up his beloved Genevieve and she would have to call the police, and then in court the next day he would have recovered and brushed his hair and the judge would find it hard to believe that this winning gentleman before him was guilty of his wife's charges, and she couldn't really believe it either, and so that job was lost and they were still together and the family would move to another town, another state, he would find another job and begin very well and his employers would congratulate themselves on finding someone so fine and solid and such a delightful person in addition and Georgia and Lynn would start settling into the new school and then his demon, his vision of himself and what he ought to be—a leader, a power, an influential force—would blind him again and the job and the home would fall apart again and Genevieve would send back the little rented piano and, packing their clothes and odds and ends, they would move once again. They, the three women around him, loved him more year after year because, for one thing, he was *not* a failure, only a man who threw away every success. He was vital, kind, funny. He was a wonderful man. Their life was an unending ordeal.

Genevieve was sustained by her music, by a kind of gypsy impulse she herself possessed, by her daughters, and by her love. She rarely complained; she had never expected or really wanted much materially, except for a concert grand piano.

At seventeen Georgia entered the University of California at Los Angeles on scholarships; she was a first-class student in the field of anthropology but finally and with great difficulty decided to concentrate on drama because she felt herself to be too restless to become a real scholar or scientist or teacher. She would have a career as an actress. Then on her USO tour, in London, she met Neil.

"I didn't marry him for his money," she said querulously, as though refuting a reproach. She felt a compulsion to be abrasively honest in this conversation, because talking about her father made her feel just now that being honest with oneself was life's first requirement. "I love him and he loves me but doesn't know what to do about it. The Irish Catholic influence, 'sure and begorra' or whatever that sickening phrase is."

Neil came out, looking almost as slim as a bachelor again, almost wolfish again in his evening clothes. He and Georgia left and Cleet roamed down the huge, dark, creaking staircase, actively alarmed. Mr. Sommers had failed, missed, thrown himself away, not gotten to the priceless core of himself and used it and made something of it, not contributed it to life and so become immortal—for nothing else would do, immortality alone, in a very minor, very modest, fragmented way, a speck of immortality alone would meet Cleet's demands on life. Otherwise it would not be intelligible, but instead it would be some kind of atrociously painful practical joke played on him, a gigantic feast placed in front of a starving man who discovers as he puts the first morsel of steak in his mouth that he has no teeth.

Mr. Sommers, so alarmingly much like himself, the only person he had ever met who even faintly resembled him—Mr. Sommers was as empty, as by-passed, as neglected as Wetherford Cove.

Cleet reached the ground floor and went up to the library doors, slid them apart, and stepped inside. Mr. Sommers was slowly turning the massive old-fashioned terrestrial globe near the window. He shot a smile across at Cleet and said, "Big world, isn't it?"

Cleet came in, his hands in his pockets, and shrugged.

"I haven't really seen much of it. You can see, you know, just a corner when you have it all in front of you like this. I've only seen a little slice here and there."

After a silence Cleet said flatly, "I've seen about half."

"I guess that was one good thing the war did."

Cleet lapsed into a disgusted silence. Mr. Sommers continued slowly turning the globe.

"Of course to someone who's done a lot of flying like you it must seem small. To my generation flying is still a sort of novelty. It made me nervous, flying here in that plane."

"Jesus," said Cleet under his breath.

Mr. Sommers glanced at him apologetically and said, "Of course flying doesn't bother you a bit."

"It doesn't bother anybody I know," Cleet growled into his fist.

"Where is everybody?"

"What kind of work do you do?" said Cleet, ignoring that.

"Me? Why, sales. I thought I mentioned that this afternoon, sales, the thing that makes the country go."

"Are you any good at it?"

"Not bad, not bad. Of course it's world affairs that are my real—"

"Do you work on commission or salary?"

"Why, on commission, as a matter of fact. As a matter of fact right now I've left the company I was working for, National Shellac—"

"Oh," said Cleet in heavy comprehension.

"Say," said Mr. Sommers with a gallant smile, "seems like you're kind of a hard man tonight."

"Me?" said Cleet, shaking his head slowly and glaring at the wall of books. "I like to know who's worth anything and who isn't, that's all."

"How about a game of pool?"

Cleet shook his formidable Indian's head slowly.

"No?" Mr. Sommers said and then added "Why not?" in a thinning tone.

Finally Cleet answered, "I don't want to cut into your work."

"My work? What do you mean?"

"Your study of world affairs. Isn't that what you're doing with the globe?"

"Just passing the time, passing the time. It's what I do as a relaxation, the same as Genevieve does playing the piano."

After a silence Cleet said, "Why don't you ask the Reardons to give her that piano? They've got about seven of them."

"Couldn't do that," he murmured.

"Wouldn't she like to have a piano?"

"Of course, of course," he said into his collar.

"That piano's on wheels, so it can move with you the next time you take off from one town to another."

Mr. Sommers squinted across at him and blinked.

"Too bad somebody who plays so well doesn't have a piano."

"Look, Cleet, are you trying to say something?"

After a sullen silence Cleet inquired with mocking elaborateness, "What does that mean?"

"I thought you seemed disturbed about something." Then turning with a show of jauntiness back to the globe, Mr. Sommers said, "What I was really doing before you came in is looking at the land masses of the world, Eurasia, for instance, which was so crucial in Hitler's planning, and wondering how the world is going to shape up now and whether the Allies will stay united. It can be strange, after wars. Funny thing. I want to make a prediction and I want you to remember it. The way this country is developing and the way the other important countries are developing, our enemies, if you can believe this, Germany and Japan, are going to be about our firmest friends someday, and not very far in the future. I know how fantastic that sounds. What do you think of it?"

"I think it's bullshit," said Cleet in his deep, level voice, turning his back on Mr. Sommers to stare out the left side of the great window.

"I don't know what's on your mind, boy, and I don't see—"

"Don't call me 'boy,'" said Cleet, dangerously softly.

"Just a way of speaking."

Mr. Sommers took a deep breath and turned back to the globe of the world. He had been through this many times before, arousing in new acquaintances an extravagant and idealized admiration only to have to endure a vicious reaction, equally exaggerated, when they discovered that he did not fulfill their idea of what a man should be, after all. Sometimes it made him want never to encounter another new person again in his life.

Cleet stalked out of the library and was walking down the long hallway leading to the newer part of the house, boiling with anger, thinking how much he scorned weak failures, men like Mr. Sommers with his mild, too mild, too kind, too understanding blue eyes, weak failures like that. Cleet had even thought they were alike! He was as different from Mr. Sommers as a horse was from a bunny rabbit. Nothing life could do would ever make him like that, he would never *allow* anything in life, never allow *anything*, to turn him into that kind of puddle of human jelly, to become a Mr. Sommers, too weak to hold a place in life or even buy a piano. He strode down the long corridor, realizing that he hated this man for his weakness and failure.

And then his brain abruptly turned its ray of truth on him, as it sometimes abruptly did, and he thought: I hate him because I'm like him.

I only hate what's similar to me. I hate seeing my weak parts in other people. That's what hate is.

That thought halted him midway along the corridor. There was a large ugly potted plant, with a long scrawny stalk and large clumsy leaves there and he stood flicking the leaves thoughtfully for several minutes, and then he went back along the corridor toward the library.

"Mr. Sommers," he said without preliminaries, from the doorway, "I want to apologize for what I said. Something just got into me. I apologize."

A slow smile breaking over his face, Mr. Sommers said, "That's all right, Cleet." To himself he said: If that had been me, I couldn't have apologized.

That night Lynn Sommers disappeared from High Farms. She left a note in her sister's dressing room.

Dear G.

I want to thank you for everything and for being so generous although I know part of it was you were so lonely and needed me and were almost paying me as your companion. But I can't be happy or even comfortable in this place and I feel ridiculous here from the minute I wake up until going to sleep, when I can sleep. I can't eat in that huge dining room, I'm afraid of it. I'm all wrong and don't fit in and most of all *can't face that party,* especially with Mom and Pop here and they're sure to stick out with all those society people like two sore thumbs. I've got to feel like myself again, I don't know any boys who will come to date me as long as I'm staying in this place, they just don't want to come up that driveway. I'm going away and probably I have a job and of course I'll be all right. *Don't show this to anyone.* Love to Mom and Pop.

Your sister,
Lynn

This had happened twice before and the Sommers family was not very alarmed. To avoid gossip the police were not notified, nor did the Reardons feel a private detective was necessary. Cleet was told to make casual inquiries and see whether he could locate her.

She had not used any of the Reardon cars nor Wetherford Taxi Service, so she must have walked to the Highway and hitchhiked. To go north meant to cross the Connecticut River and enter the kind of rural country which could only depress and baffle Lynn. Cleet therefore began driving south along the Highway. New Haven was an obvious goal, but too obvious, too obvious even for Lynn; for her to stop so close to High Farms would mean that she was not running away but merely playing hide-and-seek. The nearest town which would interest her was Bridgeport. When he got to Bridgeport he went to the library and looked up the Bridgeport newspapers for the day she ran away and the following day. In these he found the employment ads for restaurants and bars wanting waitresses, and in the third place he found Lynn.

She had simply walked out of High Farms at four o'clock in the morning, avoided setting off the burglar alarms, walked on to the Highway, already beginning to feel better as she reached this strip of diners and gas stations and drive-in movies and pennants flapping in the wind; she had hitchhiked to Bridgeport, which she knew to be a large industrial town, a haven of factories and diners and juke boxes, a place where on the undersides of tables there was chewing gum which she could touch and gain the reassurance of a blind person reading Braille, where the movie houses seemed the kind of palaces she loved, so much more magical than a real house like High Farms, movie palaces with their functionless theater boxes, tormented Vatican pillars lining the lobbies, rococo balconies encrusted with crust, lost Arabian courtyards featuring one drinking fountain, fake stars winking from the satiny ceiling; above all, their huge screens, where she could watch huge people doing huge things and be happy until the arid moment when the lights came on and she had to withdraw into her own somewhat undersized self again and step back onto the bleak, unintelligible treadmill called real life.

"I didn't like the food," she said as part of her reason for refusing to return to High Farms, and Cleet had to agree tacitly with this criticism. "I didn't like having to change clothes so many times. I didn't like all those Irish people waiting on me. They didn't fool me with that 'Yes, ma'am' line of theirs, I knew what they thought. I didn't like Geraldine because, I don't know, because she was always too tanned, because she had too many fur coats, because she never really looked at me, always over my shoulder or at my hairline. I didn't like Neil because, well, because he's just a bastard."

"No, he isn't."

"Yes, he is. He can't help it, I guess. I didn't like Mr. and Mrs. Reardon and I didn't even like those two damn dogs. And I was scared of the horses. Then when Mom and Pop showed up it was the last straw. Everyone was *laughing* at them, especially at her. At this party they're going to give everybody will laugh at *him*, everybody always laughs at him when he goes to a party. So I'm not going back. I'm twenty-one years old. I ought to have at least one boy friend. Any boys who came to visit the Reardons always thought they were too good for me. Yes, I'm telling you, they did, they really did. I'm staying here. I like it here. I don't know what to do with myself if I don't have some kind of a job. I don't *play* tennis. Give them my love—no, let's be honest, give them . . . say hello to them for me. And don't worry. I won't disgrace the family. I won't tell anybody that Mrs. Cornelius Reardon is my sister. Why should I? I never really believed it: I still don't believe it."

Cleet's feelings about women were always extremely physical

to begin with, although with time they were capable of many complex ramifications. He had always been quietly repelled by Lynn, by her lifeless skin, her chunky body, the artificially augmented blondness of her heavy hair, the bushy turtle-neck sweaters she affected, on top of which sat her face, square, sullen, pouting, muddled, like a piece of ludicrous sculpture on a pedestal. She had scuttled down the great hallways of High Farms like some pilfering cat, distrustful of everything and everyone and most of all of herself.

Now he discovered one thing to like about her: her honesty. He left her there among the glasses of beer, humming to herself, and when he had explained her situation and what she herself wanted and how she felt to the people at High Farms they all agreed to leave her there too.

The ballroom was not at all suitable for the ball.

It was the most peculiar section of this peculiar house, having been erected during the Oriental period of Victorian architecture. It was in the shape of an octagon, with a great rickety-looking brown wooden ceiling billowing improbably up to a kind of Turkish minaret. The ceiling had been meticulously and wanly decorated with paintings of Japanese waterfalls and mountainsides and moons.

The old gas fixtures around the walls, although now converted to electricity, still cast from the large round globes the vague illumination of gaslight. The parquet floor creaked. The eight glass doors with their curved arches, one communicating with the rest of the house and the others opening onto a terrace, had panes of glass tinted and distorted by age. The deep red damask wall hangings looked as though much Victorian cigar smoke had settled into their fibers. Huge baskets of white flowers, silk streamers from the minaret, and bunting shone with additional brilliance against the faded colors and brittle woodwork of the ballroom.

The society dance band was on the side of the room opposite the doorway leading into the house, the musicians looking marooned behind their blue sequined bandstand and their blank smiles.

On the other hand the party was helped by a cloud of gardenia smell in the air, new dresses shining, jingle and tinkle and laughter, flowers and jewelry and frothy music. A carefree, moneyed excitement was being released inside the old walls and sweeping over the guests.

Georgia was coming alone down the great dark stairway beside the library. She was wearing white, and with her very costly new bracelet and necklace, she knew that she looked, if not beautiful, then extremely pretty and very fashionable. She was also feeling almost uncontrollably happy. The music coming to her along the corridor, the gardenia smell, the throb and rattle and flash of this party in the old country mansion, the cars rolling along the driveways, headlights and flashlights and lanterns outside, the bustle and emergencies of final preparations, the specialness of the occasion, had gone straight to her head and all these fragments were now carrying her, almost floating her down the old staircase, toward the Octagon and the party. The exoticism and the expense of her perfume, the weight and flash of the bracelet, the feel and flow of her dress, all combined to make everything seem unforgettable. She hurried along the creaky corridor and came out into the Octagon, dazzling now, the chandelier glittering and the dancers in full, crowded motion.

From across the room Cleet Kinsolving saw her enter. He had never seen her so lovely, so happy, nor so out of place. It wasn't that she looked out of place or that she should be out of place, it was that deep in her bones she felt it; he could see this in her eager face and her clutched hands, desperately happy, momentarily, not really believing she was here, not believing, above all, that this splendid ball was being given in her husband's family's house, therefore in *her* house, and these elegantly turned-out celebrators were her guests, beholden to her, and she was the center and cynosure of all the glitter and expense and excitement of the evening.

"I hope you're having a good time!" she said gaily to someone as she passed.

Mrs. Sommers was still in the Rochambeau Suite, fixing her hair.

"There's only one way it can go," said Mr. Sommers. "The way you've got it now. That's the only way it goes."

"Shut up. It's not right."

He himself was simultaneously thinking of all the information he had ever gleaned anywhere about high finance and big business so that he could hold his own in the urbane chats he visualized going on among the successful men downstairs, and also thinking that he must do the right thing by Georgia this once, not embarrass her in any way, and he must win back the high opinion of the Kinsolving boy in some way, and he must at last show Genevieve the time of her life, and he must *enjoy* himself, forget his obsessions, have a good time, not try to get himself a job through the opportunities because for one thing Mr. Reardon had already offered to look into that in any way that was suitable.

He stood watching poor Genevieve try to make her hair look thicker and prettier: she was not going to have the time of her life or even a moment's pleasure tonight; he was going to embarrass his daughter in one way or another, fail to get along with the successful men, and all the other resolutions he was making would be unfulfilled because once, twenty or thirty years ago, he had had some unsuccessful evening somewhere, and then another and another and another; no resolution could reverse it now, it was too complex for him; his life was like a dam breaking, and if he patched one widening leak his back was turned while another opened and the fissures and the flood increased. There was not mortar enough anywhere to stop it, the water had backed up much too far, for too many years, the deluge of his failures was now unstoppable.

"What are you staring at? Go down and look after your daughter, see if she's all right."

"Don't you want me to wait for you? You can't go in alone."

"Who says I can't? Why can't I? I've gone in worse places alone, you bet I have. Don't stand there. You make me nervous."

Ken touched her hair and then went out. Genevieve looked at herself in the mirror for a while longer, gave the lowest horizontal ironlike curl a disgusted flip, and got up from the dressing table. After all, her looks had never mattered to her, she reminded herself. She had never had to rely on *them* in life, which was fortunate, for otherwise she might have died of neglect.

Passing the piano, she realized from the faint strains of the society band coming up through her window that the evening was going to be an ordeal musically as well as in other ways for her; the fake bounciness and metronomic beat of the music were going to be a ceaseless aggravation throughout the party. She sat down for a moment on the piano stool and with her left index finger touched middle C. Then with her right hand she ran up an arpeggio lightly, flightily; it was so beautiful, she thought, the tone of even a half-decent piano, not to mention the almost unendurable splendor of the concert grand downstairs, which she had played the afternoon before when everyone had been far away in some distant outpost of the house. If only people were like pianos and would let you draw out all the beauty they contained and that they themselves were passively ignorant of: if only you could play people. How often she had thought that. Ken was a beautiful and delicate instrument, a spinet, a harpsichord; if only she had been able to draw out his music before so many of the strings grew brittle, broke.

Then recollecting her flat nose, large mouth, her ridiculous tiers of curls, she thought, How could a dumb, clumsy thing like me ever have been able to! Me! I'm not good for anything but playing in barrooms, that's what I should have done. How strange to find herself the center of a family of rare people like Ken, and like Georgia. Georgia, that rare child, had gotten them all into this huge castle in wherever it was, and this big, fancy party was going on, with limousines and jewelry and a band.

Georgia was even going to provide Ken with a job that could not be lost, at last. Lightly flitting arpeggios up and down the keyboard with her left hand, Genevieve thought to herself, Of course it's wonderful for Ken to have found his place at last, but, of course, by now, most of his strings are broken.

But still, after all, you never know. Who could tell? Maybe they were only silent, waiting to be sounded.

III

THE HEIR

Neil, in his white dinner jacket, had gone up to the train room. Geraldine's ten-year-old son, Hugh Reardon Blanchard, was resetting the tracks of the great Reardon electric train with three other boys, who were overnight guests at High Farms along with their parents. The cars of the electric train were one foot long. It had two whistles, a bell, and a caboose with a back platform where a railroad man sometimes appeared; there were overpasses, trestles, stations, watertanks, a lake, signals and lights and cranes, two towns, a mountain chain. The railroad cars were heavy and meticulously accurate miniatures; the engines were powerful, and the room smelled of burned rubber, wire, and vibrated with a sense of overcharged transformers and grinding metal.

"How's it going?"

"Okay."

"You're going to move that bridge over here?"

"Yes. Then the track can go through—"

"I see."

"To change it."

"Right."

"Uncle Neil?"

"Yes."

"Did this used to be your electric train?"

"Yes, it did."

"Then where is the baggage car? There used to be a baggage car."

"That's right. I forgot that. Well, a friend of mine—you met Mr. Kinsolving—wanted to find out how the cars were made, so he took that one apart one day. We never could get it back together. The pieces might be around here somewhere still, for all I know."

"We could use a baggage car."

"I don't think they make that model of train any more, or we'd get another."

"It's part of the whole thing, baggage cars."

"Hugh."

"Hm?"

"You shouldn't say 'hm' to adults. You're practically a young man and you've got to be politer. Especially with your elders."

"All right."

"With me it doesn't matter, since we've always been friends."

"That's right," said Hugh thoughtfully, fixing the trestle in its new position.

"You can say, I don't know, 'hell' if you want when I'm the only person around."

After a pause Hugh said, "Hell," and then chuckled.

"I don't mind."

"Hum-um."

"But with other older people you should say 'Excuse me' and 'Pardon me' and 'What did you say, sir?' or something like that. When you're a young man you've got to be polite."

"All right."

Hugh directed the three other boys, who had been intimidated into a respectful silence by the grandness of the Reardon electric train, to lay a section of track up to the new trestle. They set obediently to work, pulling teeth in track sections and reinserting them as necessary to make the sections fit together.

"Uncle Neil, when are we going to stay all night in the old house by the Cove?"

"Whenever you want to."

"Tonight."

"Tonight I can't because of the party and all these guests and so on. We have to plan it in advance."

"Why?"

"So I can tell Georgia—"

"You're going to *tell* her?"

"Uh, of course not, it's a secret, naturally. I have to tell Georgia I'm going to New York for the night."

"Oh."

"Nobody else is going to know."

"I didn't think that was part of it," said Hugh.

"No, of course not."

"Can I look at those—"

"Cuff links."

"Cuff links. What are they made out of?"

"Gold, I think."

"Real gold?"

"I think so."

"I'm going to see if I can get a pair like those pretty soon."

"You like these, do you?"

"I sure do."

"I'll tell you what. When you've learned, really learned, that arm stroke I was showing you in the pool, I'll give these to you."

Hugh gazed down at the trestle, silent before the majesty of his delight. It wasn't the cuff links, it wasn't the gold, it was that they were Uncle Neil's and Uncle Neil was giving them to him. He was too overcome to say anything.

Then they all set to work completing the new section of track. By the time it was ready the three other boys had become disciples of Neil's because of his unfeigned and straightforward interest in them and his assumption that they were people who were in most ways his equal. Neil never failed with the young; within five minutes after they met him all their resistance collapsed.

"Did your mother tell you about the new Reardon?"

"Nope. What new Reardon?"

"A first cousin you're going to have. A boy cousin, I hope."

"Well, who is he? I mean—"

"He's going to be my son."

"Gee," said Hugh with fake enthusiasm.

"You don't like the idea very much."

"Sure I do. Why not?"

"I don't know. I just thought you didn't seem too enthusiastic."

"Too what?"

"Enthusiastic."

"What's his name?"

"I don't know yet. Maybe just Neil Reardon, Jr."

"Just don't call him Hugh."

"No, of course not. That's your name."

"Where's he going to sleep?"

"Come on, Hugh. There are plenty of places for him to sleep around here. You'll like him later on. He'll be too young to be your friend but you can look out for him and teach him things, help him out."

"I might if he does what I tell him."

"I'm sure he will."

The new section of track was now complete, Hugh threw the switch, the engine spun its wheels and then began dragging the eight cars along the track to a grade crossing where bells rang and lights flashed. The five people became preoccupied with switches and buttons.

Neil knew he should be downstairs and he was going down very soon. But he needed this respite from the dry world of adulthood very much. All those shrill women, all those uneasy men: why couldn't any of them ever say anything? So he had escaped up here, away from their posing and superficiality and silliness and stupidity and evil.

No adult was exempt from this indictment.

For example, there was Fred Hatch, the soccer coach at Country Day. Everyone considered Fred Hatch an exceptionally good soccer coach and chemistry teacher, a model family man, and someone who "liked people," as they said at the Kiwanis Club. Neil couldn't stand him. All that cheerfulness: it had to be concealing something, masking some unpalatable ambition; it was a device for deceiving the world, nothing else and nothing more. That open face and those optimistic eyes were further disturbing proof of the power and concentration he poured into his hypocrisy. He gave one tenth of his income to church or charity, as the accountant who helped with his income-tax return had told

Neil. He had been eliminated from military service by bad knees incurred from soccer injuries. But one would have thought the fate of the world depended on him from the way he had sold war bonds and donated blood to the Red Cross and organized collections of scrap metal and administered the civil defense program and even gone to the lengths of demonstrating the use of gas masks, on the Highway, at noon. All of this trickily manipulated appearance of compassionate humanitarianism created in Neil's mind an image which could be extremely briefly expressed: Fred Hatch was a pain in the neck.

Human males began to develop toward becoming pains in the neck for him when the first shadow of a mustache appeared on their upper lips, the first croak came into their voices, when their hands and feet began to grow disproportionately large and a general unpleasantness began to emerge in their personalities, a contrary, quirkish, fuzzy ineptitude. It was in that period that he eliminated them from his sympathies. When they crossed that frontier they ceased to be cohorts and turned into enemies. Neil now wanted not to teach but to defeat them, all of them, every single unappetizing one. An unresting competitiveness entered his feelings. It was peculiar that because of one short book and a few journalistic articles and speeches, American Youth—Neil detested such categories as American Youth and the Intellectual Elite and Informed Opinion and the Catholic Vote—American Youth looked to him as one of its leaders and spokesmen. Like all public figures, Neil did not resemble his popular reputation at all. He was considered, of all things, a kindly young man who wanted to help humanity.

But eventually American Youth would come to see him for what he was; long before that, however, he would have abandoned them. After all, a man could not lead his enemies; that only risked being shot in the back.

Neil's true vocation was with children, and his real ambition, he was finally coming to recognize, after all his efforts and earlier ambitions, was purely and simply to be the headmaster of Wetherford Country Day School. He was comfortably sure that he could attain this, in view of the source of endowment and of the individuals serving on the board of governors. The little bubble of fame which had whimsically formed around him because he had been bored for several weeks in the North Atlantic was sure to collapse. Three years from now he would be forgotten. That was very agreeable to him. He felt that fame was very irritating because of its dishonesty.

"If you don't make that curve by the lake there bigger the train's going to jump the track one of these times."

"Do you think so?"

"Yes."

"We better fix it."

"*We'd* better fix it."

"Hm?"

"We'd. It's a contraction of 'We had.' "

"Weed?"

"Yes."

"*Weed* better fix it!"

"That's right."

"I don't understand."

"It's a contraction for 'We had better fix it.' "

"*Oh.*"

"Do you know what a contraction is?"

"I think so."

"What is it?"

"Well, it's when two people agree on something."

"No, that's a contract. A contraction is two words combining into one. For example, 'I'm' instead of 'I am.' Do you see?"

"Yes." He looked at the other boys. "Let's fix it."

Neil burst into wild interior laughter at this but he maintained a completely serious mien. Hugh: what a great little person he was. And his own child—son—would have an ancestry, make-up, innate endowment, or whatever one wished to call it, one half of which would be identical with Hugh's, in view of the fact that Neil and Geraldine were siblings. So his son and Hugh might very possibly rather closely resemble each other. Neil fervently hoped so.

The other half of his boy's ancestry, make-up, innate endowment, or whatever one wished to call it, would, to be sure, spring from the Sommers line, and while Georgia's combination of good looks and intelligence was as rare as radium, there lurked behind her Mr. and Mrs. Sommers: Genevieve, to give them the cognomens which were more in their own unbuttoned style, and Ken.

Genevieve was fundamentally tolerable, Neil felt; there were no sizable degenerate strains, no recessive genes, no sub-average trends in her physique or personality. Ken, on the other hand, viewed objectively, which Neil was unequipped to do, detesting him on sight as one of those all-charm-and-failure pastel males who made Neil's flesh creep and brought out an almost overwhelming desire to punch them in their long-suffering, kind faces, Ken, viewed as objectively as possible, was a disaster. But even he possessed one or two minor positive features.

These combined Reardon-Sommers strains were even now, this very second, flowing into that fish-infant being formed downstairs in the Octagon.

Ken had to be conceded charm. Charm in a man repelled Neil: he had always been certain that he had none himself, and he didn't want any. Still, charm was useful in the world, and Grandfather-to-be Sommers had charm. He had something that for lack of a more accurate word Neil had to label fineness, and he was far from stupid.

He was also a weak drunk without guts or spine or will or drive and Neil despised him. No one could say that he, Neil, lacked guts or spine or will or drive, and if, once, so very many years ago, when he was just a boy playing along the river's edge with Cleet, or when they first started playing football, or at other odd moments—those uncontrollable, almost hallucinatory, black and silver years between the ages of six and seventeen—if here and there now and then a weakness or lack of will, a timidity and even a horror at life and its challenges had been visible in his own character, that was long ago and long buried under the callus and muscle and toughness he and his father had grown upon his body and his character. That timidity had been eliminated long ago and had merely been normal boyish shyness in any case.

Its main symptom had been nothing more than a fear of the dark, of all dark, everywhere, which had lasted until he was quite big. Sleeping alone downstairs in the Old House at the Cove, with Cleet Kinsolving on the floor above, the night of the flood, had been the last time it had assailed him, as though the risen waters had washed this stain, baptismally, away. He had never before fallen asleep in a room with no light whatever in it, and he had been ashamed to confess this to Cleet, and so he had not lighted the candle which he had secretly brought with him, out of fear that Cleet would come downstairs for some reason and see it and discover his secret and so think less of him, of his toughness. As it happened, the freshet inundated the first floor of the house and Cleet had indeed come downstairs to wake him and would have seen the candle, burning or gutted, and discovered his secret, if he had not conquered his fear that night and left the candle unlit and all the same been able to sleep.

Despite Ken Sommers, the human material flowing into his son was of a high quality, and if the weakness before life of his maternal grandfather or the feeling of what one might almost call fear his father once felt so long ago began to show themselves in the heir, then Neil would patiently, day by day, irresistibly train such weaknesses out of him as he and his father had trained their traces out of Neil himself. He already passionately loved this boy and as the boy developed into puberty, Neil dimly foresaw, his own feelings would mature at last and he would accept older males by way of his love for his maturing son.

The train jumped the track at the curve Neil had warned about.

"Hell," said Hugh.

"If you try to take a curve like that at full speed it's bound to jump."

After a concentrated pause Hugh said, "I guess that little boy will get the train."

"This train? Why, the train's for everybody—or no, I can see that wouldn't work. Not too good an idea, is it? Well, the truth is, it's my train. Now if you and my—boy get along, if you teach him things and look out for him and so on, well then I think I may give my train here permanently to you." Like his father Neil regularly practiced a certain amount of judicious bribery.

That plunged Hugh into profound reflection. Minutes passed, and then he said, "You know where he could sleep? In that room next to mine where the sewing machine is. He'd like it in there."

"It's a thought," said Neil carelessly.

Cleet Kinsolving came into the room. "Georgia said she was

going to divorce you unless you're in the Octagon in three minutes."

"She can't divorce me. She's a Catholic."

"Not yet, she isn't."

The two young men left the train room and went along the corridor, which was on the fifth floor of High Farms. Parts of the house were two stories high, most of it was three, sections of it were four, and this northern slab was five. Through a slanting skylight over the corridor the bright moonlight and star-filled sky shown down. They went down a narrow spiral stairway to a rarely used upper landing lighted by a large, gloomy chandelier with a blue and crimson glass shade. On all four dark blue walls there were large oil portraits in heavy gilt frames of former owners and occupants of the old house. Neither Cleet nor Neil had ever looked at them and they didn't now. They crossed the shadowy landing to a wide flight of stairs and went down them, between heavy balustrades with urns on the newel posts, to the third-floor hallway, wide and dim, thickly carpeted and with small tables and heavy chairs and floor-length cloudy mirrors and useless sofas and potted plants, down to the second-floor landing, where a guest neither of them recognized crossed in front of them, ducking his head in greeting. Cleet felt Neil's easygoing mood, which he had carried with him from the train room, dissipating rapidly; at the foot of the stairs on the ground floor there were three ladies chatting; both Cleet and Neil made hospitable noises as they went by them and received trills of recognition in return: Cleet sensed that Neil's feeling of well-being and trust was almost entirely drained away, and when they entered the crowded, pulsating Octagon, Neil had become his habitual pillar of controlled belligerence. "Hello," he said to someone curtly; "Good to see you," he let fall to someone else; "How are you?" he said expressionlessly to a third guest; then he began just nodding with a rather bitter-looking smile on his face to people who crossed his path or caught his eye.

"Darling, you look as though you're having the time of your life," said Georgia, smiling theatrically. "You're radiantly happy, anyone can see that."

"Is your father drunk yet?" said Neil suddenly, without the slightest intention of saying it.

Georgia recoiled as though he had slapped her face. Then she said evenly, "He's over there—yes, there by the bar. Why don't you go and smell his breath?" And she turned away from him. Cleet was standing there and he put his arm around her waist and they started to dance. "What in the world's the *matter* with him!"

"Nervous, I guess. He didn't mean anything."

"What a lousy thing to say."

"He didn't mean anything. All these people make him tense. Forget it. You've been having a wonderful time."

"Haven't I! I have been. I still am. I can't believe this wonderful party. Everything is wonderful, I *want* to become a mackerel snapper—"

"A what?"

"Mackerel snapper," she said, laughing her devastating, irresponsible laugh. "That's what we used to call Catholics back home. And there will be a baby and my life will never be anything like the first years of it, and even Pop's life is changing forever and the Sommers family is going to be saved, happy at last!" She spoke with mock dramatics, but she was very serious.

"Do you really believe that?" Cleet found he had to mutter.

"Of course I believe it. It's perfectly true. Why shouldn't I believe it?" She tilted her head back and gazed along her cheeks at him, which was a new gesture of hers and one of the few things he still disliked about her.

Georgia felt in her bones, in her stomach, that in doubting this picture he was somehow right, which redoubled her resistance. "You're not the least bit jealous by any chance, are you?" she found herself inquiring. It was amazing how fear could produce so many disagreeable things in an instant.

"Jealous? Well now I honestly never thought about being jealous. How could I? I just work here."

"Just work here," she echoed.

His anger began to rise. He couldn't stand someone as smart as Georgia telling herself fairy tales.

He was sure people didn't just live happily ever after. The Brain Truster suddenly sprang out of Cleet's memory, where sensing at that dinner so many years ago that the man's words were very valuable although incomprehensible, he had kept him ever since. The Brain Truster had said that people behave in a way very appropriate for the period of their lives that is already over, that people are like actors in a repertory company, forever performing last week's play in front of this week's sets. Now that Cleet saw this happening in life itself he remembered the words and understood them at last.

"You don't even believe that bracelet there belongs to you. You're surprised these people are polite to you, instead of saying, 'Bring me another glass of champagne' or something like that. So how can your father believe what may happen to him now? He'll go on thinking he's a big idealist and a big failure all his life. It's too late. That's why—that's why, well—"

"Yes? What were you going to say, Socrates?"

"I was going to say," he continued more definitely, "that's why people can't delay their life if they've got any sense, not wait, stall, that's why they've got to make the life they want early and soon, before it's too late, that's why I—"

She gazed at him with a slight smile. "That's why you're going to start a freight-carrying airline from Washington State to Alaska tomorrow, isn't it?"

"Not exactly tomorrow, but—"

"No," she said in her melodic voice, "not exactly tomorrow at all."

After a pause he said, "Are you trying to say something to me?"

"Mother!" cried Georgia. "Come dance with Cleet. He's a dream on the floor," and taking Genevieve's hand she put it into Cleet's. "I've got to look after my guests. After all, I'm Mrs. Cornelius Reardon, and I never forget it!"

Cleet danced the way other people moved furniture. Genevieve found herself being transferred from spot to spot across the parquet. "You're very blunt, Ken tells me. You always come out with just what you think. So I want you to tell me I'm the belle of the ball, the best-looking thing in—wherever we are."

"You're the belle of the ball and the best-looking thing in wherever we are, Mrs. Sommers."

"Thanks. The truth is, Georgia is the best-looking thing here. And pregnant too."

"Georgia looks great."

"I don't see how Ken and I ever did it. It was like opening some funny-looking old oyster and finding a perfect pearl inside. I still can't get over it."

"No."

"We can't believe it happened, that she's ours. Look at this place! It's hers! It's a terrible dump to live in, if you're like me, but I mean all the same it's a castle! To think we spent one winter in an abandoned gas station! Well," she said, "what a thing to talk about, dancing at a ball with a handsome young man like you! I guess it must be your bluntness, it makes me blunt too."

"Is it being blunt to tell the truth?"

"It's not only blunt, honey, it's an insult."

"I thought maybe it was a help. You see, listen." The music had stopped for a few minutes, and Mrs. Sommers and Cleet moved to one of the doors for some air. "All my life I have had this somewhat foggy mind, you see—that's blunt—I can't remember what the capital of Russia is or who the second President of the United States was or things like that, or trigonometry and physics and things like that. But all my life I've had a certain thing inside my head like a beacon in the fog. Once in a while it cuts right through the fog and lights something up very clearly, clearer than most people would see something because it comes out of a fog. I always thought that was a good thing and I ought to tell whoever is concerned when I see something clearly like that. I always tell myself when I'm the one concerned, no matter how bad it is."

"Good for you," said Genevieve, who had not been listening, her eyes fastened on Ken, in close conversation with three substantial-looking gentlemen at the bar on the terrace. They seemed to be listening politely to whatever he was saying.

Mr. Reardon came up and asked her to dance.

The orchestra struck up its inevitable lifeless fox trot, animated but dead, cheerful but empty, and she felt a momentary pang at dancing to such aborted music, as though she were attending the rites of some outlawed and shameful religious sect. Mr. Reardon, tall, square-shouldered, bald, with his baby coloring, firm mouth, and extremely capable-looking eyes that glanced everywhere at once all the while they seemed to be remaining centered on her, was a good dancer.

"Georgia's just as happy as a lark here. I've never seen her like this. We all love being here. What a house!"

"The heating is a problem in these old houses. High ceilings. And the plumbing too."

"It has the best view!"

"Originally this site was occupied by the Pequot Indians. They had their war hut here, according to the earliest maps of Wetherford which the Connecticut historical society has. Later the settlers had a fort of some kind near here. The reason is, of course, that it commands the river. If you'd like to read the history of the property I would be glad to have someone go through the *Chronicles of Old Wetherford* and mark the appropriate chapters."

"And your pianos! That concert grand in the . . . do you call it the Music Room? What tone! I'm crazy about it, I wish I had the talent to really play it."

"Moisture from the river sometimes affects its tone."

"What a grand party. Aren't you having a grand time?"

"We give these parties twice a year; that is, we did before the war and I suppose we will now again. I hope they're enjoying themselves and that you are too, Mrs. Sommers."

"Genevieve," she said impulsively, squeezing his hand.

He smiled at her briefly, and then said carefully, "Hugh."

"Well now, Hugh, that's the way we ought to be, first names, now that Georgia's so happy and we're related and you're planning this *wonderful opportunity* for my husband, for Ken. I know in the East people are supposed to be so formal. But you know, *our* side of the family, the Sommers side, we're just folks."

Mr. Reardon's trained face did not betray his disgust with the expression "just folks," this confession of mediocrity, this cozy lower-middle-class self-conception which by will and work he had lifted *his* side of the family, the Reardons, far above, stratospherically above anything as petty and negligible and exploited and pinched as "just folks." Nor would such a self-conception be permitted in his descendants; he would see to that. Neil's child, Neil's child by Georgia Sommers, it was never going to be allowed to cross that child's mind that he was or could ever be "just folks." This would be Mr. Reardon's second grandchild, but since it was Neil's and its name would be Reardon, he anticipated it more than he had Hugh. He saw his continuity, the continuity of his power and will, passing through Neil to the future; he saw himself living on, becoming permanent, touching immortality, by means of this driving son, of whom he was so strongly, and so silently, proud.

"I think kids should be allowed to express themselves, don't you?" said Genevieve.

"Very firm guidance, that's what parents should supply."

"Life gets serious soon enough for them, poor little things."

"A sense of responsibility certainly is a necessity."

"I mean, those are the best years of their lives."

"Good habits formed early are really invaluable."

"Carefree, carefree, *that's* what youth should be."

"It's never too early to start."

At the bar on the terrace, surrounded by September's moisture and fragrance, the scintillation of nighttime outdoors, and the heightened sensuousness people feel wearing evening clothes in the grass, Ken leaned forward and his elbow slipped off the bar and he spilled a little of his drink on his shirt front. He fumbled for a handkerchief, finally located it folded neatly in his breast pocket, and brushed at the stain. The three men had moved away and no one happened to notice except Cleet Kinsolving, who was standing on the steps just outside the Octagon.

Ken was getting very gracefully drunk. Just as an apprentice dancer will acquire grace with practice, so had Ken in getting drunk. He knew all of the paths, all of the fences to be vaulted and later clambered over with great care and finally circumvented, the bogs were all marked in his memory, the lime pits covered over and the quicksand fenced off; through all these snares and perils he knew how to wend his labyrinthine way, a strangely varied, tantalizingly circuitous trail to sweet oblivion. Sometimes, it was true, he took a misstep and then the journey was ruined, he slapped Genevieve or broke something, but with care all pitfalls could be avoided and the evening made a complete success.

"Says he wants to be a pilot, have an airline or something like that, isn't that it?" inquired Genevieve, dancing past Cleet, who was still in the doorway.

"Yes," said Mr. Reardon, "I believe so."

Ken now began to gather a personal dusk about himself, a soft and silvery cloud through which others were seen in a flattering, glowing blur, flattering not to him but to them. The percussion of the band was cushioned now, and slowly but deliberately, as though setting sail on the shining river below, his problems and failures embarked and drew away from him, were cut loose to drift off, and he was what he confidently knew himself to be and always to have been, a charming, accomplished, fine gentlemen.

"Come over here, young fellow," he called in his clear voice across the terrace to the immobile figure of Cleet on the steps. "Tell me more about what a stupid man I am."

Stricken, rooted with a mortification he could not understand, Cleet nevertheless compelled himself to walk across the grass to Mr. Sommers' side. "Tell me where I went wrong," went on Mr. Sommers, smiling slowly, his fine eyes on Cleet.

After a long pause Cleet said, "I haven't got anything to say."

For the next forty-five minutes Cleet watched as Mr. Sommers slowly and steadily unwound before his eyes like a toy airplane, the rubber band which made the propeller go, so tightly knotted and springy at first, becoming slacker and limper, the tension and power continually leaving it until there was no force whatever left. "I have to go," Cleet said several times, but Mr. Sommers always detained him, and above all Cleet was detained by the fear that if he abandoned Mr. Sommers, his disintegration would become evident to everybody. Cleet knew that, in a way he could not explain, it was damaging to himself to see this, but he wished to protect Mr. Sommers and Georgia and Neil, and so he stayed. Mr. Sommers could not be persuaded to move from the bar, and in fact the only sign of ill temper in him emerged when Cleet suggested that.

Finally however Mr. Sommers began to cry, from pleasure at Georgia's beauty and happiness, which he had been glowingly describing, and at last Cleet was able to drag him away from the terrace, around the back of the house, to the gymnasium wing. There he stripped Mr. Sommers of his clothes and put him in the steam box. Then he threw him into the Plunge. Then he rubbed him with the wire mesh glove, rolled him in a sheet, and deposited him on a cot. Mr. Sommers had already lost consciousness.

Cleet sat contemplating this man. There was no sound except the low, pleasant hum of some ventilating machinery, no smell except chlorine, no light except one bright lamp above the cot. Cleet had more or less forgotten that there was a party being given in the house. He studied Mr. Sommers, who did not move and did not even seem to be breathing, lying like the effigy of some medieval knight upon his tomb. Cleet watched. He did not really know why he was watching, what he was looking for or waiting for. Random thoughts flowed through his mind and then behind the hum of the ventilating machine he thought he heard another sound, distant but approaching, the sound of a machine, a motor, an engine, a clattering racket coming closer.

Get going, the searchlight in his mind suddenly signaled, get going.

He gazed with his level Indian stare at the waxen figure, the slain crusader, the crippled corsair, the beached privateer lying motionlessly in front of him.

How dried-out he was. Cleet had noticed that after they had been adults for a while people began to dry out, more and more rapidly, dry out in their hair and their skin and their fingernails and everywhere, and to become too thin—especially women, especially in their legs—or too fat, too coarse, their juices draining out of them.

Mr. Sommers was as parched as West Texas, at his age, whatever that was. The tiny domes of skin over his closed eyes were like crepe paper; his neck was loose and dry and ringed with lines, the skin across his forehead and temples was like wax paper through which fragile blue veins could be seen, there was a flaky quality to the skin of his arms, there was something almost prune-like about his hands, and the nails were cracking. He was like West Texas after a long drought, or a mummy, or an embalmed saint: or what Cleet himself might be someday.

Georgia came hurrying in, the heels of her slippers clicking on the tile floor, a faint rattle of beads and bracelet, a vague mist of perfume. "Here you are," she said in her low-pitched, melodious voice nervously.

"He passed out."

"Why did you let him drink?"

"I didn't let him or not let him. He just did it."

" . . . helpless . . ."

"You ought to know that by now," said Cleet.

"I'm a slow learner."

"The hell you are, you've had your whole life to learn how helpless he was."

"He. You mean Pop? Well of course *he's* helpless." A suspended silence. "I was thinking of you," she murmured.

"Oh," said Cleet unemphatically, nodding his head slowly.

"What are we going to do with him?"

There was a silence during which Cleet reviewed possible replies to this, some beginning with "You can take him and stuff–" and "I don't care if you and your father go to–" and "If I had a daughter like you I'd–"; but he controlled his feelings, for once, and replied, "Leave him here. It's the best place for him."

"He might wake up and come straight back into the middle of the party in that sheet, or with nothing on at all. Someone will have to watch him. Will you?"

"Um-hum."

"You don't sound very pleased."

Cleet looked at her, and then looked away.

Suddenly she said, "I'm sorry if I seem like a witch tonight. I'm scared with my family here that something will go wrong."

"Relax."

Georgia did not leave, lingering in the distant hope that her father would wake up and say it was all a hoax, that he had had nothing to drink, that he was ready for the opportunity of secure work which his daughter had provided for him, that he was going to be happy, that the past and its failures and scars had all been expunged, that they were all going to be happy now.

"I wish you'd hurry up and have that baby."

"*You* do! How do you think I feel?"

"I don't know. How do you feel?"

After a pause she said, "Scared, to tell the truth. That's funny. I haven't told anybody that, not Neil or the doctor or my own mother. Why did I tell you?"

"It's because I'm not Albert Einstein."

"That's a mysterious answer."

"Why are you scared?"

"Because, I don't know, nature's got possession of me. It's like being caught in a current that's too strong to swim against, and wondering where it will carry you and is it going to hurt, is it going to be dangerous, and how much is it going to change me, things like that."

"Well, I wish you'd hurry up and have it."

"Why?"

"So I can get out of here, take off, *start.*"

"What has *my* child got to do with *your* starting something?"

"Everything. I told myself I'd stay until you and Neil were through with this, and after that I'd take off."

"Take off? Where?"

"Well I told you, to start that little air freight service—"

She was looking studiously down at her father. "That's out," she muttered.

"Huh?"

"I mean I heard—"

"What do you mean, 'That's out'?"

"Why I thought everybody had agreed not to go . . . I . . . don't ask me, I, I really do feel nervous tonight. Pop here—"

Cleet, seated on a stool next to the cot, with Mr. Sommers prone in front of him and Georgia now moving restlessly back and forth on the other side, put his two hands on the seat of the stool, the edges biting into his fingers, all the muscles of his arms locked, and across the cot he glared at her with a force that made her almost flinch.

" 'Pop here!' " he said with a level violence. " 'Pop here!' I'm asking you and you are going to answer the truth. What did you mean when you said, 'That's out'?"

"I don't know what I meant, I mean I had Pop on my mind—"

Cleet got deliberately up and walked around the cot; Georgia drew back a little but then faced him, blinking. He stopped in front of her, balancing on the balls of his feet as though about to spring forward, his green eyes hanging expressionlessly in his strong, square, expressionless face, his stare fixed on her as though he could control her by his eyes alone. He grasped her arm with his left hand. "I want an answer out of you." She suddenly realized that her father was unconscious and that everyone else in the house was twelve or fifteen partitions and seven or eight hallways away from where she confronted Cleet Kinsolving. "What did you mean?" he said with now a querulous kind of gentleness, which was more frightening than ever.

Georgia, feeling her position nevertheless both innocent and truthful, faced him. "I don't make decisions here, why ask me? Ask Neil, ask his father."

He stood looking at her as though she were a conjurer who at any second was going to produce another rabbit from her hat, or pigeons would come fluttering from her sleeves, or she might even disappear entirely. She was a source of revelations and he waited second by second for the decisive one, ignoring, not hearing, anything unrelated to such a revelation, such as, "Ask Neil, ask his father."

"They're not going to give me my chance?" he finally inquired hesitantly, almost shyly, like someone so shocked at attributing evil to another that he hesitated to suggest it even in the face of stark proof.

"I don't know," she murmured.

He turned like an automaton away from her. "Stay here," he said in a quiet, ordering tone.

"Why should I?"

"You want your father to wander into the party naked? No? Okay, stay here."

Then he walked out. Georgia took a deep, shaky breath, feeling both better and worse. She gazed at the thin, lined, sallow-skinned figure prone before her under the white illumination of the single light. In her moment of terror just then, before the blind-seeming rage of Cleet, her father had been of no help, he had been unconscious, as dependent and helpless as an infant.

He slowly opened his eyes. "What'd he say? Where'd he go?" he said in a vague manner which Georgia recognized. He had been only pretending to be unconscious so as not to become involved, not to have to defend her if she was attacked, safe and scared, hiding as always, a charming man who would let his own daughter be attacked and not lift a finger to help her because it simply wasn't in him.

"I think he's gone to assert himself," she said bitterly.

Mr. Sommers looked up at her and smiled.

Cleet walked, setting his feet firmly, along the long lower hallway to the back stairs, up to the kitchen wing, through the green Music Room, through the dining room, along the short, dark passage beneath the stairs, and out into the hall in front of the library doors. Surprisingly, light was shining beneath them, and he crossed to the doors and slid them apart. Neil was standing at the desk in front of the huge bay window, the desk lamp illuminating some papers before him; there was no other light except a little wall fixture high up along the catwalk, which cast a grayish light over that section of the room.

"Where are the copies of that thing I wrote about brotherhood?" Neil said without looking up. "The editor of the Hartford paper is here. He thinks they'd like to run it."

Cleet stood motionlessly in the doorway.

Neil finally glanced across at him over the tops of the shell-rimmed glasses he had put on. "Hm?"

Cleet stared at him a moment more and then taking a step forward he said, "Do you want me to help you look?"

"Hm?" Neil glanced at him over his glasses again. "Sure. Naturally."

After a pause Cleet said, "But I can't keep it up forever."

Neil was rummaging in a drawer stuffed with papers. "Why not?" he remarked, frowning at the confusion of papers.

To that Cleet answered quietly and carefully, "I've got my own life to lead."

The tone of voice in which this was said penetrated Neil's inattentive mind. He straightened up, still frowning, a bunch of papers in his right hand, and said, "What are you talking about, anyway?"

The two young men stood facing each other in the dim library, wearing their black ties and white dinner jackets.

"I'm talking about my . . . career," answered Cleet, ending the sentence in a tone of slight uncertainty. Neil felt his stomach contract as he forced himself not to burst out laughing. Cleet's career: somehow it sounded the same as if Hugh had said, "I'm talking about my voting rights."

"Well, what about it?" Neil asked soberly; he now knew what was at issue and so he proceeded to act his part, thinking always of his own advantage, as he had been trained from birth to do.

Cleet began to circle slowly in front of the big desk, then over toward the globe and the ladder, "Well," he suddenly blurted violently, "it's time I started, that's what about it!"

"Take it—"

"I'll miss the boat if I don't, I'll be finished, I'll be another Mr. Sommers, I'll be your office boy, I'll be a derelict, I'll be nothing, that's what!"

"I see."

"All right," said Cleet evenly, pivoting his torso as he always did, confronting him. "What are you going to do about it?"

After a pause Neil raised his eyebrows and said, "Me?"

Cleet felt a frigid paralysis moving across his brain. Trying to resist this with all his will he went on in an even tone, "I am asking you to lend me the money to start a little freight air service." Then he was silent and looked unblinkingly and motionlessly, as though cast in bronze, at his friend.

Neil twiddled a pen in his left hand. "Well I'd forgotten about that," he murmured, "and—"

"I haven't," said Cleet, his voice coming forcefully, although he hadn't raised it, across what Neil was saying.

"I'd forgotten about that," Neil repeated with emphasis, "and in any case I've talked it over with Dad and we've decided it's a bad idea."

Something rattled somewhere, perhaps a loose shutter in the wind.

"You've decided it's a bad idea," repeated Cleet cogitatively, as though these words were in Latin and someone had asked him to translate them. "You've decided . . ." pondering the sentence, he continued slowly moving in and out of the pool of light cast by the large Victorian lamp on the desk. Then the meaning of the words reached him and glancing over at Neil he said quietly, "I'm going to do it myself."

"Cleet, listen," said Neil, his voice for the first time, now that he did not feel guilty about what he was going to say, becoming a little warm. "We've looked into it. It's very chancy, very speculative." He circled the desk and came up next to Cleet. "Besides," he said in his sincere tone, "we've got to be honest." He started to put his hand on Cleet's shoulder but decided that would be too patronizing in view of what he was about to say. "We don't think you could run it. We don't think you're qualified. It's very complicated, running any business today. You fit in here, you can be a tremendous help to me." Neil went behind the desk again and sat down.

Cleet looked at him and slowly nodded his head, as though recognizing some long-concealed truth he had never allowed himself to recognize before. It was the first cynical reaction of his life.

"Yeah, um-hum, I see what you mean," he said, turning slowly away so that Neil could not see tears spring into his eyes. "Well, good luck," he said.

"What?"

"I, um, resign, thank you for everything . . . I wish you never came to Kansas because you see I had made a little start there and might have been crop dusting or something like that on my own by this time and now I've got to start from scratch, which is always hard. You've never done it, so you wouldn't know about that. Scratch, scratch the ground or the streets of some city or the door of opportunity or whatever you want to call it, hold on and get a chance with nothing but your fingernails for grip! You wouldn't know about that and I don't blame you and I don't envy you, I'm just explaining something you wouldn't know about. Because when somebody like me has to start from scratch it's very hard and very—delicate, starting from scratch, and if some small things disturb us and throw us off, well then maybe we'll never get started at all! You threw me off when you showed up there in Kansas and talked me and pressured me and bribed me into coming back to this God-forsaken town and this crazy house and all the things I wanted to get away from. Now I've got to get down there and start scratching with my fingernails again and hope that I can get a grip on something. And this time," he faced him directly, confronted him with the point-blank power of his presence, "leave me alone, will you. Don't uh do me any favors or anything. Don't help."

"Aren't you forgetting about the plane?" Neil suddenly said in an offhand tone.

"The plane? The crop duster? I'm sure as hell—"

"Our plane," he said casually. "The *Flying Folly*."

"What do you mean, forgetting about it?" said Cleet roughly. "Why shouldn't I forget about it? What's it got to," infuriatingly he had to pause an instant for breath, "got to do with me?"

"Don't try to fake out your old football partner," said Neil, leaning back in his chair and tapping his thumb with the end of his pencil. "You wrecked it and you know it. I just touched you on the back and you fell all over the pilot and the instruments and everything. You wanted to cause it and you caused it."

Cleet stared at him, his face twisted into a mask of exasperated rage. "Why?" he demanded, his mouth curling contemptuously. "Why would I do that? Do you think I'm crazy!"

"Oh," answered Neil almost airily, "you knew enough about flying to realize it probably wouldn't be a really *serious* wreck, so you thought you'd get the pilot fired—that worked—and get his job yourself. You've always been obsessed with being a pilot, haven't you? Since you had to work for us, you decided to . . . make a place for yourself." Neil gestured vaguely in front of his forehead. "Some foggy notion like that."

There was a long, heavy silence and then Cleet said, "You're wrong. That's what I guess you would have done if you'd been me. You think everybody's like you, including me. Well, you're wrong." And Cleet saw that this interpretation of Neil was correct and in any case there was not a shred of evidence to support the accusation and he had only to leave the room and the house and no problem about the plane would ever confront him.

But he did not leave. After a while he decided to say: "But

maybe I did in a way half cause the wreck. Something in me was trying to stop me from coming back to Wetherford and back to your family, and it was like a force in me. Maybe that force had something to do with causing the accident."

"The wreck. It wasn't an accident."

"The wreck."

There was another protracted silence and then Neil said, "Don't you think you owe us something for that? For wrecking our plane, for risking our lives?"

"Nobody was hurt but me, so I don't owe you anything for that. And the plane, well, Neil, the plane is insured."

Neil turned in his swivel chair and looked out the window.

"I can't think I owe people something for being myself."

"What does that mean?" said Neil in a tone of controlled contempt, turning back to look at him.

"If you don't understand it, I can't explain any better."

"I think you owe us something, but I also think we owe you something and I want you to sit down and listen while I explain."

Cleet let an expression of his disgust show on his face, and then said, "No, there's nothing to explain. I understand why you don't want to put up some money for my idea. I was even stupider than I usually am, not to understand it before. You're afraid to. I should have seen that back in Kansas in the tourist cabin. What the hell, I've known you all your life. You've always been scared, I knew that when we were seven years old." Neil's arms were resting on the profusion of papers before him, hands clasped. He looked at Cleet with the fixity of someone being sentenced. "You were afraid in the river and in the Cove and you were afraid the night of the freshet. You've always been afraid. Why didn't I think of that before!" He struck his forehead. "How dumb can you be! Naturally you wouldn't back my idea. It might fail! We might lose! You just said it was too speculating or whatever you said." Cleet frowned at him. "You're scared to fail. You have to win all the time, you always did. You think if you don't win you might starve to death. A hundred million dollars isn't enough for you. If you lose one of them, then the ninety-nine million nine hundred and ninety-nine thousand nine hundred and ninety-nine other dollars you've got might go too. My idea was too risky for you. *I'm* too risky for you!"

Neil's face wore the expression of alert impassivity both he and his father instinctively assumed when an adversary had probed to their weakness. "You're making a mistake," he said soberly: both believed that when a weakness has been located, attack. "You are better off here and now than you will ever be anywhere else, much better off. You've got security, you're surrounded by friends, familiar town, you're safe. Outside . . . well, you just seem to be some kind of crazy guy who isn't very bright. I'm sorry to have to say things like that to you. I grew up with you and the people here in Wetherford watched you grow up and we all know you and all your good qualities and we want you to stay here where you belong. That's Dad's whole feeling about it too. Do you mind that I'm so blunt? We're old friends, and what are they for?" Cleet continued to direct his unwavering stare at him. "And," Neil continued, "we know you can be safe and content and secure here and be a big help to me and to everybody and so that's our plan."

Cleet went up to the desk, put his fists on it, and staring across at Neil said quietly, "I don't like the plan. You know what it is? It's a way of slipping around life instead of going through it, it's too safe, it's too dead, it's all dried up. I'm supposed to go through life, maybe getting killed and maybe, maybe having the most wonderful life anybody ever had! You've only got a hundred million dollars, so you've got to take all the precautions in case you're ever destitute or anything like that. You always will work hard and you're real competent and you've got a brain, but you still want to take all kinds of precautions. I'm not too bright a lot of the time, you just reminded me of that, thanks a lot. I've got four hundred dollars in war bonds and twenty-five dollars in the bank, but the hell with this. I'm not that scared, yet, so while I'm not, I'd better use it. Right? Anyway, I uh quit, Neil."

He walked out of the library.

Neil did not follow. He began carefully and methodically thinking what steps were necessary to prevent Cleet's departure. Several possibilities occurred to him. Now, more than ever, Cleet had to be forced to stay, now Cleet had to be where Neil could demonstrate to him daily that fear, if Neil had ever experienced it, was completely conquered now. Of course, he wasn't *afraid* to underwrite the air-freight service. It was simply that all the evidence pointed to failure and he couldn't do anything as stupid as deliberately failing, not even to placate his friend. Someday Cleet would have to grow up; he must not be indulged, humored: it was time for him to face life. Another reason he had to be made to stay was that Neil had decided that was what he wanted to happen, he and his father had decided it that way and told others of their decision, and there was something faintly obscene about flouting with impunity a decision publicly announced by Reardons senior and junior.

Cleet walked slowly up the huge old staircase, in the light of the frosted globes which used to be illuminated by gas and looked as though they still were. He felt a sensation of sickness in his stomach and sweat broke out on his forehead. He could not believe Neil and the Reardons had gone back on their word. He was not frightened of the future; he was frightened of the past. This friend and this family, the closest people in the world to him after his brother and grandmother, were nothing like what all his life he had assumed them to be: as good as their word. No treachery or cheating or betrayal in the outside world could any longer surprise him. But betrayal at the hands of the Reardons amazed the Cleet Kinsolving of seven and twelve and sixteen years old who had first learned to trust and even in a way love them, for Cleet as he grew older had never thought to re-examine or question that early feeling; it was this intact early faith in this family which suffered the blow, unprotected by all Cleet had learned about human nature since. That was why tears had come to his eyes; that was why, infuriatingly, there were still tears in his eyes.

He reached the small wood-paneled bedroom he often used at High Farms, with its balcony and spiral staircase going down to the South Lawn. He turned on the light and its projection instantly created a bright rectangle on the empty grass below. He took the pillowcase off the bed pillow and started to stuff the few belongings he kept in this room into it: a toothbrush, toothpaste, razor, shaving cream, deck of cards, volumes one and three of *The Life and Loves of Frank Harris,* two cigars taken from Mr. Reardon's private, reserved humidor. Then he noticed two figures step into the rectangle of light on the lawn, Georgia leading, with her father, wearing pants and a shirt, stumbling along beside her;

his right arm was across her shoulders and she was holding that hand firmly with both of hers, pulling him along. Looking up in surprise toward the source of this sudden light on the dark lawn Georgia saw Cleet through the wide glass doors of his room and motioned to him to come down. He went on stuffing things into the pillowcase. Georgia glared up at him, then led her father to a stone bench in an inset in the high privet hedge, and hurried back across the lawn, up the spiral stairs, across the little balcony, and pulling the sliding glass doors apart began a little breathlessly, "Honestly, Cleet, I wish you'd help me out for just a little while. Can't you? I have got to get back to that party, I have got to. My mother-in-law must already think I'm crazy, or dead. Come down and take care of Pop."

Cleet fired a single glance at her and turned his attention back to the pillowcase. "Cleet?" She leaned against the glass doors, folded her arms, and watched him, the expression on her face growing progressively more sardonic. She said, "What are you doing? Robbing the house?"

After a pause he looked up at her and said, "No, but it's a thought."

Another silence followed. Although part of her mind urged her to go back to her father before he disgraced her, another part held her immobilized in Cleet's room. It was as though the rather comical spectacle of his stuffing a peculiar assortment of items into a pillowcase was some kind of series of signals which she felt an almost hypnotic urge to interpret. She stared at him with torn fascination, furious with him, herself, her father, and life, but caught, her deepest curiosity binding her to the sight of these possessions disappearing into that pillowcase. It was as if she was about to learn something, and if she did not learn it now, she would never learn it, because a half hour from now would be too late.

"It's no use standing there," he said without troubling to look up. "I'm not going to waste time with that drunk."

She went on watching him. He was going through some drawers and had found a pair of socks. She had divined what was happening: he was leaving, and a feeling of desolation swept over her. "They decided not to go along with your idea," she said.

"That's right."

In Georgia's mind the question of exactly why she was tarrying to watch him pack continued to trouble her. Something was about to escape, her opportunity to help him. "Don't you understand the Reardons after all these years?"

He shook his head.

"The Reardons are very rich, so they change their minds all the time. They're always changing their minds. Nothing ever satisfies them. They feel people are taking advantage of them. They feel their fortune isn't respected enough. They're perfectionists. Whatever they have, they feel they've made a mistake, they should not have that, they should have something else. They feel imposed on and impatient, and they don't care who knows it. Neil *meant* to go along with your idea and so did his father. But they just lost interest in that, they thought another solution would be fairer to . . ."

He was listening now. "Yeah?"

"Well, to themselves."

"Oh," he said flatly.

"They can only think of themselves, they're afraid that if they don't, constantly, other people will take advantage of them. They feel a duty to be selfish. Otherwise, they'd be undermining the free enterprise system. You've got to be patient with them."

"Patient!"

"Yes. You've got to wait. If you leave now—" and then Georgia could not finish her thought aloud. Her thought was that there was simply nowhere for Cleet to go except down, if he left High Farms; he would never be so well off nor so secure again, she believed, because the world had become too mechanized for his kind of nature, he asked too much of life, and he had, as America started into the second half of the twentieth century, too little, speaking strictly practically, to offer. What a pity, what a waste, what a tragedy. How it must baffle him. He was like a beautifully armored warrior facing a tank. He was also one of the few remaining heirs to a far older tragedy. Leaning over the pillowcase now, Cleet's strongly formed face with its high cheekbones and straight strong nose was as unconscious as ever of its significance. The face, the fixed expression of the eyes, and the impassivity he often exhibited were the last vestiges and relics of his Indian blood, mingled and swamped in him by his three-quarters-European ancestry but still unchangeably there, that persistent strain in his nature making him sometimes utterly bewildered by this America today, an alien who however felt in his blood that this was and always had been home, and somewhere far back in his mind he kept asking what had happened, what had happened. She saw that deeply buried in up-to-date Anglo-Saxon Country Day School Army Air Force slang-speaking football-playing Cleet, was that aboriginal American, bound and affronted. She was very moved, gazing at him.

"What's it to you anyway?" he suddenly asked, cutting into her thoughts.

She hesitated, recalled what she had been saying, and then said crisply, sensing some snare being prepared for her, "I'm thinking of Neil, and he needs you." But she did not say this quite crisply enough, and Cleet's shrewd mind, uncluttered by learning or information, cut through her words and tone, and he told himself: I'll be damned. I attract her.

He looked carefully across at her. Georgia was glancing over her shoulder down at the lawn, where her father still sat motionlessly on the bench. I attract her, he said to himself, and she doesn't know it. "What do you care," he said slowly, "if I leave?"

"I just told you."

"Yeah, but I didn't believe that reason. That's not a reason. What do you care if I leave?"

"I don't want you to throw this chance away, maybe throw your life away. I'd hate to see anybody do that."

"Would you?"

"I don't understand that tone in your voice."

"Don't you?"

"No," she said querulously.

He lowered the pillowcase slowly to the bed and very deliberately released it. Then he advanced around the bottom of the bed and came up to her. She was leaning against the glass door, watching him with total incomprehension. "Yes you understand that tone in my voice," he said to her, "yes you understand. You understand yourself all of a sudden, don't you. Hm?"

"Why are you trying to scare me? Cleet?"

"Does what you feel scare you?"

"I don't know what you mean."

"Do you want me to show you what I mean?"

A frantic bolt of excitement seemed to cut through her; something was cutting off her breath.

"Do you want me to show you what I mean?"

"I think I'm going to . . ." she mumbled. "I won't understand . . ." and Cleet said contemptuously, "Yes, you will understand." His eyes hung before her, she smelled some lotion he wore, and that he had been smoking. "Cleet, you've got to help me," she heard herself say before his mouth closed over hers and everything became unthinkable; everything was a lie, everything was true. "That's it," he said.

She felt his tongue shoved into her mouth and his charged body around hers. There was the smell of him, piny lotion and perspiration; her dress was pulled from her shoulders; the warm and tough-skinned palms of his hands slid over her breasts and along the sides of her body, and her veins were pounding and pounding and her brain was paralyzed, stark; he was like some very intelligent animal; she was out of her clothes and on the bed and his wide-shouldered body was on top of her and her hands slid down his back and felt the two ridges of muscle separated by his spine, not like Neil—Neil! Neil!—her paralyzed brain took no action; she felt Cleet warm and naked on top of her and between her legs and as his thick tongue thrust itself again and again into her mouth she felt him enter her between the legs with the same irresistible force; her veins were pounding and pounding and her feelings were drowning her; his warmth and his vibrant body were everywhere and he was entering her again and again. The smell of his perspiration intoxicated her, and the warm roughness of his hands; her paralyzed brain was flooded. And they finished together.

"What are we doing?" he finally mumbled. "What are we doing?"

Georgia, drawn and wide-eyed, stared at him.

"What are we doing?" he repeated.

Georgia stared wide-eyed at him.

"I have to get out," he said, standing up and pulling his clothes together. "I have to get out." He moved disheveled across the room, out onto the balcony, and down the circular stairs.

Georgia lay nearly naked on Cleet Kinsolving's bed, staring at the glass wall of the room, staring, staring.

On the lawn below, Mr. Sommers opened his eyes and squinted up at the single bright rectangle visible on the side of the old house. Two figures had been together in the middle of the brightness; in the vagueness of his mind he recognized one of them as his daughter and then let the recognition slip away. Someone came down the stairway and went off toward the river.

He continued sitting there for an indefinite stretch of time, his mind drifting mistily over his family and their past and California and ski lifts for automobiles and air pumped down from outer space and other marvelous possibilities for the human race which he would like to implement someday; realizations of life floated shimmeringly across his thoughts in all their perfection, and he wondered how long it would be before some of these came to pass, and what he might do himself to hasten that day, what contribution he could make at this time to hurry the day of their realization, the day on which he would be so happy for others, not for himself, for these dreams were purely selfless, concerned with the well-being of other people, of all other people, whom he hoped to benefit; pulsations of happiness passed through him at the thought of his hopes for others, of the beauty and goodness he so ardently desired for them, of the day, soon now, very soon, when he would be able to endow them with this great heritage.

Sometime later Mr. Sommers became aware of another presence on the lawn, a sturdy figure standing off on the brow of the hill leading down to the river. His mind was a little clearer now and he thought that he recognized the Kinsolving boy, who seemed to be just standing there in the moonlight alone, looking down at the brilliant waters of the Connecticut.

The water scintillated dizzyingly in the moonlight, millions of agitated specks oscillating rapidly, wildly, an uncontrolled splendor of ceaseless motion, staccato darts of reflected moonlight quickly creating networks and instantly altering them, forever in motion, unstoppable, haphazard, blinding. The figure watching them was Cleet Kinsolving, staring down at this pageantry of nighttime, not moving, not even blinking.

He was not and had not ever been attracted to her. What he

had done was take animal revenge, driven by his instincts, not his mind or even his will. Still, no one had seen, no one would know. He stared at the river, thinking in amazement of the vengeful animal inside himself and how it had tried to wreck him and her and everything. It, the animal, was powerfully and deeply pleased that it possessed what was all too accurately called animal magnetism and that its power held sway over Georgia, mate of Neil, enemy. It had forced the use of that power.

So he had had his revenge. Neil, the Reardons, his job, Wetherford, the freight airline, everything else was lost.

However, he thought, drawing a deep breath, he was twenty-three years old and God knew he was *healthy:* there had to be something for him somewhere out in some town or country somewhere someday; he would have to find it, that was all, he would have to.

He stood cogitating all of this very vague future, his eyes on the mad complexity of moonbeams on the river, thinking about all of this, all the while his eyes on the unending silver motion, noticing that at the heart of it there seemed to be something moving forward, something more solid than moonbeams moved over the surface of the Connecticut River. He seemed to see, he thought he saw, he was almost sure that slowly swinging into view around the bend in the Connecticut River was the long, upward-tilted bowsprit of a great sailing ship.

It seemed to be a square-rigger, and as he watched transfixed the foremast passed in front of his eyes, its sails reefed, and then the mainmast and the mizzen and the aftermast; there were banners rippling and streaming from the topgallants; figures were lashing the great sails of the topmast to the spars; the jib, just released, flapped loosely in the wind; in all of the gunports on the quarter-deck cannons stood at the ready; a landing net hung over the side and trailed in the water; great hemp cables lay coiled on the foredeck, attached to the anchor, which was next to the bow, since the ship seemed to be coming into its mooring at Wetherford; in front of the hatch, on the afterdeck, there was a long windlass and a water cask, and a smokestack coming up through the deck from the galley; as all of the ship swung into view he thought he saw the high transom stern, its gilded cabin shining with many small-paned windows, the railings around it a brilliant yellow and red. Behind this great man-of-war there glided slowly around the bend a brigantine, its two masts under full sail, ballooning proudly up the silent river so long empty of all fighting craft, of almost any craft at all; into the great bend around Wetherford Meadow there now crowded, coming slowly along behind the man-of-war and the brigantine, a lighter and a pinnace, and even an ancient wallowing shallop, barges and ketches, one of them carrying on its stemhead a beautiful figure of an angel, its wings flung back against the great oak hull, gliding seraphically above the waters of the Connecticut River; all of the rigging was busy with figures preparing the ships to come into the mooring, figures moving swiftly up and down the rope ladders and working the halyards, furling the great ghostly sails, moving the anchors into position, executing the final maneuvers of their long voyage with care, home, the flotilla coming skillfully up to this last mooring before his eyes alone.

It was a vision which he was seeing, really almost seeing, and it crowded his heart with hope.

Neil Reardon woke up the following morning and bitterly regretted it. He usually got up at seven A.M. and ran a mile, outdoors unless there was a blizzard, in the gym on those occasions. Today he woke at eleven-twenty.

One of the housemen, whose face he suddenly realized he detested, brought him breakfast, his mail, the Hartford *Courant,* and *The New York Times.* Two fried eggs stared him in the face, vibrating faintly. They were undercooked. He pushed them irritably aside. The first letter he opened was an invitation to address a political science conference at the University of Connecticut. The University of Connecticut! *Was* there a University of Connecticut? Certainly no one anyone had ever heard of had ever gone there. He dropped the invitation on the floor. There was a letter from a priest in Samoa requesting that any unwanted or duplicated books in the famous young Mr. Reardon's library be sent, in the slowest and least expensive way, of course, to his hospital in Samoa. If Mr. Reardon would take the trouble to sign just one or two it would be very exciting for the patients. From this letter the boredom he always felt with people dedicated to good works settled over him like a cloud.

He tossed that letter aside and opened one written on silver-gray stationery, scented, the handwriting telling him that this correspondent could have been educated at only one of five girls' schools. She asked questions about his work, which he instantly interpreted as an intellectual subterfuge: she was making the first overture toward having an affair with him. There was a request for an interview from the Boston *Globe.* Why the hell should he *give* his opinions to some hack reporter instead of *selling* them in articles by himself? What kind of moron did people think he was! There was a long letter from one Gil Manchester, full of jokes and clumsy attempts to compliment him on his success. Gil Manchester was a shadow from Country Day School, who had played the bugle, he seemed to recall, or was it that he recited? Perhaps he had been a cheerleader. The letter aroused a kind of energy in him because of its crude assumption of intimacy and cordiality where none had ever existed. Neil decided he would reply to this letter and began to compose the opening sentences in his head: "Dear Gil Manchester, I have received your long letter and note that I 'sure didn't look like a national leader in the shower room.' I'm sorry I can't visualize what you look like; otherwise I might be able to say what you did or didn't resemble in the shower room. I don't recollect you at all, as a matter of fact, although the style of your letter is very familiar, 'sophomoric' as we used to say in the shower room," and so on.

His correspondence disgusted him so much that he picked up the Hartford *Courant.* Its front page shrieked provincialism. He threw it away. He picked up *The New York Times.* He felt that morning that its pomposity might cause his first ulcer to break out. Mornings like this occurred rather often to Neil.

He got out of bed and went across to the bathroom. The full-length mirror on the door gave him a view of himself which was the final affront: mussed hair, freckles, bony face, sour and hopeless expression, Neil Reardon tried for a second to stare down Neil Reardon. He wanted to defeat everything. If only he knew how, he would have defeated himself that morning.

He heard a kind of choking sound coming from the other side of the door. It was Georgia. He opened it. "Neil," she began, gasping, "Neil, I think . . ."

Georgia was still in severe pain when they reached the hospital. A little before noon, it was all over. It had been a boy.

The doctor told Neil that "some profound emotional disturbance" seemed to have been responsible for the miscarriage. He also told Neil that it was questionable whether, after this, she would ever be able to have a successful pregnancy.

Georgia lay motionless and unspeaking in her room, and Neil was not permitted to talk to her. He and Mr. Sommers left the hospital together late that afternoon.

Neil was mute with a dry, unquenchable fury at this human wastebasket ambling along beside him, since he was sure her father's drunken, disorderly behavior the night before had been the profound emotional shock which had killed his son.

"She looks a little better," said Mr. Sommers mildly.

Neil didn't speak. They reached his car and got in.

"She's always been healthy," he added.

Neil started the motor, and the car shot around the hospital driveway and out on the road.

"Just so she's all right, that's the important thing," he glanced hesitantly at Neil, "isn't it?"

Neil took his eyes from the road—they were traveling at eighty miles an hour—long enough to shoot at Mr. Sommers the sort of glance he would have directed toward a decomposing corpse.

"We're all," Mr. Sommers went on, "going to have to give—"

"Don't speak again," Neil said in his most razory voice. "I'll tell you when to speak."

"Am I bothering you? I am—"

"You caused it. You ought to be put away."

Mr. Sommers sat aghast in silence for several minutes, and finally he said, "I was a little, more than a little, well, *very* drunk, but Georgia's seen that, I have to admit it, hundreds of times. Nobody saw me except her and the Kinsolving boy. What could shock her in that? Nothing, nothing, I swear to you. Why, the Kinsolving boy took me straight to your gymnasium and then Georgia took me for a walk and when she went up to his room I sat on a bench quietly and nobody saw me. If you knew how hard I've been concentrating just now to remember what did happen. And that's what happened."

Neil had been on the point of hitting Mr. Sommers in the face when he started to speak, but as his story continued he had listened, steadily slackening the speed of the car. "Went up to his room?"

"Pardon?"

"Georgia went up to Cleet's room last night?"

"Why yes, while I was, you know, getting my head cleared out on the back lawn overlooking the river. He was up there doing something and she went up and they were inside together, talking I guess. I—"

Neil stopped the car with a jerk next to the Green. "Walk to the highway. Take a taxi home."

Mr. Sommers looked blank.

"Walk. Get out. Taxi."

Mr. Sommers got out of the car; before he could close the door the car leaped ahead, but its momentum slammed the door shut.

Cleet was practicing golf chip shots on the side lawn of his home. He was waiting for a long-distance call to Kansas to go through.

Neil's car halted in front of the house. Cleet saw him across the hedge. Neil came through the gate and crossed the lawn. His first words were said with studied pleasantness. "Hi, Cleet."

"Hello, Neil."

"What are you doing?"

"Hm?"

"I mean, is everything all right? Do I—don't I owe you some back salary?"

Cleet cut cleanly under a golf ball, and it arched through the air and dropped close to the birdbath, which was his target. Then he said, "You don't owe me anything."

Through his teeth Neil was forced to say, "I think I do." Then he tried to smile again and said, "What happened to you at the party after I saw you in the library?"

"I wandered around."

"Where?"

"Well, first I went up to my—that bedroom I used at your house and got some things of mine."

"Did you?"

"Yeah, yes I did. Why?"

"How long were you up there?"

Cleet had the golf club at the end of his backswing when this question was asked, and its deep undercurrent of rage froze him into this position for an instant before he was able to swing through and hit the ball, which he topped badly. Neil noticed the moment of rigidity. Cleet glanced at him and said, "Twenty minutes or so." Clamping the firmest control upon his feelings and mobilizing all his will power he then said in passing, "Georgia dropped in for a minute," his face curving into a smile which he hoped was not like a death's-head, "I guess she wanted to console me about the airline."

There was a short silence and then Neil said, his voice going hoarse and his eyes frozen, "And did she console you?"

"Oh you know, women, that idea of mine, I'm going to Kansas, did I tell you?" Cleet said, glancing winningly, he hoped, at Neil.

"I've just come from Georgia at the hospital."

Cleet's body was more intelligent than his brain. It congealed now into a state of preliminary fear although his brain supposed that she was having only some checkup.

"She has had a miscarriage and she has just lost our son!" Neil's voice starting quietly but ending in a shout.

After a silence Cleet heaved a deep sigh and just said, "Oh." He closed his eyes and said again, "Oh."

Neil grabbed Cleet by the arm and swung him around, sending the golf club flying across the lawn. "What did you do to her!" he shouted, wrenching him more and more violently. "What happened in that room!"

Cleet thought Neil might try to strangle him. He roughly shook himself free. They stared at each other.

Then in a soft conspirator's voice Neil asked, "What happened?" his eyes bright and strange.

Cleet stared at him and blinked and started to say, as indignantly as he could manage, that nothing at all had happened and how could Neil suspect him of such a thing, how could he suspect that he would make any advance to his wife and how could he moreover suspect that his wife would involve herself in any way with him; all the plausible lies crowded his mind, and he set out.

"Did Georgia say something?" he began in a swift undertone,

trying somehow to ask this question and get an answer without Neil's noticing that it had been asked and answered. He saw from Neil's face that she had not. "No, because nothing happened, how could it with that huge window and anybody could see in—even if you think I'm capable of that, or she is. She didn't even come in the room."

Neil was speechless: from the formidable position he occupied he didn't know which gun to fire first. "Her father saw her go in the room."

Cleet shot one glance at Neil, saw that he was possessed as if by some devil in the ancient days of Wetherford, someone due for the stake and the flames, outside safety, and he was filled with fear, more for Neil than for himself or Georgia, filled with fear for everybody. "That silly drunk," murmured Cleet. "You've been listening to him babble. He was out cold."

After a long, cold silence, Neil said, "Did you assault her?"

"Are you crazy?" Cleet shot back, and instantly regretted it because he saw that at that moment Neil was indeed crazy, shaking like someone with a high fever.

"You always were a bad liar," Neil said hoarsely. Then looking around erratically, "Your golf," he suddenly added, "isn't getting any better, is it?" turning to stare with an expression of stony inquiry at Cleet. "It's the backswing, it goes too far."

"Neil," said Cleet.

"Too far back, too far. Do you want to try it again?"

"Neil!"

"I'm better than I used to be at golf myself. We'll have to play a round. I used to be lousy, but I worked on it. I'm better than I used to be, now."

Then Neil sat down on the grass. He was silent, staring at his hands.

"This is what insanity is," flashed through Cleet's mind. Not enough love or trust or warmth or juice in Neil's life; those things were like dikes against the flood, and in Neil, poor Neil, impoverished Neil, they were very, very low.

And Cleet grasped at once that he himself was profoundly sane, in spite of his vagaries and visions, protected by all the years of love he had lived, all those girls and women and places and things and people he had so passionately loved all of his life;

every one of those feelings had been adding to the protective dike raised against the uncontrollable currents and floods of life, the freshet which would break out one day and challenge all that he had been, and test mortally what he had done, as it had this minute tested and engulfed Neil.

Then the appalling realization broke over him that this summer, for the first time in his life, he had not been in love with anybody. It was like discovering that his spine had been quietly amputated one night while he slept. He couldn't believe it; something had to be done right away.

He looked down at Neil, his head buried in his arms, and thought how quickly he had to get back to safety.

Neil looked like someone in the corner of an asylum. Love was the wall against insanity; the only segment of wall in Neil's life consisted of Georgia. Cleet, by reflex, without enough time to calculate the consequences, decided to tell half the truth.

"Neil," he said, "I have to tell you that I think I may have—I think maybe I did uh upset Georgia last night."

Neil lifted his head out of his arms and turned slowly to look up at him. "I made a pass at her, out of revenge against you, I was out of my head, but when she slapped me," he lied, "I got hold of myself and that was the end of it but I guess I might have had something to do with upsetting her."

He watched as Neil's face slowly settled back into an expression closer to his usual self-possessed competence and calmness, overlaid now with the vigilant look it had acquired when Neil first caught sight of a new enemy in life.

He got up, and facing Cleet, said all the things Cleet expected him to say, all the devastating indictments and the vows of enmity and the abuse and the oaths and menaces; Cleet just nodded his head slowly and said nothing.

After Neil had left, Cleet walked around the lawn of the house, and then at last the telephone rang.

Ten days later Georgia, in her bedroom at High Farms, sat depressed at her dressing table, absorbed in the dismal suspicion, which had just occurred to her, that Neil would probably divorce her eventually, if it proved true that she could no longer have a successful pregnancy. He had the obsessive need of a lonely man for children. He has to have them, she thought to herself, he's always wanted a large family, he's a Catholic—

My God, he's a Catholic!

Georgia got up, finished buttoning herself into her dress, and went out of the room. It opened on the wide, gloomy second-floor hallway, with its aura of misty green isolation, gray and mahogany and red wine, wide enough for a car to be driven down it. She went along to the main stairway, to the first floor, through several living rooms, and finally opened the ornate red wooden door and stepped into the Mexican chapel.

Ugly as sin, she reflected as usual as she moved amid the crude baroque bends and knobs, all gilt and fire-engine red, an Indian's attempt to make something Viennese.

She sat down in one of the pews and stared at the garish altar. Then she knelt, self-consciously, and began to say the prayers she had so recently and so mechanically learned, listening to the words for the first time, to see whether they meant anything: "I believe in God the Father Almighty, Creator of heaven and earth, and in Jesus Christ . . ." If she did not believe that at all, she now wanted to believe it. The Catholic Church, repellent, moralizing, shanty Irish, gloomy, antihuman, totalitarian, death-obsessed Catholicism, had suddenly turned a dazzling new aspect to her. It powerfully and fundamentally supported her life, by reinforcing with all its baleful strength the indissolubility of her marriage to Neil. And Neil was a believer. I think I believe too, she said hesitantly to herself, to see how it sounded. She could not make up her mind at once as to how it did sound.

But if Neil hadn't been a Catholic, with all the sexual fears and complexes which being an Irish-American Catholic implied, their love together would have been happier physically and she would not have been left vulnerable, entirely unconsciously, to her own excitement, to being betrayed by her body into responding to a crude sexual provocation. Those fears and complexes were Neil's part in the death of their child.

Taking a deep breath she forced herself to look at the better side of her life; that was why she had come to this hideous chapel. There were certain other, good facets to Catholicism. There was Aunt Ethel, cheerful, busy, constructive Aunt Ethel, with her shawls and good works and pilgrimages—and nothing else—filling her life. Why wasn't she a bitter or silly or useless or listless old maid? What gave her her energy and optimism and purpose and support? Catholicism.

It really isn't such a *bad* religion, she thought to herself, and at the word "bad" the sense of her own actions came flooding through her again and she felt herself totter spiritually before the enormity of what had happened.

Did I really want that baby? she suddenly demanded of herself for the first time, emboldened somehow by being in church to confront herself with that question. Did that have something to do with losing it? she demanded. Wasn't I afraid? *Is Cleet Kinsolving right!* Do I *still* somehow feel I'm a penniless little actress and not able to have the responsibility of a child! Did the simpleton at the core of my character think there wasn't enough *money* for this child! Didn't that have something to do with it! Oh God, oh God, she cried over and over to herself. What other words were there to say?

Oh God, she said fervently to herself, will I ever stop feeling I'm a penniless little actress, will Neil ever stop thinking he's a schoolboy and the entire world is hostile to him, and will Pop ever stop thinking he's nineteen years old and destined to change the face of the world?

We're out of phase with life; we live our lives out of season.

Cleet Kinsolving was the only person she had ever met who didn't, who lived it as it was now, who knew how old he was. That was why he was so urgent about the airline, for otherwise he would begin to fall behind too, like everybody else, into an Indian summer of brief, too late, doomed flowering.

The Reardons, the Reardons, she said to herself, the poor Reardons. They're such a lonely family, and so eager, and so powerful, more powerful than even they realize. When they find somebody who interests them, somebody who seems able to relieve some of the loneliness and to fill this haunting house a little more, they just pull him up by the roots! They don't even realize they're doing it. And then everything is wonderful and they change that person's life and it's the most wonderful thing for them and for him, and then someone else catches their interest, four other people maybe, and they start to lose interest in that person who's rootless now, that Buddy Ashcraft, that Cleet, and the poor guy gets desperate, and retaliates, and then the Reardons to their amazement have a Buddy Ashcraft persecuting them, have a Cleet . . . Only Cleet had more—more life in him than any of their others, so his desperation was worse and hurt them more than any favorite of theirs had before, hurt Neil more, hurt me.

At the thought of him her rage began to rise and she recalled the contemptuous way he had attracted her, the humiliating assurance of his magnetism, offhandedly stripping her self-ignorance away, hardly noticing that he was devastating her, and not quite bothering to complete the wreckage. So nature had done that for him. She coursed with rage, kneeling rigidly in the ugly little chapel, succumbing to wave after wave of hatred for Cleet Kinsolving. The fearful onslaughts seemed never-ending, and she asked herself despairingly how she would ever be able to live with these tides of poison flooding her.

And then this thought entered her mind: I can't surrender to this hate. I've only got so much emotion and I've got to use it for love, love for Neil, who needs it so desperately, for Pop, who needs it so desperately. I can't give in to this, I've only got so much emotion. If I let myself feel all this hate it will grow and grow and love will get more and more crowded and thin and diluted in me and the people who must have it from me won't get it.

I do not hate Cleet Kinsolving. God, listen: I do not hate Cleet Kinsolving. I do not.

Charley Kinsolving was going to be able to continue as a freshman at Yale University after all, because he had obtained a scholarship and a bursary job and a loan from the university. Cleet was leaving for Kansas. It was a propitious moment to dispose of the house, especially in view of the sharp postwar rise in real estate values. The sale would settle practically all the claims on the estate, cleaning up all loose ends, closing the file, all lawyers' and executors' problems removed, and the Kinsolving boys left without home or money.

Miss Ethel Reardon was putting little stickers on pieces of furniture which in her opinion merited professional examination for their possible value as antiques. She was privately dubious that any of them had value.

Cleet said goodby to her and to his brother and went out the front door, his huge duffel bag once more on his shoulder. It contained everything he owned. He had packed the atlas, because Kansas might be only a stage in his journey. Outside, there was an absolute autumnal stillness, and looking up one final time at his bedroom windows he thought of the hallucination he had had of a pursuing plane about to slice into that very room. Walking on toward the Highway he thought to himself that he planned not to have any more of those visions and hallucinations from out of the past.

Suddenly he had never felt better in his life. He didn't know why; it seemed to be merely the rather formidable weight of his own duffel bag, on his own shoulder.

ABOUT THE AUTHOR

JOHN KNOWLES, born in Fairmont, West Virginia, was educated at Phillips Exeter Academy and Yale University. He worked as a newspaper reporter and then as an associate editor for *Holiday* magazine. His first novel, *A Separate Peace,* received the Faulkner Foundation Prize and the Rosenthal Award of the National Institute of Arts and Letters. Since its publication in 1960, *A Separate Peace* has become, along with *The Catcher in the Rye* and *Lord of the Flies,* one of the most influential books in schools and colleges throughout the country. A second novel, *Morning in Antibes,* and a work of nonfiction, *Double Vision: American Thoughts Abroad,* came out of Mr. Knowles' stay in Europe and the Mediterranean. He now makes his home in New York City.